MRS. LOWE-PORTER

Praise for *Mrs. Lowe-Porter*

I was completely seduced by the story, the recounted life, and the personality of the main character. How does Helen retain control of the central challenge of being Mann's translator without losing herself in his overwhelming grandeur as a world-famous novelist? Jo Salas brilliantly captures the shifting depths underfoot. Despite the strictures of sticking to some semblance of biographical truth, however elastic, she maintains the pact between her subject and the freedom to stray and invent.
—Adam Thorpe, author of *Ulverton* and *The Rules of Perspective*

Helen Lowe-Porter, like the talented women who came before and after her, faced dilemmas that men have rarely needed to consider. As the woman behind two larger-than-life men, Helen's desire for her own creative expression will resonate with readers. Jo Salas skillfully depicts Helen's milieu and her rich inner world in this wise, engaging, and touching novel.
—Nava Atlas, creator of LiteraryLadiesGuide.com

I gave him my creative spirit, my conscientious, painstaking labor.... I was just the translator. I was not an inventor of worlds." The deep contradiction between "I gave him my creative spirit" and "I was just the translator" defines the driving dilemma of Helen Lowe-Porter, the first English translator of Thomas Mann. Jo Salas's engaging novel, based closely on the life of this admirable woman, is a must.
—Suzanne Jill Levine, author of *The Subversive Scribe: Translating Latin American Fiction*

An exploration of the complicated life of the translator of Thomas Mann—who is a writer in her own right. Salas asks difficult questions about work and gender—whose words should take precedence? Whose work? Whose needs? Salas

uses the real life of Helen Tracy Lowe-Porter as the foundation for this fascinating novel.
—Roxana Robinson, *Dawson's Fall*

Mrs. Lowe-Porter beguiled me in its nuanced and insightful depiction of the dilemma common to so many women: how to balance one's own ambition and need for self-expression with the demands of families within a culture that neither values care nor prizes women's work equally. The author not only deftly commands the details of an earlier time and place but imagines Helen Lowe-Porter's interior life and struggles with such sensitivity and verve that I found myself moved to a deeper understanding and profound appreciation of a woman I barely knew, my own grandmother.
—Anneke Campbell, writer and documentary filmmaker

MRS. LOWE-PORTER

a novel

Jo Salas

JACKLEG PRESS

JackLeg Press
www.jacklegpress.org

ISBN: 978-1956907056

Library of Congress Control Number: 2023933889

Cover photo: Image of Helen Lowe-Porter, courtesy of the author
Author photo: Dion Ogust

For Jonathan

My painting absorbs me more & more every day. I am slowly settling down to an oldmaidship, and I have only one prominent idea and that is that nothing will interfere between me and my work.
—Frances Hodgkins, *Letters of Frances Hodgkins*

Thou'rt a bold, spirited wench and I like thee for it. Yet forward as thou art, thou art still a woman; we must all come to't, niece.
—Helen Tracy Lowe-Porter, *Abdication, or All is True*

Contents

Author's note

Mrs. Lowe-Porter, based on the life of Helen Tracy Lowe-Porter, the translator of the great twentieth-century German novelist Thomas Mann, is fiction. I've used Helen's and Mann's real names as well the names of their publishers Alfred and Blanche Knopf, Mann's wife Katia, Helen's husband Elias Lowe (born Loew), their friend and neighbor Einstein, Helen's aunt and mentor Charlotte Porter, and Charlotte's partner, Helen Clarke. None of the other characters have real people's names, and in most cases they are not close counterparts of the people in Helen's world. The lives of her children and grandchildren in this book are not parallel to the lives of Helen's actual family members.

To portray Helen (in my subjective understanding of who she was) along with the dilemma of her multiple roles, I've imagined thoughts, conversations, and events. I've tweaked chronology at some points. However, nearly all of Helen's story here does follow the historical record, including family members' written and verbal recollections.

Part One

Helen and Elias

Meeting Elias
1906

She found him waiting in front of the massive entrance to the Alte Pinakothek with its arched windows repeating themselves endlessly on each side. Helen knew him immediately, though they'd never met—an American informality, a concentration of energy, in contrast to the leisurely burghers of Munich and their wives in their decorous Sunday clothes.

Elias Loew evidently recognized her as well and bounded toward her, hands outstretched.

"The clever Miss Porter!" he said, smiling broadly. His handshake was warm and forthright. "Your sister spoke so much of you." He seemed very young, like a boy dressed up as a professor in shabby black and wire-rimmed glasses.

"Well...clever!" she responded clumsily. "I believe you're the clever one."

From her sister Elizabeth's letters Helen had imagined a taller man. Elizabeth had described Elias's air of confidence, his brown eyes, his black wavy hair, his formidable intelligence. Helen had looked forward to meeting this interesting person once Elizabeth had come home and it was finally her own turn to sail to Europe.

Helen followed Elias into the museum's cool interior with its marble floors and high ceilings, their carved detail lost in the dimness. A young child's shrill voice echoed in the vast space before he was hushed by his parents. People clustered in front of paintings in heavy gilt frames, gazing contemplatively or conferring in whispers. I'm in *Munich*, she thought, in *Europe*. To learn everything about everything. Since she had stepped off the ship in Hamburg she had felt her senses opening wide; even her skin felt translucent and porous.

"Come!" Elias said over his shoulder, striding into one of the galleries. He led her to one masterpiece after another—she recognized the names but not the paintings. Van Eyck, Rembrandt, Vermeer. In a trance she followed Elias's short black-clad figure, the murmuring voices washing over her, the paintings rising up like the pages of art books leaping into life, enormous and vivid, the paint thick and glistening as though the painter had just left the room, brushes in hand. She would give this experience to Ruth, the heroine of the novel she was writing: the provincial American artist face to face with the Old Masters. Her little notebook was tucked into her purse as always but she was too self-conscious in the presence of her new acquaintance to reach for it.

Elias stopped in front of a painting of a naked young woman holding a fur around her body, happy enough, judging from her mischievous gaze, to display her round breasts.

"One of my favorites," whispered Elias. "What do you think?" He stood with his arms folded, contemplating the painting.

Helen stepped closer to peer at it. She found it embarrassing but did not want to say so. "Her arms seem unusually long, don't they?"

Elias laughed. "Rubens wasn't the greatest of draftsmen, it's true." He talked about the painting's unashamed sensuality: the breasts pushed up by the woman's arms, the suggestiveness of the fur against her belly. "I suspect that fur was on the floor the minute Rubens put down his brush."

She braced herself a bit, as though his frankness held some danger for her, knowing at the same time that the idea of danger was absurd. This is what I *want*, she reminded herself, this kind of bold conversation. I want to speak this language. I want to get fluent in it. Why should I not enjoy imagining this young woman in the studio and the man looking at her?

2

But she couldn't yet find a response to Elias's comment.

"Beauty is very important to me," he said. He turned and looked at Helen appraisingly, to her acute discomfort.

Helen returned to her pension flushed and stirred by the encounter, by the roomfuls of brilliant paintings, by the novel sense of being plunged into a world she had imagined and yearned for all her life. I won't hear from Elias Loew again, she told herself. I'm not sophisticated enough for him, nor beautiful enough. Then reprimanded herself: I am not here to become acquainted with young men.

But the next day there was a note: "Dear Miss Porter, won't you join me for a walk? I would love to show you Munich." They met under the Rathaus glockenspiel, this time falling easily into conversation as though they were already old friends. After the bells had finished their recital and the bright-painted figures paused to rest, Elias took her arm and guided her around the Old Town, pointing out landmarks in his quick way. When they parted it seemed natural to plan to meet again soon.

"There's a concert on Friday," he said. "Mahler and Wagner. Shall we go?"

In the warm darkness Helen sat beside Elias, washed in the lush harmonies, transported by the woodwinds' melodies. Mahler himself conducted, his dark hair flying.

They met often after that, drinking coffee together between her language classes and the lectures that he was already giving at the university though still a student himself.

"You sprechen very well," Elias said, after listening to Helen slip comfortably into German with his friend Willi, who'd appeared unexpectedly at their table by the lake in the Englischer Garten. "Could you help me with a translation that I'm working on? If you can stand it—a paleographic paper, dry as old bones."

He'd been told, he confided to her, that as soon as he had his doctorate he would be offered teaching posts at more than one university. "I've had my eye on Oxford ever since I can remember," he said. "Can you imagine? From the shtetl to the dreaming spires!"

Helen was curious about his origins, which he rarely referred to. "What was it like—the shtetl?" she asked. She knew no one else from that world and had never said the word aloud before.

"I don't remember much," he said. "You can ask me about growing up in New York." So she did, and he told her about being befriended by the children's librarian at the settlement house when he was still new to America. "An extraordinary woman, Hal, and she took a great interest in me. It's thanks to Miss Evans that I'm here. Miss Evans and the people she introduced me to." He looked at her earnestly. "I don't want to sound boastful. But they recognized something in me, different from other boys."

Helen believed him. It was easy to imagine Elias as a bright, charming, immigrant child, eager to be taught, inspiring pride and optimism in his idealistic benefactors.

He looked out at the lake beyond the café terrace where they were sitting. Yellowing willow branches trailed in the water. A family of ducks paddled by, the mother circling back to herd a wayward duckling who was heading for shore. "I've been extremely fortunate, always," he said.

Elias wore a blue scarf wrapped around his neck, a fetching contrast with his brown eyes, Helen thought. In spite of herself she had indulged in a flicker of a romantic dream before they met. Perhaps after all she was not too old to find a soulmate, and this Elias Loew...But the fantasy receded quickly once she was in Munich and observed Elias's appetite for curvaceous "Blondkopfen" as he liked to say.

He touched her hand on the table for a second. "What about you, Hal? What is your dream? Love and marriage, like your sister?"

Helen winced inwardly at the nickname he'd endowed her with. "I won't marry, Elias," she said, wishing she'd never mentioned the young man who'd briefly courted her during her last year of college. "I told you. I'm going to write. And you?" she went on, wanting to poke him a little in return. "Are you going to sweep some lovely Bavarian lady off her feet?" She was pleased with herself for producing this worldly banter.

"Oh," Elias said, winking, "I already have. More than one, actually. The frolicking Fräuleins of München." He shaped an exaggerated hourglass figure with his hands, his eyes dancing. Again he seemed like a boy, not an almost-professor.

He leaned forward and squeezed both her hands. "See, that's what I like so much about you, Hal. I can say anything to you, as though you were another lad."

He'd already told her how much he relished her mind—like a man's mind, he said. She knew he meant it as a compliment to her intelligence and was flattered.

Helen had not yet told Elias about the novel that she worked on each morning before classes began. Being far away from home had unleashed imagination and momentum, instead of the opposite, as she'd feared.

"Traveling will most certainly make you a better writer," Aunt Charlotte had assured her when Helen visited her in Boston to say goodbye. "It will bring great richness to your work. But"—poking Helen's shoulder for emphasis—"only if you absolutely *insist* on writing every day while you're away. Otherwise your novel will retreat into the shadows and may never emerge again."

Charlotte's unkempt living room was the headquarters of the poetry magazine she and her partner had founded and still edited, bringing European writers to American readers, sometimes in Helen's translations. Piles of copies rose from the floor like stalagmites. A solemn portrait of Shakespeare oversaw all operations.

"Now, dear girl, I want you to write to me every Friday describing to me what you are seeing, what you are doing, whom you are meeting, and how the writing is coming along. And let the German soak into your skin. I'm counting on more translation from you."

In the heady whirl of European life Helen was grateful for Aunt Charlotte's demand. The assignment sharpened her eyes and ears and her pen. She barely mentioned Elias in her letters, knowing that hinting at his place in the foreground of her Munich experience would trigger a suspicious interrogation. Charlotte, alone among her relatives, did not smile on friendships with eligible young men.

"Companionship, by all means, my dear," she'd once said, wrapping her arm around her partner—Helen's namesake—who shared her home and every facet of her life. "Marriage and children, I'm sorry, no. Unless of course you're not really serious about your writing, which would be a waste of ability, not to mention education. Anything is within your grasp, Helen. All you have to do is decide."

In her Munich pension, fresh from her dreaming self, Helen summoned the spirit of her heroine Ruth, an ambitious young artist of twenty-five who intends to make her mark on the new century with her art. Ruth has studied with a master—his only female student—but she's left his cautious brushstrokes far behind. Ruth paints muscular women with strong teeth and splayed toes: modern paintings, not entirely realistic. She herself has a dazzling smile, a flexible and powerful body, a confident stride. Her auburn hair flows down her back in a loose braid, sometimes crowned by a floppy green velvet cap. She attracts young men in spite of her scorn of womanly wiles. The men tell her that she would grace their parlors, their bedrooms. They tell her, believing that they are flattering her, that her artistic talents will be an asset as a wife and a mother. But Ruth despises the domestic arts: flower arranging, choosing tasteful silks for a new dress, gestating and doting on beautiful children who will pose wide-eyed in their frothy christening gowns. Her own parents have accepted with reluctance that their wild girl will not marry.

Ruth's younger sister Nellie is to be married in four months. Ruth loves and admires her but she shudders to imagine stepping through that weighty matrimonial door and pulling it shut behind her. Slam! Ruth is determined to say nothing to Nellie about her revulsion. Let Nellie thrive in wifehood, or make her own disappointed discoveries, at which point Ruth will give her every support.

Ruth will encounter troubles of a different kind in the future, her creator thinks. A problem with alcohol. A crushing and scandalous love affair that tests her resilience to the limit. Perhaps a child out of wedlock, forcing a terrible choice. How the story will end is unknown.

The daily revelations of life in an unfamiliar city jostled Helen's mind. New ideas and insights flew out like birds flushed from cover. Helen found herself suddenly sure of the next steps in Ruth's life. Her heroine would spend a year, two years, in Europe, and meet people who were nothing like the inhabitants of her provincial hometown or her women's college. On the threshold of the Old World, so new to her, Ruth would discover a different scope of existence. She would haunt the museums. Her own painting would transform. She would move further away from realism, immersing herself in pure color and design, striving to close the tantalizing gap between the visions in her mind's eye and the images on her canvas. As any artist does, thought Helen. As I do myself, only with words instead of paint. That maddening gulf between what I want to say and what I am able to say.

She read over the last ten pages that she'd written, struck by their sureness and flow—pleased to have gone a little further than she'd thought toward bridging that impossible gulf. But it was probably an illusion, a self-serving illusion, which would dissipate next time she looked at it. She could ask Elias to read a chapter. Or not. The idea of his piercing eye on her work attracted and scared her.

By the stream
1907

Because they were not in love and because they were free agents, far away from the conventions of home and family, Elias and Helen decided to have an adventure together, camping and fishing in the Bavarian woods like two lads, as he said. Elias's friend Willi knew of a trail that led to a stream and a field where they could set up camp.

"Just us?" she had asked when Elias raised the idea. She could not help a frisson of shock—traveling alone with a man. But the idea had charm. And after a year in Europe her new self had left the old Helen far behind.

"Just us!" he said. "Who's to know or care?"

"Yes!" she said. She'd never camped in her life but she and Elizabeth used to fish with their cousins in the Poconos.

The forest was silent except for the shuffle of pine needles and the snap of twigs under their feet, and an occasional squawk from a blackbird annoyed by their intrusion. Sunshine lit the feathery branches but the air was cool and earthy. Ferns curled at the edge of the path and occasionally a blue wildflower that Helen did not recognize. She had borrowed a pair of Elias's golfing knickerbockers and the freedom of her legs gave her pleasure. His sturdy figure ahead of her was almost hidden by his rucksack, filled, like hers, with camping supplies and books to read, as well as notebooks for their thoughts and observations. And, in her case, poems. She had already thought of a couple of lines to jot down as soon as she had a chance.

At first they talked as they walked, Elias turning so she could hear him. They were discussing women's rights, prompted by Helen's claim to be a suffragist. "Of course! And so you should be!" he called over his shoulder, a little out of breath. "But the franchise won't change the fact that woman's first duty is to her family."

Helen wanted to debate this point: why shouldn't women's roles and responsibilities, and men's, be examined and changed for the betterment of all? But the path led steadily uphill, narrower now, with rocky outcrops on one side and a steep slope on the other. Talking became difficult. Helen could feel her heartbeat in her ears. The heavy rucksack pulled on her shoulders. One foot after the other. Watch for roots. Breathe in, breathe out.

Elias stopped and wiped his face with his handkerchief, then pulled Willi's map out of his pocket. "Here's where we are," he said, pointing. "And here's our spot." It was the other side of the ridge, not far ahead. He offered her his canteen. "Another half hour, perhaps. How are you faring, Hal?"

"Quite well, thank you!" she said. "I'm faring quite well." And she was. Her body felt strong and able. The woodland air was intoxicating.

He leaned toward her and gave her a quick kiss on the cheek. "Good fellow! Onward, then."

It was late afternoon when they reached a small meadow edged by a fast-running stream, almost a river. The water caught the sun's oblique light. Elias and Helen put down their rucksacks. The sudden release of weight made her feel as if she might levitate. She sat down gratefully on the grass, which was cool and slightly damp, rougher than it appeared. She looked around. Only the larches in the distance, the field with its waving grasses, the water splashing noisily over rocks. No sign of human life.

"How lovely!" said Helen, turning to Elias with delight. "How lucky we are!"

"We must bathe," he said, already beginning to unbutton his shirt. "Before the sun gets any lower. Wash off our travel stains."

He flung his shirt on the ground, untied his boots and kicked them off, and began to unbuckle his belt. Helen wanted to stop him, she wasn't ready to see the whole man, she'd never seen a man's body. But it was too late. He stood before her, his pale body with its abrupt patch of dark hair and the extraordinary configuration of brownish-pink male genitals, quite unlike the colorless marble curlicues of the statues she'd observed in shy glances. He grinned at her consternation and did a little dance, making the genitals bounce. "This is what we look like, Hal!" She clapped her hand over her mouth, laughing at the ridiculous sight. He ran down to the stream and plunged in—it was deep enough to submerge himself lying down. He lifted his head out of the water, bellowing with the shock of cold. "Come and join me, it's wonderful!"

Reckless, she threw off her own clothes, not letting herself think. The cool air on overheated skin felt wonderful. No one had ever seen her body, not even she herself. She avoided looking in mirrors when undressing. She did not know if it was an attractive body or not. She held her blouse around her like the fur in the Rubens painting, slipping it off at the last moment before stepping into the water. The coldness took her breath. Then she felt Elias's arms around her, his cold solid flesh pressed to hers.

The tent smelled of crushed grass and musty canvas. In the darkness he showed her how to make love. "I've never…" she started to whisper. "I know," he said. "Don't worry." He was tender and patient. It seemed astonishing that, after all the stern prohibitions since girlhood, no less implacable for being indirect, there was now nothing and no one to prevent her from jettisoning her virginity. She felt a little dizzy, as though she'd cut a thick rope and launched into free fall.

Her flesh awoke slowly to sensation: the pressure of the bumpy ground underneath her, the cold air on her skin when the blankets slipped away from them, the pleasure where he touched her, the wholly unexpected and exquisite fullness inside her when he had eased himself in. She heard him cry out and was startled, then understood that it was a cry of joy.

Afterwards they opened the flap of the tent to look up at the clear sky.

"Look, Elias—Cygnus the Swan," said Helen, grasping his forefinger and pointing it at the constellation straddling the Milky Way straight above them.

"Good evening, Cygnus," he said. "Helen Porter and I have just made love."

She blushed and was glad of the dark. In the tent she had crossed a divide that she had thought she would never cross. Suddenly she had become a Helen who felt sure of herself and knowing. It occurred to her that her writing would benefit. Not that she would ever write about this. But a writer must know about life.

She positioned her head more comfortably in the crook of Elias's arm. Her body felt both charged and relaxed—had she ever in her life felt so relaxed?

"Ah, Hal," he said on a sigh. "Sex is the life force. Did you know that?"

She didn't.

"Hal."

Her eyelids were closing. "Hmm?"

"We belong together, Hal. Our minds belong together and so do our bodies."

She did not open her eyes but she was no longer sleepy. She waited.

"I want you to be my wife."

Helen sat up and pulled the blanket around her against the cold night air. A proposal of marriage. She tried to rally a response but could not find one. They'd talked about marriage only in an oblique, ironic way, not in reference to themselves. She had not revealed to him her private debate: for her writer-self, marriage meant danger, compromise, even extinction. Yet on the other side, companionship, children, a family, as other women had. And now this marvelous thing, sex.

Elias sat up beside her and tugged the other side of the blanket around him. He turned her face towards his and kissed her lips. "Your blue eyes, Helen, your beautiful clear blue eyes," he said, his voice deepened and soft.

They could hardly see each other in the dark. She thought perhaps she loved him. Marriage...Her thoughts skittered in all directions.

But a great tenderness had been unleashed in her. "I have to think, Elias—let me think about this," she said.

In the morning Elias strode off with his fishing rod to catch trout for their breakfast. Helen sat at the edge of the stream with the sun on her back, feet bare, pen and notebook in hand. The extraordinary night was still with her and demanded expression.

We have crushed the ripe pomegranate and laughed as we drank,
Where the blood leaped up like a flame and the spent seeds fell.

She knew the lines were overwrought—she could hear Aunt Charlotte's theatrical groan. I'll tone it down later, she thought. The dramatic images presented themselves without invitation—how else to evoke an experience so revelatory?

We have numbered the spawn of this fig, the crimson, uncounted.
We have walked with the moon, we have waked with the sun, we have made
With the morning star our brave antiphonal music.
The winds are our breath, in our veins are the tides of the sea.

3

A feather
1963

Her daughter was coming to visit. Helen decided to wear her favorite black silk pants, so loose and airy around her legs, like pajamas. Oh! Silly! She already had them on, from the night, and from yesterday too, she thought. Perhaps the day before as well. She loved the silk for the way it sat so lightly on her skin, the little strokings when she moved. She scratched at a spot where she had spilled something and the silk had dried stiffly. It was wintertime—yes, she could see snow on the ground, and bare trees. Too bad. She would have liked to wear the matching black silk sleeveless top that the dressmaker had made for her, even though Marjorie disapproved of revealing her loose and wrinkled arms. But it was too cold.

She touched her hair, still plentiful. It amused her that to her fingers her hair felt brown, when in the mirror it was white. She rarely looked in the mirror, discomforted by its gaunt crone with her own sharp blue eyes under drooping lids.

There was a knock on the door. "Breakfast!" called Mrs. D's cigarette-thick voice. She no longer tried to persuade Helen to eat in the dining room with the other half dozen inmates. ("*Residents,* Mother!" said Marjorie's voice in her head. "You mustn't call them inmates.")

Helen sat motionless, grinning to herself. If she didn't answer, perhaps Mrs. D would think she was not there. That she had run away during the night in her black silk pajamas, darting along the moonlit road to the train station, slipping onto a train just as it was about to leave.

But to where? What should she tell the conductor? She was suddenly unsure. Was she in America again? Or England? Or somewhere in Europe? She'd gone back and forth so often, a nomad, a refugee, shedding belongings until there was almost nothing left.

The door handle turned and the door opened a sliver. Mrs. D's hennaed head appeared around it. "Go away!" said Helen before Mrs. D could say anything.

"I'll just leave your breakfast here, then." She left the tray on the table by the door and withdrew quickly.

Helen was not hungry. She would let the coffee grow cold and the omelet congeal. When Marjorie arrived she and Mrs. D would mutter together. Marjorie would shake her head and apologize for her mother's behavior. She pretends to be a serious grown-up, Helen thought. Somewhere inside she's still funny little Miss Hedgehog scribbling her poems. Except she's not scribbling any more. A spike of guilt assailed her. I did something unkind, Helen reflected. The memory disintegrated.

She comforted herself by imagining Marjorie in the distant future, freed from the rich husband, her hair as wild as when she was a child, writing and drinking with other unruly elderly ladies.

We could be friends again, she thought, then corrected herself. When Marjorie's old I'll be dust.

If it weren't for Marjorie and the boy she'd have no one.

Helen softened at the thought of Marjorie's boy, with his limpid brown eyes and satin skin. The dark tendrils on the nape of his neck. She loved nothing more than the sweet weight of him on her lap. Had she held her own children like that? Were they as enchanting? She wished she could remember but all she could summon was a blur of small warm bodies, the smell of wool and talcum powder. She was always so terribly busy when her daughters were small: the mounting stacks of pages on her desk, the all-absorbing work itself, impatient letters from the publisher, manuscripts sent piecemeal by Mann himself, only to require retranslating after his revisions. The muffled bleating of her own unfinished writing, hidden in the bottom drawer. Not to mention Elias, who had perfected the art of making demands without having to say a word. No, not much time for babies on laps.

She hoped the boy would come, with his mother. Then she and the child could cuddle and talk nonsense, saving her from straining at adult conversation. We were fonder of each other once, Marjorie and I, she thought. When she was a girl.

Yes, she hoped very much that Marjorie would bring the little boy. She got off the bed and hunted in her chest of drawers for a gift. Last time–but she could not bring the last time into focus. She had given him something that he had loved. What was it? A game, yes. An old box of ivory dominoes. She stopped, picturing an older child absorbed in balancing the dominoes in a precarious geometry. "Look, Grandma!" She was confused. Was there another grandson? There were granddaughters, she was sure, but far away, and older. She went on with the search. Tucked under a pile of folded clothes there was a long feather. She drew it out and held it up, letting the light catch its iridescence. He will like this, she thought.

Helen stood at the window to watch the driveway, holding up the feather by its stalk and closing one eye so that her perspective was distorted and the feather became an exotic tree in the grove of bare maples between the house and the road. She liked the monochrome landscape. She liked austereness, after a half a lifetime of immersion in Mann's dense, elaborate, long-winded German, transforming it into language that would keep English readers turning the pages.

Her eyes flicked to the bookcase with its empty top shelf. She had instructed Mrs. D's husband to get rid of the long set of broad-backed books that had lived up there. Twenty-two of them! Mr. D, not a reader but aware of Mann's stature and Helen's integral role, had exclaimed in consternation. "But these are your books, Mrs. Lowe! Your name's on all the title pages— you showed me!"

"You'd need a magnifying glass to see my name, Mr. D."

"Well, but—what about donating them to the library, then, if you don't want them?" he said. Helen did not care, as long as they left the room.

Inconspicuous on the third shelf, among poetry books and orange Penguins, was the only one with her own name on its narrow spine. Well, not quite the only one. The other, even narrower, barely counted. Neither of them counted at all, to tell the truth. But she loved them, her literary offspring, the only ones to survive gestation.

"Mrs. Lowe!" called Mrs. D, rapping on the door. "Your daughter's here."

Marjorie must have sidled in without Helen noticing, even though she'd been waiting at the window. She opened the door. There stood a slim, middle-aged woman in a fur-collared coat who after a moment turned into her daughter, smiling at her. Helen accepted a kiss on the cheek. She looked all around, but Marjorie was alone.

"I was hoping you'd bring the baby."

"What baby?" A frown. "You don't mean Nick?"

Nick. Nicky.

"Mother. Nick's nineteen years old. He's in college." She shook her head, looking worried.

Oh dear, thought Helen. I've made a mistake again.

Marjorie put down her shopping bags and hung her coat on the hook on the door. She had on high heels and one of her smart suits.

"My goodness, you're in those floppy old pajamas again!" Marjorie's eyes narrowed. "They need a wash, Mother—couldn't you let Mrs. D wash them for you?" Her gaze fell on the unmade bed. Helen watched as Marjorie tucked in the sheets firmly and straightened the blankets, her long thin legs just like Helen's own. Marjorie shook the pillow and pulled up the dark green coverlet. "There!"

What's the point, thought Helen. I'm only going to untidy it again.

"What happened to the Mann books?" Marjorie was staring at the empty shelf.

Helen smiled at her. She couldn't think how to explain.

"Where are they, Mother?"

"I didn't want them anymore. Mr. D gave them to the library. I think."

Marjorie flushed. "Why didn't you give them to me, if you didn't want them? They must be valuable, surely."

A useful memory came to her, a little gift from her old pragmatic self.

"I sold all the valuable books and papers years ago, don't you remember? To the university. They paid quite well."

"But those books are a record of your life's work!"

"Yes." *Quod erat demonstrandum.* I do not need a reminder of my servitude. I am not likely to forget, am I? I gave him all those years, I gave him the very best of my capacities, I gave him my creative spirit, my conscientious, painstaking labor, for which his thanks were never more than equivocal.

Marjorie sighed. "I'll talk to Mr. D. He probably still has them. Here, Mother, I brought some things for you."

Helen watched without interest as clothes and food items emerged from Marjorie's shopping bags and were displayed on the taut bedspread. A gray-green scarf. Dried figs in a round packet. She despised dried figs, which bore no relation to their fleshly incarnation. A tin of shortbread. No books.

One time Marjorie had brought her a book of poetry by a young woman. "You'll like these poems, Mother," she'd said. "And look." She pointed to the short biography on the back. "Like you, when we were little"—a young American writer transplanted to England, with small children and a celebrated husband. The poems were astonishing. But recently she'd heard—Marjorie must have told her—that the young poet had killed herself, defeated by the irreconcilable burdens of writing, motherhood, and a sexually incontinent husband. Or at least that was Helen's interpretation. She grieved for the young woman and for her children.

How could Nicky be nineteen? And yet she knew that he was. His young-man self appeared in her mind, sleek as a young cat, confident and charming. But something disquieting about him. In her mind he turned into Elias, dark hair and twinkling brown eyes, certain of himself. She thrust the image away.

Marjorie held up the last item from the bag, a bottle of dry sherry. Ah! Something she needed, finally. Helen did not like to run low on sherry.

"Brava, Marjorie!" she said, patting her arm.

"It's from Daddy."

Helen's face stiffened. She touched her throat with the feather, which she was still holding, ready to give to the baby.

"Mother—he would so much like to see you."

Helen picked up the scarf and examined it. It was soft, with the drape of raw silk. She wrapped it around her shoulders and then around her head, peering at Marjorie from under the fringed edge.

Marjorie sighed. "Couldn't there be some kindness between you two, Mother?" she said, her voice gentle.

She wants me to forgive him, thought Helen. Of course she does. Daddy's girl all her life. I wonder what he's told her.

"I am not going to talk about Elias," said Helen.

4

Early Latin minuscule
1909

Her life now braided with her young lover's, Helen found herself peeking into the dim world of paleography where scholars like Elias pored over ancient manuscripts to decipher their secrets. He spent weeks at the monastery of Monte Cassino in southern Italy, one of the lighthouses of Western culture, as he said, studying medieval Latin manuscripts in Beneventan script with its tightly spaced letters and ligatures, indecipherable to her eye though she could translate the Latin if he transcribed it. He wrote to her with excitement about his growing conviction that the calendars he was studying were centuries older than they were thought to be. If he could prove it—and he was confident that he could—his dissertation would assure his place in the field.

As each chapter of his dissertation was completed Elias handed it to Helen, who, he'd learned, would add style and clarity to his writing, even in German, as the thesis had to be. She crossed out some of the throat-clearing phrases he was fond of, suggested a stronger word here and there, drew arrows to show where a paragraph might fit better. He praised her bilingual editing skills and urged her to offer her services as a translator for German academics, which she did, with the help of Elias's connections. To her surprise, she was soon busy with articles and conference presentations, earning a trickle of money to replenish her dwindling funds.

In the little park across from their pension Helen sat with her notebook in hand. The sunlight was about to disappear over the roofs and treetops. She had just finished translating a research article about Austrian forestry and now she rewarded herself with thoughts of her long-neglected novel. She held her mind still, waiting for the door into Ruth's world to swing open. Wait. Listen. She stepped over the threshold and the artist Ruth emerged in front of her. Ruth, who is now attracting attention in the New York art world for her bold painting and her even bolder behavior. An indiscreet love affair with a respected older painter. Scandal endangers her career but also puts her in the spotlight. Ruth knows she has to ride this moment like a skier on the steepest slope. Peril as well as momentum.

Helen started making quick notes—a word, a question, a visual image to flesh out later when she had a chance to sit down and write. Where did these ideas come from, swooping in like a flock of birds as though they'd been perched on the tops of the trees waiting for her invitation?

She felt Elias's hands on her shoulders and then his kiss on her neck. Without looking up from her notebook she reached up to touch his hand. He sat down on the bench and sighed heavily. His arms were full of the final draft of his dissertation—all two hundred and seventy pages.

"I do hate to ask you this, Hal," he said. "Could you bear to...?"

She knew what he was asking. The dissertation had to be submitted next week and Elias was ragged with anxiety. Helen put her hand over her notebook. Ruth, Ruth, I'm sorry, I'll come back to you, I promise. She reminded herself yet again that she could open that door whenever she wanted. Elias's need was pressing.

She suppressed a sigh. "Yes, Elias. Don't worry. I'll retype it for you."

He seized her hand and kissed it extravagantly. "You are my angel!" he said and promised to feed her peaches and cream, fresh figs, chocolates, cognac, anything.

The typing took far longer than she expected—it was laborious, typing accurately on Elias's old German typewriter, following the university's stringent requirements for layout. No corrections permitted. The dissertation convincingly argued that the famous Monte Cassino calendars were written well before 800 AD, the date that scholars until now had asserted. She ignored the call of the crystalline September days and stayed at her desk until the task was done. She did not let herself think of Ruth.

On the day that his doctorate was granted Elias and Helen celebrated with dinner in a fine French restaurant, a rare extravagance. She gave him her gift of congratulations, a new fountain pen and a poem that she had written out on parchment as beautifully as she could "in Helenic minuscule," she told him. The candlelight glinted in his glasses as he read it. He looked up with a smile and reached a hand to her across the table. "Hal— you helped me more than I can say. My dearest." He took off his glasses and lifted the white napkin to his eyes.

Elias had a gift for her as well: a framed page of Beneventan script, illegible to her, but the meaning didn't matter. It was visually beautiful, a work of art, with its gracefully formed letters, the first "O" illuminated in gold, a three-sided border of delicate flowers in red, yellow, green and blue. An anonymous monk created this, she thought, with his quill and brushes and his pigments made from cinnabar, turmeric, indigo. A thousand years ago. An artist, who did not need to sign his name.

5

Fictional Ruth scolds her creator
1910

I don't mean to make demands, Helen. But are you aware that you have not paid attention to me for months? Do you have any idea what I've been up to?

I know, I know, I know. I'm sorry. I do think about you. More often than you'd believe. It's just...

Yes. You have other things to think about now. You have *him*. You're living a rather interesting story yourself. Perhaps you don't need to write one any more.

Ruth! I do! Desperately! You have no idea. I long to sit down for four hours, five hours, and enter your world, and discover what happens next, and make my best efforts to describe it. I miss it so much, slipping into that world, *creating* that world. I *need* it.

So why don't you do it?

Ah...

Why, Helen?

It's hard to explain. It's hard even for me to understand. It's not that he stops me, I can't blame him at all. It's just...

Have you shown him your work?

I did, finally, yes.

And?

He liked it. He had some excellent critiques and suggestions.

I'm pleased to hear it.

It's just that...I can't help comparing my efforts with his. I've read every word of his dissertation, more than once. It's magnificent. Solid as a rock, and already recognized as a substantial contribution in his field. In comparison my scribblings are nothing but wisps of the imagination. So how can his work not come first, Ruth? And how can I not help him in any way possible? Then the second priority is anything I can do to earn money. I don't have a lot in my coffers, you know. Which means translating scientific talks and articles for agricultural journals or whatever else comes my way. And limping along, half a mile behind, covered in dust, one shoe missing, is my own fiction writing. Barely in sight!

Oh dear. But it's hardly a surprise, is it? What has Aunt Charlotte always told you? And isn't that what *The Artist* is about? My courageous willingness to forgo love and family for my art. In contrast to Nellie's acquiescence to wifehood.

I have hardly "acquiesced to wifehood," Ruth! At least not like Nellie. Do you see me collecting hemstitched linens and sending out engraved wedding invitations? Yes, I'm going to be married, but not like that. No guests. No tiered cake. I'll wear my brown silk costume that I've had for five years.

Helen. Be honest. I'm not talking about the wedding. Let me ask you this: what would happen if you said to him, Dear, I can't see you for a few days, I'm working on my novel.

Yes, well, all right, Ruth. I'll be honest. This is what would happen. He would pat me on the head, metaphorically speaking, grant me permission with a cheerful smile, tell me he hopes I enjoy myself. Then he'd remind me about his deadline, but don't worry, he'll manage fine without me, and I would feel sheepish, and selfish, and I'd probably say, oh, never mind, I'll do it another time, it's really not important, compared to your work, our conversations, our excursions. And it certainly won't earn us any money. I can't say it's any use at all, in fact. Elias's dissertation will be published, you know. And very well published—the Clarendon Press at Oxford, no less. He'll need me to help prepare it. And Oxford's going to offer him a position as well, we're almost sure. Whereas me...

Oh, please. Spare me your self-pity. If this is your attitude, how am I ever going to do what I need and want to do in my life? I'm drinking rather a lot these days, Helen, what are you going to do about it? Am I doomed, or not? Do you know what I did last week? I drank too much wine at Harry's opening and I insulted him, I called him a paint-spattered poseur—I was so drunk that I could hardly pronounce the words—and then I kissed him on the mouth, in front of his wife, in front of the press, and all our colleagues and friends. Are you going to write that?

Of course I am, it's all in my notes already. Just give me time. A little more time.

The longer you stall, Helen, the harder it's going to be. But you don't need me to tell you that.

No, I don't. Whenever I manage to gather up my accumulated pages they feel heavier and heavier. I have to scrape off layers of guilt and neglect and ambivalence before I can regain any momentum at all. Every time it gets harder. It's not him I'm fighting, it's myself. All I can manage is the odd poem. Poems don't take long to finish.

I'm going to be harsh here, Helen. Imagine yourself ten years from now. What will you say to yourself if you have not finished and published your novel? Think about it. Take your time. I'm not in a hurry.

Well, Ruth, I've succeeded in endowing you with a forthright personality, haven't I? That's one success I can claim, at least. Yes, that is a harsh question. The truth is I don't know how to imagine my life ten years from now. I'll be the wife of an Oxford don. I might have children. I'll probably be doing bits of translation here and there. But. If I've given up on you I will judge myself more harshly than you could. I will be horribly disappointed. And I don't want to make you jealous, but it's not just you and Nellie. There's so much more I want to write—stories, poems, plays. More novels. I haven't made much of a start, have I?

Helen, this is the question—

You've said quite enough, Ruth.

6

Life Force
1910

They lay side by side, overheated, top sheet and eiderdown tumbled to the floor. The room was cold in the Oxford winter night and soon they would have to cover themselves again. Helen was suffused by a physical contentment that her younger self could not have imagined. Bliss. Yes, bliss is not too strong a word for it, she thought. Why does no one talk about this? It was like a secret kept from the uninitiated. She was curious about her parents—she could not imagine her mother surrendering like this to the extreme joy of the body. Especially when pregnant. Helen raised her head to look down at the curve of her belly in the clouded moonlight. Elias noticed and reached out to stroke the taut skin gently. She felt the hidden child respond to his touch, flipping like a fish in her warm depths.

"I wonder if he will be like me," Elias said.

"Short and bespectacled," said Helen, turning on her side and wrapping her arms around him.

"No, I was thinking about the life force. Will he be over-endowed with the life force, like his father?"

She let go of him and rolled onto her back again. This was something that she did not like to discuss.

Elias had raised the topic a week after their wedding in Munich, early one morning when the midsummer sun had woken them in time to make love before the busy day began. "Hal," he said, holding her hand as they lay together afterwards, "you know about the life force, don't you? It's part of the sex drive, but it's more than that. It's the force that makes us who we are, that propels us to fulfill ourselves, to fulfill our calling. The *élan vital,* if you will. Some call it Eros." He looked at her to make sure she was paying attention. He's giving a lecture, thought Helen, trying not to giggle. The boy-professor, post-coital. "Now, the thing to understand," he went on, "is that the life force is stronger in men than in women, both in our sex drive and in our work. The equivalent in women is the desire to nurture."

"How interesting," she responded innocently.

"And in me," Elias continued, "for better or worse, the life force, in particular the sex drive, is more pronounced than in most men. You might not realize that, since you don't have past lovers to compare me with." He dropped a kiss on her cheek. "My virginal bride."

He propped himself up on his elbow. There was evidently more to divulge.

"And Hal, here is what I wanted to speak about. I've given this a great deal of thought, now that we're married."

"Yes?"

"I don't want this imbalance to become an obstacle between us. And so I propose an arrangement: that I may sleep with other women if the life force demands it."

Helen stared at him.

"Only," he added hastily, "when I'm traveling, of course. And I'd be completely open about it. I'd never want to deceive you, Hal."

She shrank away from him, the sheet clutched around her.

Elias went on. "We're not like other couples, you and I. Not bound by the old rigid conventions. Why shouldn't the physical side of marriage benefit from emancipation as well?"

Helen shook her head, still dumb.

He misinterpreted her silence. "And of course, I would sanction the same freedom for you."

The idea of another man repelled her. The idea of Elias with another woman repelled her. "*You're* my lover, Elias!" she burst out at last. "And I'm yours. Why would we let anyone else into--this?" Her gesture included him, herself, the rumpled bed, the sun-filled window. She pulled the sheet up to cover her face and willed herself not to cry. She was desperately confused. How could she refuse her bridegroom a freedom that he was willing to grant to her, even if she didn't want it? And how could she deny him something that he claimed to need, even if she didn't understand it? She loved him. She had promised to love him always.

On the street below a woman shouted at her child, "Wait for me, little devil!"

He caressed her shoulder. She flung herself out of the bed and grabbed her robe. "Go away. Leave me alone. I can't possibly answer you right now." She walked out of the room.

"Don't be afraid, Hal," he called after her. "Remember that we love each other. Nothing can change that."

His preposterous words echoed in her mind throughout the day as she swept the floor, edited a translation, walked to the shops. The proposition sickened her. I *cannot* say yes to it, she thought, only then to argue with herself: but I love him. Perhaps it will be all right. Perhaps I will get used to it.

When Elias came home after his evening lecture Helen was sitting in the bay window, an unread book in her lap. Their supper of bread and cheese waited on the table.

He sat at her feet and looked up at her. "Did you think about it?"

"Of course I did." She looked out the window. "All right," she said eventually. "All right. I don't like it at all, Elias. But if it's so important to you, then—yes."

Elias reached up to embrace her. She turned her face away.

"You'll see, dearest," he said. "It will benefit us both. I don't want to burden you with my need. We're making a sensible accommodation."

She told herself again she must trust him. Elias knew much more about these things than she did. In time she might come to understand. Meanwhile she would put it out of her mind as much she could. She avoided the thought of what her feminist friends at Wells College might say, and Aunt Charlotte, and her bold invented Ruth.

A year later, more confident and worldly herself, Helen wished she had not acquiesced. Her own life force, or libido, as she had learned to call it, did not seem to be at all lacking. And surely a modern marriage meant more than just sexual license—it meant mutual respect, equality in decision-making and family life, fulfillment in work for both partners. She resented having to wonder, each time Elias traveled, if he would return with a report of a tryst. So far he had not. Perhaps it would never happen. Perhaps knowing he had the freedom was enough in itself.

In the cold moonlight Helen lay still, willing herself to recapture the wellbeing of a minute ago. Elias seemed to sense her unease and stroked her forearm. She reached awkwardly down to the floor and pulled the covers up over both of them. "This baby might be a girl, you know."

Elias curled into her body and fell asleep. I hope it's a girl, Helen thought. She pictured a baby, a little girl, a young woman who would be her and Elias's shared creation. In her drowsy mind her future daughter melded with Ruth the artist. Strong-willed, energetic, beautiful in her own distinctive way. Her life force second to no man's.

Helen sank into a dreamlet of a woman, herself perhaps. The woman is absorbed in something, she's making a musical instrument, fitting delicately carved pieces of wood together with infinite care, oblivious to a crowd of men outside the locked door who call to her that they need her.

7

Baby Rosalind
1911

Helen sat on the carpet with the little girl, who was studying a red and yellow knitted ball with absorption. Her back was as straight as a sapling, her chubby wool-clad legs folded in front of her. Tiny fingers poked at the stripes on the ball, then brought it up to her face for another tasting and biting with four new teeth.

"You're going to have a little boy, dear, with brown eyes just like his father," the English midwife had said to hearten her during the long labor. But then out came this blue-eyed Rosalind, who was now looking up at her mother with a beatific smile.

"Dear little thing!" Helen exclaimed. The baby dropped the ball and waited to be picked up. "Come here," encouraged her mother, "come to your mama!"

Rosalind had recently taken to rocking on all fours but had not yet launched into motion.

"Come!" said Helen again, holding out her arms. But Rosalind just smiled enchantingly. Helen picked her up, nuzzling the warm round cheek before scrambling awkwardly to her feet and positioning the child on her hip. She glanced at her pocket watch. The young nursemaid would be here soon, and she would be able to get back to her study and close the door. Her pages lay there waiting for her like a secret lover, hidden inside a dull brown folder.

As soon as they'd moved to Oxford she had written to offer her services to a London publishing house, suppressing her doubts—could she honestly claim to be a professional translator?

Elias read the draft of her letter and shook his head. "Here, give me the pen," he said, crossing out phrases and adding new ones.

She looked over his shoulder, aghast. "Doesn't this horribly overstate my qualifications?"

"No, Hal, it does not. One has to put one's best foot forward. You have to tell them what a gifted and experienced translator you are."

The publisher, Quest, was known to be eager to cater to the British reading public's newfound interest in German literature. "Your offer has come at exactly the right time," wrote Gilbert Brooks, the editor. "I am taking the liberty of sending you the enclosed short novel in hopes that you will agree to work on it." She was pleased to work on something narrative instead of a technical article. To her surprise the work also engaged her artist self—the aesthetic, creative challenge of making a story in English that would honor the intention of the author, that would draw in a reader and leave a mark of beauty in his or her mind.

Mr. Brooks was delighted with her translation and promptly sent the modest payment they had agreed upon. Two weeks later there was another book: "If you are available, please consider this essay collection, which deserves a translator of your caliber."

But it was not translation work that awaited her in the study. She'd sent off the most recent manuscript to Brooks a week ago without mentioning the fact to Elias—an omission, not exactly a deception. His respectful support for her translation work did not extend to her own writing, which, she'd realized, he viewed as a hobby. He'll change his mind, she thought, once I start publishing.

The nursemaid still came daily, two hours each afternoon. Enough for a delicious week of dalliance with Ruth and Nellie, with four chapters revised and a new section taking form in her mind and urging her to get it on paper. Ruth was now twenty-eight, growing older more slowly than her creator—her privilege as a fictional woman. Her life sometimes took turns that surprised Helen: Ruth was now secretly, wretchedly pregnant. There was no husband, nor the prospect of one. Despite her staunch independence she was in panic. But there was something else as well, altogether unexpected, a profound, peaceful fulfillment; a sense of her female body bearing fruit as it was meant to do. Her paintings had become coded for anyone to see, if they thought to look. But no one did.

This pregnancy will fail, Helen decided. There will be a late, dangerous miscarriage, just as the baby starts to quicken. Cold looks from the doctor and nurses who suspect that this unmarried woman is relieved at the loss of her baby, or, worse, ended her pregnancy deliberately. Ruth will refuse to explain or apologize, her grief masked by her stoic manner. There is a long recovery in the hospital. Her lover, unaware, brings sunflowers and a sketchpad, ready to accept Ruth's vague story of "woman trouble." He does not want to know the bloody details.

Later, perhaps in Ruth's late thirties or early forties, there would be another pregnancy and a child this time, forcing Ruth to a grim choice: she must neglect either her child or her art. Helen did not know yet which it would be. She hated to inflict this grievous dilemma on her heroine. But she must.

Ruth's taunt a few years ago had taken on the force of a deadline. Seven of those ten years were up and Helen was nowhere near finished.

She tried to hold the rush of creative thoughts in her mind. As soon as she could close herself into her study she would write against the clock, scribbling in note form the thoughts and ideas that poured in the minute she allowed them to; slowing down to describe a scene, detail by detail, line by line of dialogue, before the girl knocked on the door to say she was leaving or she heard Rosalind crying in a way that only Mama could cope with.

And tomorrow or the next day another translation would arrive.

She carried Rosalind into the cold kitchen and filled a bottle for her, standing it in a pot of water on the stove to warm. The baby chirruped and reached for it. "Oh, you love your milk, don't you!" said her mother. "Here, how about this?" giving her a crust of bread to gnaw on with her little front teeth. She watched the child with fascination while part of her mind dwelt on pregnant Ruth, who was staring at a fresh canvas, waiting for an image to come into focus. It was not the image of a child, nor a woman, but abstract curves with the suggestion of life burgeoning in watery darkness.

Helen looked at her watch again. Where on earth is the girl?

The astronomer
1912

When her next payment from Quest arrived, Helen reported the amount to Elias as usual. He noted it in his pocket diary with a nod of approval. She'd take it to the bank and—why not?—indulge in a visit to the bookstore. She had Rosalind, so it would be a brief visit. She parked the pram on the sidewalk and carried the child inside in her arms. Rosalind had learned to walk but her mother did not dare to set her down on the dusty wood floor. Havoc would ensue in a moment, with all those lovely big reference books to pull out from the bottom shelves. Helen smiled placatingly at a frowning customer—an elderly man in tweeds who no doubt had never had to run errands accompanied by a small child. Helen was looking for Chekhov's short stories, to learn from the master of the form. Other titles caught her eye but she had to ignore them. One day, she told herself, she'd have enough time and money to pluck anything off the shelf that took her fancy, browse through it, buy it, and take it home to read at her leisure.

Outside she put Rosalind back in the pram and tucked the satin-edged blanket around her. The little girl in her knit bonnet held onto the sides of the pram and looked around, entertained by the bustle on the street. Helen opened the green covers of her purchase and leafed through its pages. For about eighteen seconds she was in Chekhov's Slavic world. Then Rosalind summoned her with a wail—she had dropped her toy pony overboard.

Helen picked it up and walked on. There were more errands to be done, the greengrocer, the cobbler for Elias's shoes. High

Street in mid-morning was populated by women with shopping baskets over their arms. Some were pushing prams. The younger ones did so with a proud look; the older ones—her own age, since she was old to be the mother of a first child—with lines of weariness in their faces and other small children in tow. Helen thought of the irritated professor in the bookstore. In a tearoom, when she was eight months pregnant, another man had looked up from his soup and muttered, "They breed like rabbits around here," his disgusted gaze going from herself to another woman drinking her tea with a toddler on her lap and an infant in a pram. Flushed with humiliation and rage, Helen had gathered up her bags and fled. With her visible pregnancy she was seen, she knew, as a biological entity only. A mother. A breeder. Not a person, not a thinker or a worker.

Walking along with the pram Helen wondered if she was guilty of the same prejudice. Sternly, she set herself a thought experiment: she would imagine every woman she saw as someone with an active life of the mind, someone who was observing and thinking as she went about her business; an educated person, a political person, a courageous person, an artist, perhaps, or a scientist. A person whose children had not reduced her to motherhood alone, any more than a man was defined by fatherhood alone, his other identities and accomplishments occluded the instant his child was born.

A woman pushed a pram toward her. She was short, plump, young, wearing a paisley headscarf against the fresh spring wind. She squinted with absorption, breaking into a quick smile when she leant down and murmured to her child, whom Helen couldn't see. All right, Helen thought, as the woman drew nearer. You were studying astronomy before you became pregnant. You intend to complete your degree when this little one starts school in a few years, and you hope that the next baby does not arrive before then. Meanwhile you devour articles in your field and attend public lectures when you can. You have a telescope in your backyard and you look at the sky on clear nights when the child is asleep. You look forward to telling your daughter about the stars. You'll teach her that women can be scientists, or anything they want.

Helen was ready to nod and smile at the feminist astronomer as they passed but the woman did not see her.

She turned the corner onto St. Aldates and paused to look at the entrance to the Town Hall, where notices of events were posted. As if in response to her train of thought, a sign caught her eye:

National Union of Women's Suffrage Societies
Oxford branch.
OPEN MEETING
For all interested men and women.
Wednesday, April 24, 8:00pm.
Tea provided.

"Well!" said Helen aloud. The baby looked up at her. "What do you think about women's suffrage, Rosie?" Rosalind babbled earnestly in response. "Shall I go along? Demand the vote for all of us?" She was curious to know who attended such things: perhaps the young astronomer would be there.

9

Aladdin's cave
1913

The burgeoning British taste for German fiction was a stroke of luck. Elias was paid little in spite of the academic recognition he continued to receive. Flattering invitations to lecture and research at hallowed European libraries were seldom accompanied by more than a small honorarium. Elias did not consider refusing them. The reward for these invitations was not monetary.

"It is like being shown into Aladdin's cave, Hal," he said to her. He placed another block on Rosalind's wobbly tower. "There! High as the sky, Rosie!" His task was to keep the little girl amused while Helen folded shirts and stacked them in his small leather suitcase, already festooned with travel labels. Elias was soon to leave for another stint at the Biblioteca Vaticana. "Imagine! A huge high-ceilinged room with dim lighting to preserve the manuscripts, stained glass windows, the librarians with their hushed voices and solemn manner, like priests. They bring me one treasure after another—these magnificent documents written by someone who's been dead for a thousand years. And I'm free to penetrate their secrets as deeply as I want, for as long as I want."

Helen paused in her folding, arrested by his choice of verb. Elias did not notice, still savoring the image he had created. What else—*who* else—might Elias penetrate while exploring those treasure caves? The librarians are men, she reminded herself. Priests, as he says, or monks, many of them. But she knew that Elias in his exalted state would meet a woman somewhere, a serious but attractive assistant perhaps, or an Italian graduate student with a sultry voice, and the life force would engulf him. And then he'd come home and report to her.

"Hal," he'd begun in a tender and solicitous tone after his last trip. She knew what was coming. "There was a moment, dear. A life-force moment. A red-haired young lady from Scotland, very bright, doing her own research at the library. There was a sudden downpour. I had an umbrella, she didn't, and ..."

Helen held up her hand. "Thank you," she said. "You don't need to explain more." And he stopped, his pleasurable memory evident on his face. Helen poured the tea and cut slices of homecoming cake, the familiar pain flaring.

The fellowships were in her interest as well as his, she admonished herself. It was an article of faith that they shared: that his research would eventually lead to academic success and financial security for their family. He was not naive or passive about it. As often as he could he met with people of influence—senior professors, eminent writers and intellectuals—to learn where there might be sources of support for a scholar engaged in the kind of major research he wanted to carry out. No one had ever attempted the comprehensive cataloguing of ancient Latin manuscripts that he planned. He studied the huge American foundations and slowly, patiently, he courted them. "It is a matter of time and persistence," he told Helen. "I have every reason to believe that my work merits support."

Elias's horizons were vast. She must not fetter him with mundane jealousy.

And his absences freed her. Alone with baby Rosalind, who was happy as long as her mama was in sight, she could let her mind branch and meander. There was a sort of sequence, she had understood, an alchemical process that starts with a vision, a perception, followed by the painstaking effort to find the words that would communicate it to others, and finally, an offering, a gift to be given. The effort required courage and blind faith—foolish faith, perhaps. One could fail wretchedly at any point along the journey. The vision could be unworthy. The right words could elude capture. A finished work might never reach its audience, the gift ungiven and unreceived.

It's my fate, she mused. I don't have a choice, however talented or not I might be. I simply must do it. And surely this is an expression of the life force, this imperative to do one's chosen work. Elias is wrong. It's not only men who have it.

10

Pre-prandial sherry
1963

It must be nearly lunchtime—time for a little pre-prandial libation. With an effort she yanked the cork out of the bottle of sherry. She didn't want to think about where it came from. She held the bottle up to the window and squinted at the label, which said nothing about Elias. Well then. I'm drinking the sherry of Mr. Ximenez. *Gracias, Señor. Me gusta mucho.* She poured half an inch. In the stemmed glass the sherry glowed in the dim sunshine. It was very good indeed. She took another sip in order to examine its taste, the feel of it in her mouth. Cool and warm at the same time. A layer of pungent sweetness above a deeper layer of astringency. She patted her pockets for the index card and stub of a pencil that she kept close to hand. There was something already written on the card, from yesterday. She squinted at her cramped handwriting.

> *How old does one have to be before one stops wanting?*
> *The woman who cries for her mother at night.*

Oh yes. She remembered the crying. Sometimes it woke her in the dark, for a moment thinking she was in Bedlam again. And then remembering, her heartbeat steadying, that Bedlam was years ago, in another country. It wasn't Bedlam, they insisted. A nice place, a nice hospital, for people like you who just need a little rest, Mrs. Lowe. All right, not Bedlam, but bad enough, she thought. Bars on the windows. Wretchedness on every side.

She wanted to describe the sherry. *Like dark brown silk,* she wrote. *Silk charmeuse, lustrous and sinuous.*

She had a blouse of that brown charmeuse once. Elias had given her an amber necklace to wear with it and kissed the nape of her neck when he fastened it on her.

> *Like warmed wildflower honey.*
> *Like a field of autumn wheat in Spain.*
> *Like the viola in the Sinfonia Concertante.*

She poured a little more into the glass. Her replenished supply imparted a sense of expansiveness, wealth almost. But if Elias thought he could ingratiate himself with sherry he was mistaken. Poor Elias. He's been trying for years. He doesn't understand. He never did understand, not at all.

Helen made an effort to hold onto lucidity, after her mistake about the baby. She remembered the last time she'd seen Elias, when she'd agreed to receive him for a visit. She was shocked how old he was–bald, shrunken, frail. But still wearing his mantle of fame and success. Still the fulcrum of attention. No doubt he still had young women at his feet. She had no wish to see him again.

A knock on the door startled her. Mrs. D put her head around the door. Her lipstick was painted outside the edges of her lips like a clown. Helen mentally added a bulbous red nose. "You must be hungry after missing your breakfast, Mrs. Lowe. Come and have lunch with us. We've got a nice baked fish for you in the dining room." She looked beyond Helen toward the windowsill. "You've had a little drink, I see."

Helen ignored the admonitory note in the woman's voice. She considered the idea of baked fish, finding it rather appealing, and weighed it up against the distinctly unappealing prospect of sitting in the dining room with her toothless fellow-inmates.

"With potatoes or rice?" she asked.

"Potatoes. Baked."

A baked potato, steaming hot, butter melting into it. Her stomach gave a sudden growl.

"All right," she said, and followed Mrs. D down the hall.

The others were already crouched over their plates raising slow forks to their mouths when she came in. No one was talking. She ignored them and sat down at the smaller table.

The old man to her left cleared his throat lengthily and put down his fork. "Mrs. Lowe?"

She turned to him, surprised.

"Helen? May I call you Helen?"

Some inkling of manners returned to her. "Yes, of course." He was holding out a trembling hand. She shook it. He seemed to think she should know his name. But he did not seem familiar and no name came to her.

"I'm sorry..."

"Clifford Sims. We met a few times. At the Institute, years ago."

"Oh yes, of course." She still had no recollection of him. "How nice to see you again."

"Yes, I've recently come here to Mrs. D's. How is your husband?"

She forced herself to smile, as though she had a husband and knew how he was. "He's very well," she said, hoping this would shut him up. And, fortunately, Clifford Sims returned to his plate of fish and white sauce. Eating takes all our concentration, she thought, us old crocks. The logistics of it. The regressive pleasure of it.

At least he didn't call me Hal, she mused, releasing the baked potato from its foil jacket. It was enormous, far more than she could eat. She applied a generous lump of butter to each half and murmured the two names aloud while maneuvering a chunk of potato onto her fork.

Hal.

Helen.

No one heard, too absorbed in their masticating and swallowing, and most of them deaf as posts as well. The buttery potato was delicious.

She did not feel like a Hal. She never had. It was Elias's determined fantasy of her, a person who was a good sport and had a mind like a man's, and also, conveniently, the physical attributes of a woman. A sort of custom-designed hermaphrodite. She frowned and shook her head. "Is something wrong?" said the young helper, starting to clear away the plates. Helen smiled to reassure the girl, her mouth full.

"Who's ready for dessert?" asked Mrs. D. "Apple pie à la mode!"

Helen pushed herself to her feet, ankles creaking. Clifford Sims put down his fork and wiped his mouth with the mauve napkin. "Helen, a pleasure to see you again. Perhaps I'll see you again at dinner. Or the crossword this afternoon."

She nodded with what she hoped was a gracious but noncommittal smile and escaped back to her room. Crossword puzzles as a group activity was a foolish pastime in which she had no intention of engaging. Besides, the other inmates considered her unfair competition, with her exceptional vocabulary and general knowledge. That was clear, from the glares she'd earned the one time she'd participated.

And no, she wouldn't appear for dinner. The fish and potato were more than enough sustenance for the day.

11

Hyde Park
1913

Helen arrived at the station just in time to find the last seat in the ladies' waiting room. She smiled at the grey-haired woman who had gathered up her skirts to make space for her—Mrs. Melrose from the Suffrage Society meetings.

"Good for you, dear," said Mrs. Melrose. "I don't think I'd be doing this in your condition."

"I'll be all right," said Helen. She looked around. Women of all ages and sizes, respectable matrons and working women, a few female students. No one else visibly pregnant. Many of the women were dressed in white, some with large signboards clasped awkwardly to their chests or under their arms. Helen tilted her head to read one of them, carefully written in an ornate script:

> *Over the Pass of By-and-By*
> *You go to the Valley of Never*

She nodded, liking the presence of poetry. And whoever had written that was absolutely right, she thought. Those men would pat us on the head forever, promising that the day will come. But it never will unless we demand it. Unless we disturb their comfort. Other signs were more direct: "Votes for Women" repeated on the sashes that diagonally crossed coats and dresses.

The door kept opening. Women stepped in and looked around, some smiling, some with solemn determination, others shy and uncertain. There were no more seats. The spaces between the wooden benches filled up with women standing.

Conversations multiplied, voices raised in order to be heard. The room grew stuffy and hot. Someone opened the one small window.

Mrs. Melrose took out her pocket watch and frowned. "We've still ten minutes to wait," she said to nobody in particular. She dabbed her forehead with her handkerchief. "I'm going outside."

Helen watched her inch her way to the door, squeezing between backs and bosoms, stepping carefully over boots and skirt hems. Two more women were entering as she reached the door.

"Ladies!" Mrs. Melrose called over her shoulder, loudly enough to pierce the jumble of conversations. "Let's wait on the platform!"

There was a startled pause. Then a chorus of laughter. "Yes! And why should we not?"

They poured out into the fresh morning sunshine, past the large framed sign that instructed ladies to stay in the waiting room.

At Paddington, rivers of women were converging from every platform, now holding their signs aloft in triumph. There was an unmistakable smell of victory in the air. How can we not win, Helen thinks, so many of us, so righteous a cause. Gaining the vote in England would not mean a vote for herself, an American citizen. But in America the women were marching too.

Along the arteries of London, a female tide flowed towards Hyde Park. Helen felt like a cell in an immense body, her individuality subsumed in it. The streets seemed transformed from their usual selves, trams and carriages and cars replaced by women walking six or eight abreast down the middle of the road, as far ahead and as far behind as she could see. A treble chant rose up: "Votes for women! Votes for women!" The chant pealed for a while and then died down, replaced by a marching song that

45

Helen had learned at the meetings. "Shoulder to shoulder and friend to friend!" she sang, her voice lost in the voice of the crowd.

Elias had not wanted her to go. The absurd words "I forbid you!" quivered between them, almost but not quite spoken. "You are the mother of a small child, Hal! You are nearly seven months pregnant!" This he did say aloud, his face flushed.

Was he really concerned about her welfare, or was he disturbed at the idea of women taking political action?

"I'm going, Elias. This is important. For our children too. Nancy will come at nine o'clock and stay until I get back. You won't have to disrupt your day." She tried to keep her voice free of sarcasm.

Now, walking a little more slowly along the packed streets, she was grateful for her own determination. He will recover, she thought. Once I'm back safely. Sometimes he just needs firm handling. She glanced around, wondering how many of these women had had to argue with their menfolk. A few lucky ones had their husbands with them, supporters, presumably, of votes for all men, not just property-owners, as well as for women. She could not imagine Elias out on the street, for this or any other cause.

A chant rose up again. She became aware of someone beside her shouting lustily and turned to look at her: a tall, well-built woman perhaps ten years younger than herself, hatless, frizzy reddish-blond hair falling out of its pins. "*We demand the vote! We demand the vote!*" she shouted in iambic unison with the others. Helen could not join in—her breath was already a little short. The young woman caught her eye and grinned. "Don't worry, love, I'm loud enough for the both of us." She glanced quickly at Helen's round belly. "Keep your breath for baby." Helen felt the girl's arm thread through hers. The intimacy from a stranger startled her. But the arm imparted strength. It all seemed part of this extraordinary day, where the usual rules and customs were suspended. Women bursting out of station waiting rooms and onto open platforms. Women pouring down the middle of Sussex Place, shouting and singing in public.

"Helen Porter," she said, turning to offer her hand and trying to make herself heard over the chanting. She hadn't spoken her name without the "Loew" for nearly three years. The young woman bent down to hear, then shook her hand, smiling.

"Pauline Mackie from Carlisle," she said. "We've been marching for nearly a month. Look!" She pointed at three women on horseback. Behind them others carried a tall banner: "Suffragists Pilgrimage: Carlisle to London." Miss Mackie had a red haversack on her back with the same slogan. Helen had read about the women walking to London from all parts of the country, through towns and villages. People came out to cheer them, but others to insult them, even attack them physically. She looked at her new companion with increased interest.

"And what about you, Mrs. Porter? How long have you been fighting for the vote?"

" 'Helen,' please." She started to speak about her belief all her life, fostered by Aunt Charlotte, that women were equal to men and deserved equal rights, including the franchise, and now, as the mother of a little girl.... She stopped, seeing her new friend grinning at her in delight.

"You're an American!" said Pauline.

When they reached Hyde Park Pauline shouldered her way to the wide plinth of a statue already covered with suffragists. "My friend here needs to sit down," she said, and the women made room for them. Helen found a surprising pleasure in surrendering to this bossiness. The marble felt cool and solid beneath her. It was good to sit.

Pauline drew a paper bag from her haversack and offered it to her. "Toffees, dear," she said. "To keep us going."

Far across the park, across an ocean of women and a few men, they could see the small figures of the speakers in front of a huge banner proclaiming "Law-Abiding Suffragists" lest anyone mistake them for the militant, upper-class suffragettes. Their voices were lost, but their rallying cries were repeated in waves:

"Votes for women!"

"Votes for women!"

"We demand the franchise!"

"We demand the franchise!"

And then at one point: "Sisters, we are fifty thousand strong!" The number was repeated by hundreds of raised voices. Fifty thousand suffragists! Helen looked up at Pauline, her eyes shining. "This is how we will win!" she said. "So many of us, gathering peacefully, all kinds of women together! Much better than rich ladies burning houses and smashing shop windows."

"Oh, I don't know," said Pauline. "We need it all." Then she laughed at Helen's expression. "No, love, I wasn't with that lot on Regent Street, with a silver hammer in my muff. Can you see me with a fancy fur muff?"

Helen could not.

12

Elias and the beanstalk
1915

Elias was in New York, not only lecturing but meeting with someone at the Rockefeller Foundation—a triumph, to get this appointment, but he had little hope yet of a grant. "They make you crawl to them on your knees for years before they part with a penny," he'd complained.

Now there were two little girls to feed, amuse, soothe into sleep. When all else failed Helen told them a story, her soft, singsong voice beguiling them.

"Once upon a time, children, there was a clever young man called Elias—just like your daddy—who decided that he wanted to grow a very large beanstalk, the largest beanstalk that had ever been seen. He had exactly the right seeds for it, rare as they were. They'd been given to him because he was so very clever and good. And he had a patch of ground with just the right kind of soil. All he needed was some magic fertilizer, and lots of it. That means food for the seeds. Special food, sometimes called money. Giant beanstalks take a great deal of feeding. (Here, Rosalind, here's your Teddy, look, he's almost asleep! You could pet his head, just like this.)

"Elias was eager to see his beanstalk grow. He searched everywhere for the storehouses of fertilizer. At last he found one. He knocked on the huge wooden door. After a few minutes, the door opened and a giant stood there. Politely, using fine words polished like rubies, Elias asked if he could have some of the magic fertilizer. The giant looked into the distance and tapped his bristly chin thoughtfully. 'Hmm,' he said. 'Those are very fine words.' Then he then shook his head. 'No,' he said. 'Not yet.

49

Keep working hard. Perhaps later.' And the giant closed the door with a click.

"So Elias kept working hard, and every now and then he went back to ask again. He looked for other storehouses of magic fertilizer as well. They were all guarded by giants, and they all said the same thing: 'No. Keep working. Ask us again in a few years.'

"Once or twice they were kind enough to hand him a small bag to take home. It wasn't enough to help even an ordinary beanstalk grow, let alone a very large one, but he was grateful and encouraged. If they're willing to give me a little now, he would tell his wife, they will surely give me more later on.

"His wife was proud of him and made him a cake each time he came home empty-handed, to make him feel better. Their little girls sat on his lap and kissed him tenderly. (Yes, that's you, dearie! And you too, my little Alice!)

"Elias knew that one day he would get the magic fertilizer that he needed. He deserved it, and he was not a person to give up. All he had to do was keep working and keep asking. One day they would say yes, and his beanstalk would burst up from the ground and soar to the sky, with a trunk like an oak, broad green leaves, and fat, long, juicy green beans. Such as the world had never seen."

She looked from one little face to the other. Both sets of eyelids were closed tight. She tucked the covers around them and tiptoed downstairs. Elias would get his magic fertilizer one day, of that she had no doubt.

13

Wartime crossing
1917

It was like a ghost ship, not a living soul visible, not a scrap of light escaping from any porthole, the only sign of life the mighty engines pulsing below the swirling sea. Passengers were forbidden on deck after dark—"For your safety, ladies"—but Helen crept outside when the two little girls were sound asleep in their bunks. Safety, she thought—there is no such thing any more, neither at home with the ground shaking from the shelling across the Channel, and bombs falling randomly anywhere, in London and outside it; nor out on this vast ocean where any second an enemy submarine might nose above the surface. No one ever spoke the word "Lusitania" but it hung in the air between the tense faces of the women and over the heads of the children they were shepherding back to America.

She stood holding the railing, her dark coat billowing around her. The restless salt-smelling air and the ship's oily tang exhilarated her. She watched the churning greenish-white wake as the ship cut through the black swells. It had sailed in the darkest week of the month and the splinter of a new moon had set already, but the stars were out, brilliant in a vast sky. Helen shivered, but not from cold or fear. Far behind was her little house in Oxford, and Elias in his study, and the children's room left lifeless and tidy. A thousand miles ahead was her sister Elizabeth's safe world on the banks of the Hudson River. But here, half way between, there was nothing. In the windy dark, without the children in constant orbit, without a husband at her elbow, without her anxious fellow-passengers and their self-interrupted sentences, Helen felt herself a neutral being, not a mother, not a wife, not even a woman, just a consciousness, eyes, skin, and ears, akin somehow to the stars wheeling above and the roiling sea below.

Inside her the new child stirred. She pressed one hand to her six-months belly and felt the child push back. You'll be a little American, she said silently to him or her. A Lowe, not a Loew, thanks to Elias's recent adroit anglicizing of the name—Jewish and German connotations both purged with the switch of two letters.

We'll go back to England, little baby Lowe, when this frightful madness is over, if it ever is. No one had thought it could possibly go on so long. Perhaps it will end soon, with the United States finally sending troops.

Helen thought of Pauline, her comrade in the suffragist battles and now a dear friend. Pauline was now in Serbia looking after wounded soldiers. She thought of the terrible funerals in Oxford, one after another, the next generation of thinkers and leaders blasted to bits in the trenches. She thought of the aging generals, safe in their fortifications, who would keep ordering the cannons to be fired until they'd used up the last young men in the world. In Kings Cross she had watched a battalion of soldiers singing heartily as they marched, bursting with life and youth and pride, on their way to being slaughtered at the front. She tried to push aside her fury, for the child's sake.

When she picked up the newspaper from Elizabeth's doorstep and saw the headline from England, Helen inexplicably thought of apple pie. It was not until later when she read the article aloud to Elizabeth—the five older children playing upstairs and baby Marjorie asleep—that she remembered. She and Pauline were at a suffrage society meeting in London, before the war. The speaker, an excitable Scottish lady with red cheeks and a contagious energy, challenged them all:

"Ladies, what are you going to do when the franchise is finally passed? Because that day will come, I promise you!"

"Bake an apple pie!" shouted Pauline without a moment's hesitation.

Helen gaped at her—Pauline was the least housewifely woman she knew. She'd never known her to cook anything more ambitious than toast and scrambled eggs. Pauline had stared her down with mock defiance until they both burst into laughter.

And now Pauline was somewhere in the hellish chaos of Europe. If she was still alive. In any case, she would not be baking any pies. She probably wouldn't even know that this momentous thing had happened, that the British Parliament had at last granted the vote to women, at least partially. In the face of women's valiant service during four years of war it had become unthinkable for them to refuse yet again. It was an enormous victory, if not yet complete.

"Do you have any apples?" she asked her sister, the embodiment of housewifeliness.

Elizabeth had apples from her own small orchard, stored in her cellar since the fall.

"Lizzie," said Helen as they peeled and chopped together, "do you remember the hammock?"

Elizabeth stopped, her paring knife aloft. "Yes! You were forever down there in the apple trees. Mother used to shout herself hoarse trying to get you to answer her."

"Poor Mother! I was rather a disobedient girl, wasn't I? But I loved those apple trees so much. And in the springtime…" She paused, picturing clouds of pale blossom, trying to summon the delicious fragrance. "All I wanted was to lie in the hammock and inhale."

Elizabeth made the pastry. She produced a few spoonfuls of sugar from a secret supply and stirred it into the sliced apples, supplementing with maple syrup. "From our neighbor," she said.

They sprinkled in nutmeg, clove, cinnamon. The pie smelled divine as it baked, making their mouths water. It emerged from the oven enticing and perfect, the crust slightly brown and crisp, aromatic steam rising through the little vents that Elizabeth had cut in the pastry.

Helen pulled off her apron and played a drum roll on the kitchen table with two wooden spoons. The children clattered down the stairs. "Ooh!" they chorused when they saw the beautiful apple pie. Helen and Elizabeth settled them into chairs around the table, the two little Lowes and Elizabeth's three, William and the twins Essie and Jenny, all of them bouncing with excitement. Sweet treats were rare in wartime. Baby Marjorie woke from her nap and Elizabeth retrieved her, murmuring in her infant niece's little ear.

"This is a notable day, children!" said Helen. "In England, women finally have the vote! Do you know what that means?"

They did not, of course.

"Well, my dearies, it means that women and men, not just men by themselves, are going to make all the important decisions together from now on. At least in Britain."

"And very soon here as well, I'm sure," said Elizabeth. She did not march in the street but she kept a close eye on the campaign for women's suffrage.

"You and your kind," Helen went on, pointing a wooden spoon at 10-year old William, the only male in the house—"will no longer have to do it all on your own. Isn't that a wonderful thing?"

"May we have some apple pie, Mummy?" asked Rosalind.

"Yes, you may!" With a knife Helen cut the pie in half. "Men," she said, pointing to one side of it. "And women." She pointed to the other side. Then she sliced a section of the women's half. "Is that about forty per cent, do you think?" she asked. The children looked at her, puzzled. No one answered. She sliced the smaller section into six slivers and gave one to everyone except William. "You, William, get the rest!"

There was an indignant outcry from all the girls.

"Don't worry, girls, don't worry! I'm just making a point." Helen cut the rest of the pie and distributed it with utmost fairness. "Yes, women in England have the vote at last, and that is excellent news. But not all women. Just forty per cent of them—not even half! Only women over thirty"—"Like you, Mummy!"—"and only if they own property or their husbands do." She looked around the table. Mouths blissfully full, the children were listening. She wanted them to remember this. "On the other hand, all the men over twenty-one can now vote. *All* of them."

"That's not fair!" said six-year-old Alice. "No, it's not fair," echoed the twins. William, reaching for a morsel of pastry that had fallen onto the table, said nothing.

"Are you going to make them fix it?" asked Rosalind.

"Yes, indeed!" said Helen. "Once the war is over we'll start fighting again. Until every woman and every man can vote."

She wrote in triumph to Elias, still in Oxford: "At last! So you see, we didn't march in vain."

He wrote back: "I do congratulate you! But surely you realize that Parliament's vote had little to do with the suffragists and everything to do with the exigencies of wartime." There was a handwritten postscript under his typed letter: "Hal dearest, I miss you very much, body and soul. And the children too." He had not yet met his youngest daughter. "The war must come to an end soon, and you'll come home."

At the station
1921

Helen was to meet with Gilbert Brooks to discuss a new book, the first one since the war. Gilbert thought it was time to begin investing again in German writing, though it was a gamble. "I am willing to try it," he wrote, "as long as we have your fine translation. Let us be hopeful about the open-mindedness of our readers." Helen had become fond of Gilbert, especially since learning that he'd been a militant suffragist who put noxious chemicals into pillar-boxes to disrupt the Royal Mail.

She and Elias took the train to London together. Helen would return to Oxford in time for supper with the children while Elias traveled on to the Continent. The green Chilterns sped by, blurred by the fogged window. Three full weeks before he would return. They were silent in the carriage. Elias pressed his thigh to hers. His hand found her gloved hand and held it tightly. Paddington was dim with the diffused light of the great translucent ceiling. Passengers bustled past. On the platform, the tall engine spewing steam and din, they clung to each other, not caring who might frown at their demonstrativeness or be perplexed by this couple, much too old for passion. Did that tight-mouthed woman under the purple hat imagine that they were adulterers?

The train was ready to depart. Elias held her face between his hands. "My dearest," he said, his eyes damp behind his glasses. "My darlingest," she whispered.

In her study she found the gift he had left for her, as he always did: a glass bowl of fruit, fresh figs if they were in season. It was a language between them. She read in it what he meant her to read, a wordless homage and promise.

The package
1923

Helen recognized the postman's sharp rap on the front door. Something for Elias, she thought, too big to put through the slot. Marjorie scampered down the stairs, dragging one-armed Browny Bear behind her. "Who is it, Mummy?"

The large package, half covered with stamps, was addressed to Helen. "Quick, open it!" said Marjorie, pulling at the string and sealing wax that held it together. She'd learned that stamp-covered packages occasionally contained lovely things from Aunt Elizabeth in America—a children's book, or matching pinafores for Marjorie and her big sisters. But Helen had already seen the return address in New York. "Go and play, dear," she said. "It's nothing exciting." Not exciting for the child, but Helen's own heart was tumbling. The little girl hovered beside her. Helen laid the package on the tapestry that covered the dining table. She found scissors and cut it open it carefully, revealing first a long cream-colored envelope bearing the distinctive Knopf colophon, a slender dog leaping inside an oval.

"Just a letter," said the child, disappointed. "What's that?" She pounced on two books underneath. Helen pushed her hand away. "Wait, Hedgehog," she said, taking up the letter.

"Dear Mrs. Lowe," it began. "Thank you for your patience during our recent correspondence. At this point we are very happy to engage your services to bring the enclosed work of Thomas Mann to an English-speaking readership, at last."

She stopped reading and stared out the window. Next door Miss Butler was hanging out sheets in defiance of the threatening rain.

Thomas Mann!

"Knopf in New York has bought the rights to Thomas Mann's work," Gilbert Brooks had told her a few months ago in London. "They're looking for a translator. I'm going to recommend you, if I may." She had expressed flattered willingness though immediately a debate erupted inside her. Was she in fact equipped for such a task? Her translations of lesser writers had been well received. And she had become confident of her skills. Translation engaged both her meticulous mind and her artist's bent.

But Mann! He was a literary giant. The responsibility would be immense, not to mention the amount of work—his novels were massive in length as well as importance. She had read some of his work, though not the novel, *Buddenbrooks*, now lying on her dining table in two volumes. She knew of it: a portrait of a family and an era, possibly autobiographical. It had been published twenty years before but never in English.

It was like being asked to bring Shakespeare to readers who did not yet know him. An overwhelming honor. An enormous challenge. And irresistible.

Helen sat down at the table. She put aside the letter and opened the first volume's stiff covers. Lively dialogue, minutely detailed description, short chapters and lengthy paragraphs. The two volumes together must be close to eight hundred pages, far more than she'd ever tackled in a single work. She tried to calculate: it would take her well over a year. What would they pay her? Helen looked again at the letter, but in his gentlemanly way Mr. Knopf did not specify— "...commensurate with your experience..." She hoped it would be a reasonable sum. She knew she would not ask for more.

Marjorie now clamped to her side, Helen turned back to the first page and read the opening lines, drawn instantly into Mann's invented world. It was the unmistakable voice of a master. I would learn so much, she thought, he would teach me about writing. But *can* I do it? Can I take this on?

She was surprised by a yearning in herself, akin to the creative yearning to write her own stories. She could even bear—she realized with surprise—having to put Ruth and Nellie aside for a while to immerse herself in this translation; to engage with the prodigious mind that had produced these pages.

Helen gathered up the package and carried it up the steep stairs, Marjorie prattling at her heels. Elias was bent over his desk and did not immediately turn when they entered his study. The room was chilly and he was wearing his tweed jacket and a scarf. His hair, thinning now, stood up in tufts where he had rubbed at it furiously—she had seen him do it a thousand times. Helen held out the books to him without a word, then the letter. He raised his eyebrows at her with a questioning smile, then read the letter. Marjorie tugged at his waistcoat. "Can I read it, Daddy?" She'd recently learned to decipher a few words in her storybooks and believed she could and should read everything. Elias ignored her.

"Hal," he said. "My cleverest girl. This is quite a coup." He leafed through one of the books, peering at the text. "You're going to be very busy indeed."

"But Elias—do you think I should say yes? Really? Do you think I can do it?"

"Of course, you can, Hal! And you must! This is a tremendous opportunity. You'll see." Elias pushed his chair back and stood up, giving her a hearty kiss. He stretched his cramped shoulders. "We'll have a cup of tea to celebrate. And a cream bun for Marjorie." He rumpled the little girl's hair and she squirmed in pleasure.

The headiness of signing the contract was soon replaced by the sheer intensity of the work. Every day she grappled with Mann's language, his precisely chosen verbs and nouns and adjectives, his metaphors and allusions, his surprising wit and satire. She strongly suspected the characters represented his own family members—how did they feel to be depicted here, not always kindly?

It was painstaking work. Often she consulted her shelf of German dictionaries to gain a parallax view of a word's possible meanings and connotations, parlaying a phrase into literal but infelicitous English, then, later, coming back to lift it into a literary style that she hoped did justice to Mann's.

She turned to Chapter 3, still describing the large family gathering that opened the book:

> Der jüngere Hausherr hatte, als der allgemeine Aufbruch begann, mit der Hand nach der linken Brustseite gegriffen, wo ein Papier knisterte, das gesellschaftliche Lächeln war plötzlich von seinem Gesicht verschwunden, um einem gespannten und besorgten Ausdruck Platz zu machen, und an seinen Schläfen spielten, als ob er die Zähne aufeinanderbisse, ein paar Muskeln.

Clear enough. Something on that piece of paper—the reader does not yet know—is seriously bothering Herr Buddenbrook. She wrote the exact English for Mann's phrases:

> The younger master of the house, when the general departure had begun, had grasped the left side of his breast where a paper was rustling, the social smile had suddenly vanished from his face to give way to a tense and worried expression, and was playing with his temples, as if clenching his teeth, a few muscles.

I need to remind readers who "the younger master" is, she thought. "Left side of his breast"? Breast pocket, surely. And let's make it clear that they're all headed to the dining room, as we know from the end of the last chapter. No need for the "as if". We know he's indeed clenching his teeth, poor man.

When she had the whole chapter translated she came back to the beginning. She relished this more creative step—rendering it in English that readers would actually follow.

> As the party began to move toward the dining-room, Consul Buddenbrook's hand went to his left breast-pocket and fingered a paper that was inside. The polite smile had left his face, giving way to a strained and care-worn look, and the muscles stood out on his temples as he clenched his teeth.

She felt it in her own body, on her own face: the Consul's worry, the burden he carried and had not yet shared.

Slowly, slowly the novel in English took form, a weighty saga of pride, ambition, and relentless tragedy across generations of this bourgeois family in the city where Mann was born. She became fond of some of the characters: the flighty sister who makes one disastrous decision after another; the tiny humpbacked schoolmistress whose moral stature gradually becomes apparent; the gifted youth who meets a tragic end.

Helen marveled at Mann's skill and his boldness. The sheer scope of the novel would daunt most writers, certainly herself. I know I'm learning a lot, she thought, steeping myself in his words and his narrative confidence. And yet there was something that repelled her as well, an analytical coldness towards his characters. It made her yearn for her own. Oh, dear Ruth! Oh Nellie! I'll come back to you soon.

The work left her with a laborer's sweaty, satisfying fatigue. But with every page she wondered if she was doing justice to the original. The author's own anxiety was all too palpable in her imagination—his forced dependence on the integrity and skills of someone he doesn't even know. How awful it must be for him, she thought, how dreadful! Her translation would either enable him to reach a vast new audience or miserably, publicly fail to do so. The stakes could not be higher.

It was not long before Mann's letters to the publisher and then to herself bore out her fears. He wrote in formal, diplomatic German of his doubts and his impatience. Why could she not produce the translated pages more quickly? Some of the locutions in the novel were highly sophisticated—was she quite sure she had understood? At one point he rewrote a lengthy passage that she'd already translated and sent it without apology, even urging her to hurry with this revision. In exasperation she complained to Knopf. Mrs. Knopf, his wife and business partner, responded with respectful understanding. Helen allowed herself to be placated.

Helen Tracy Porter. My original name, my maiden name, my maiden self.

Hal. Elias's invention of an androgynous partner.

Mrs. Lowe. Elias's wife, my children's mother. It will do, if you are a neighbor, a grocer, or a headmistress. Don't, however, try "Mrs. Elias Lowe," the obliteration of my personhood.

Helen Porter Lowe. A demure assertion that I have not forgotten my origins.

Helen Lowe-Porter. A less demure assertion.

H.T. Lowe-Porter. Writer and translator. My gender is none of your business.

> Dear Mr. Knopf,
>   I trust this finds you well.
>   As to the matter of my name in the published translation (and any subsequent): I ask to be identified as H.T. Lowe-Porter. I think it better,

and I'm sure you'll agree, to obscure the fact that Mann's translator is female.

For our private correspondence, I do not object to your addressing me as "Mrs. Lowe." (Though I invite you to call me Helen if you wish.) But I prefer "Lowe-Porter" as my professional surname.

Yours,
Helen Lowe-Porter

Dear Mr. Knopf,

Thank you for accepting my request.

To answer your question: my husband has no objection to "Lowe-Porter" rather than "Porter Lowe." Though it would be immaterial to me, and I trust to you, if he did.

Yours,
Helen Lowe-Porter

16

In the mountain's shadow
1963

Helen woke up on the bed, on top of the covers. She had kicked her shoes off and her feet were icy. A nap, evidently. A consequence of sherry and then lunch, which she thought she recalled eating in the dining room. She sat up on the edge of the bed and bent down stiffly to wriggle into her shoes. She stared at the bookshelf, her gaze moving slowly past the novels and poetry and essays in four languages—a fragment of her lifelong collection, now strewn in her trail like scat; past the two small volumes with her own name on their narrow spines, up to the empty shelf. So soothing it was, that emptiness. Like silence after stentorian music. Let Marjorie have Mann's books, if she managed to retrieve them from Mr. D. Marjorie had driven off in her large black car, back to the husband who dominated and indulged her. Visiting her father on the way, perhaps, in his enclave of great minds. Was he still in the house they'd shared at one time, with its comforts and discreet help, and that ridiculous garage no doubt inhabited by his latest expensive car?

"Daddy would love to see you, Mother," Marjorie had tried once more, her voice casual, buttoning her coat and patting her hair in the mirror. "You could let him come, just a cup of tea, perhaps."

Helen ignored this. "Take the shortbread for your drive," she said, thrusting the tin at her daughter.

She'd got rid of Elias. More or less. Though it had not exactly liberated her. There was still Mann, the other Man, towering over her for thirty-six years, casting his broad and inescapable shadow. Her tormenter and friend. His words the fulcrum of her days and hours, the playing field of her mind, her pathway to praise and ignominy.

Until he died and left her alone. She had left him first, tearing herself away in their shared old age in a final effort to let some light fall on her own work before it was too late. "Of course you must," he had said, when she told him, with apology and trepidation, that she was retiring as his translator in order to attend to her own writing. Once, much earlier, when she dared to refer in a letter to her own attempts at fiction, he'd told her that she was not "a literary bird." She did not argue with this dismissal and even had quoted it to others with doleful humor. How could he know she was indeed a literary bird? He'd never seen her aloft. No one had.

They'd been bound together for half a lifetime—she was shaped by it, and surely he was too. It was like a marriage, a bloodless wedlock. Booklock. She snorted. How did I, who never wanted marriage in the first place, spend my life shackled to two men, she thought. And two such men!

But now Mann was gone, and she missed him. She missed both the struggle and the rich fruitfulness of their work together. "*Our* work? Together?" she heard him repeat in his cautious English, both amused and irritated. She was mortified for daring, even in her unspoken thoughts, to place herself alongside him. "No, no, no, dear Thomas!" she said hastily to Mann's shade. "I don't mean that. Forgive me! I was just the translator. I was not an inventor of worlds, like you. I didn't snap the reader's head off his shoulders and attach it again facing the other way. As you did. No, Herr Doktor Mann, my dear Tommy. All I did was translate. A lazy job for a person of finite abilities. All I did was study your sentences and find their English counterparts."

Was she being sarcastic? Yes and no. It was so confusing. Was her work massive or trivial? Who would judge, in the end?

The clouds had thinned and the sun was low in the sky. A stream of sunlight illuminated a patch of the floor. Helen slid down the wall and laid her hand on the bright oak boards, faintly warm to the touch. The plaster exterior wall was hard and cold behind her back. Her fingers, spread on the floorboards, were thin and sallow, swollen at the joints. Age spots on the back of her hand, the veins dark and prominent. The nails not perfectly clean. Good thing Marjorie did not notice that.

The patch of warmth on the floor disappeared. "Sun's over the yardarm!" Helen announced aloud. Permission to drink, as though she hadn't been tippling all day. She levered herself onto her hands and knees and then clumsily to her feet, poured a little more sherry into the glass that was still on the windowsill, then lowered herself to the floor again, managing not to spill. "Cheers, then," she said aloud, raising the glass. "Here's to me."

17

Chickenpox
1923

"Dear Mr. Knopf," she began, then stared at the blank page, frozen by the necessity to finish the letter quickly before she was summoned upstairs to the children. She forced herself to go on.

"Thank you for yours of April 18. I am mortified to have caused you concern. I must apologize for the delay in getting the pages to you, and assure you that I am moving forward with all possible speed without jeopardizing the integrity of the work. Unfortunately—" but here she had to stop writing and rush back upstairs to the darkened bedroom where Alice and Marjorie lay in small parallel beds. Marjorie was wailing. "Hush, dear, hush," said Helen, kneeling beside her. She took the washcloth and moistened it again in the bowl of cold water, holding it gently against hot, itchy skin. She lifted up Marjorie's pajama top and sponged the angry rash on her chest, careful not to irritate it further. "I'm thirsty," said Marjorie hoarsely, and Helen propped her up and held a glass of water to her lips. The child's poor face was swollen, her eyes glassy. Alice watched from the other bed, waiting for her turn. Helen went to her. Alice's dark hair was stringy and matted. Helen thought the rash was fading a bit. She put her hand on the girl's forehead. Feverish still.

"Mummy, can you read to us?" Alice said, as though she were seven years old instead of thirteen. She'd been patient and quiet since she and half of her classmates were sent home sick from boarding school. Marjorie succumbed just a few days later. Rosalind, thank goodness, had so far resisted. Helen picked up Marjorie's *Doctor Dolittle* from the nightstand, but the room was too dim for reading and their heads would ache if she raised the blinds.

"I'll tell you a story instead." Both girls sighed and closed their eyes. Helen perched on Alice's bed, which was close enough to Marjorie's that she could hold both their hands.

"Once upon a time," she began, "there were fourteen little girls who lived in a coal cellar, but managed to keep their pinafores so clean that no one ever guessed." She continued, making it up as she went along. Alice's hand slipped from hers, then Marjorie's. Helen thought of the letter downstairs, waiting to be finished and sent. It had to get into this afternoon's post. She couldn't bear to think of Knopf being worried or disappointed and wanted to reassure him as quickly as possible, which meant at least another week while her letter crossed the Atlantic.

"Mummy!" said Marjorie, tugging her skirt. "You stopped telling the story."

"So I did!" Helen said. "What were the girls doing when I stopped?" The story was so silly and so unplanned that she had no idea. But Marjorie, in her sleepy, fevery state, couldn't remember either, so Helen made up the rest of it without concern for logic.

She crept out of the room when both girls seemed peaceful, perhaps sleeping. Poor little things, she thought. She hoped Rosalind would be spared.

Helen opened the back door and stood on the step for a minute. The sky was overcast, the air fragrant with pennyroyal from the newly mown lawn.

Back in her study she stared out the window, her hands motionless on the typewriter keys. She knew what she could not say—*Dear Mr. Knopf, you simply have no idea what it is like to be a mother with sick children who need you constantly, with every bit as much urgency and justification as Mann's novel.* No, that would cook her goose, once and for all. They would confer, Knopf and Mann, and regretfully conclude that, all things considered, perhaps a translator without such pressing family responsibilities would be a more sensible choice.

But she wanted to explain why she was behind schedule. She tried to find a suitably light tone, while assuring him that she was fully committed to the work and would complete it in a timely way no matter what. "Unfortunately, we've had the chickenpox here, which rather tends to compete with the diligent translator's daily word count!"

Too flippant? she wondered. She did not know if the Knopfs had children or not. Even if they did, Mr. Knopf, like Mann, who had six, would hardly be the one to look after them when they were sick, nor when they were well, for that matter. The girls' chickenpox had not interrupted Elias's work for a second. And men wonder why women don't achieve greatness, she thought, struggling not to fall into the familiar resentment.

Mrs. McDonald flung open the front door when they returned from their morning walk. "Visitors," she whispered. "Foreigners. I put them in the drawing room."

A man was standing by the mantelpiece when Helen and Elias entered. He stepped forward, his hand extended. "Frau Lowe-Porter," he said with a slight bow, and she realized with a shock who it was, though he did not look anything like her mental image of a white-bearded sage. This man now shaking her hand and smiling stiffly below his dark mustache was tall and good-looking, middle-aged like herself, wearing blue pinstripes. He looked like a businessman. Behind his shoulder, a head shorter, was a somber dark-haired woman.

"Herr Mann. Frau Mann." The formulas of politeness all but deserted her. "This is my husband, Professor Elias Lowe." She repeated the introduction in German, to her horror stumbling over the perfunctory words. Her mind was speeding like a train. Soon after she'd begun work on *Buddenbrooks* Mann had referred in a letter to a possible visit to Oxford with his wife, not mentioning a date. She forced herself not to look wildly around the room—had Mrs. McDonald finished tidying it before the Manns arrived? Was Marjorie's jigsaw puzzle still on the floor? Herr Mann had probably had time to study the bookshelves and would have noted the gaps in their collection, works of poetry and fiction far outnumbered by tomes on paleography, of no interest to a literary man. She prayed that the door to her study was closed: Mann's half-translated work was spread out on her desk, no doubt resembling a dreadful jumble to anyone besides herself, particularly the author.

And now I will have to talk to them in German, she thought, and Mann will see how poorly I speak. She hadn't conversed in German for years. Helen was stricken again by the idea of a genius like Mann forced to depend on someone as flawed as herself. Poor man, and it's too late to dump me.

Elias, on the other hand, was in his sociable element.

"Do sit down, Herr Mann, Frau Mann," he said, gesturing to the couch, free, thank goodness, of newspapers and splayed books. "We'll have some tea. How wonderful to meet you both. May we show you Oxford? We'd be happy for another walk, wouldn't we, Helen?" His own German had many more mistakes than Helen's but he endowed it with charm and lightness.

Helen excused herself to make the tea, hunting for something—anything—to accompany it. She cursed her failure to keep the cake tins filled. Bread and butter, that nursery standby, would have to do. With relief she remembered the mandarin oranges that Elias had brought from London, an indulgent treat. She placed them in a bowl, then trickled filberts and raisins around them. Her heart rate was returning toward normal by the time she brought the tray into the room. But she let Elias carry the conversation. She could not get over the strangeness of having this abstract figure in her house, not to mention his silent wife who, Gilbert Brooks had told her, was a formidable and wealthy personage in her own right and the overseer of Mann's career. It was not just Mann's literary stature that daunted her; it was his non-corporeal presence in her daily thoughts, on the pages she studied so carefully, in the letters that they exchanged with increasing frequency. She was not ready for him to also possess a body, a face and an audible voice.

Elias raised his eyebrows in appreciation when he saw the oranges in their still life arrangement. The Manns accepted the tea but ate nothing, even when Elias carefully peeled a mandarin and ate it with hearty enjoyment, as though offering an example. What did they want, Helen wondered. Why had they come? The conversation, largely between the two men, remained banal, as though they were four strangers sharing a train compartment— German and English strangers, with the unmentionable war between them. Yes, they had enjoyed their time in London, yes, the weather was ideal for traveling.

"Well!" said Elias when the teacups had settled back on their saucers and remained there. "Shall we have a look at Oxford?"

They walked along the city streets, Elias recounting the historical and architectural significance of the beautiful old buildings. When they paused to gaze up at the thousand-year-old tower of St. Michael's the visitors nodded and listened but did not comment. After a while, as she recovered from the shock of meeting him, Helen found herself wishing that she and Mann could talk about the novel—what an opportunity, after all, to discuss the translation in person! But she was far too shy to bring it up, and Mann made no allusion to the fact that the two of them were intimately engaged in a project of the greatest importance to them both. She wondered if he was as shy as she was, or perhaps too stunned by the fleshly reality of his translator, as unsettling for him, surely, as his was for her.

The Manns said goodbye with what Helen imagined was relief akin to her own. They were staying one more night, they said.

"But you must join us again!" said Elias. He glanced at Helen for a quick endorsement. "Our friend in the German language department is hosting an evening party tomorrow night. How wonderful if you would come!"

To Helen's surprise Mann accepted without hesitation. His wife nodded minutely. They shook hands again and disappeared into their hotel.

As soon as they were gone Helen turned to Elias.

"Are you sure, Elias? Shouldn't we have asked Baxter first?"

"Of course they'll want the Manns to come! What an honor for us all!"

But to their enormous embarrassment Professor Baxter, after consulting his colleagues, declined to invite Herr Mann—simply too uncomfortable, he explained. As a defeated German, Mann had not yet displayed the remorse that the Oxford community thought was fitting. He was known to be a nationalist, after all, and an ardent supporter of the Kaiser. And the war had ended only six years ago. They felt it was too soon for hospitality. With great regrets, Professor Lowe.

Elias was astounded and angry, Helen chagrined.

As compensation Helen and Elias found one eminent couple who were delighted to host the great writer and his wife for afternoon tea. Yesterday's mild spring weather had turned blustery but all was calm and peaceful in the Yardleys' pale green drawing room where the bookshelves were as redolent of literature and Ancient Greek drama as any modern literary legend could wish.

Helen interpreted for Mann, her tongue now loosened. He sat back in his leather armchair, legs crossed, a well-shod foot dangling, teacup in hand, laughing with evident enjoyment as well as politeness. Frau Mann melted with the attentions of the little dog who snuffled around her feet and then alighted on her lap. Lady Yardley in her innocence or boldness asked about the translation. Helen translated the question and held her breath.

"I have seen enough pages to know that it is going extremely well," he said, smiling at Helen. "We look forward to publication soon."

Helen managed to get this into English, something warming inside her.

18

"Autumn wind"
1925

Marjorie's mother was away in London until tonight and only Daddy was home. But he wasn't really looking after her, he was upstairs in his study, which wasn't fair. Marjorie had to play by herself downstairs. She worked for a while on the jigsaw puzzle on the floor in the drawing room. It had a picture of two girls picking flowers—Marjorie thought they looked like her two sisters, who were away at boarding school. She wished she could go to boarding school too. Mummy said she'd go when she was eleven.

A piece of the puzzle was missing. It had to be greenish with just a tiny strip of white. She searched everywhere but it was nowhere to be seen. Someone else must have dropped it and didn't bother to find it and put it back. Marjorie would never do such a thing herself. She gave up looking and abandoned the puzzle. In the kitchen she found the bread and butter that Mummy had left out for her before she left in the morning, while Marjorie was at school. She wished there was raspberry or plum jam as well but there was no jam at all.

What to do now? She would like to go upstairs to visit Daddy. Sometimes he let her sit on the round brown rug and read, if she was quiet like a statue. Would he be cross, she wondered, if she came in now? She liked being with Daddy. When he wasn't staring at his books or writing they had fun together. Sometimes they played a game where she had to close her eyes while he moved one small thing on his desk, like a pencil or a bottle of ink. Then she had to guess what he'd moved. She was clever at this, but when it was Daddy's turn, he was extremely bad and they both laughed.

Marjorie wanted to show him her new poem. It had a very good title: "Autumn Wind." The poem was almost finished. She got her red notebook and lay down on her tummy. The last line had to end with a word that rhymed with "water." "Umm," she said aloud, screwing up her eyes and reading imaginary words in the air. "Daughter!" she exclaimed, pleased, and then worked out what the line could be. It had to make sense, of course, not just any old line.

The moment she'd written it she ran up the stairs. She opened the door a crack. "Daddy—can I show you a poem that I've just finished?"

He said without turning, "Just a moment." She waited, her hand still on the door handle. In a minute he swung around and beckoned her in. "What have you got, Miss Hedgehog?"

She handed him her notebook, open to the new poem. It was about the weather in the autumn, wind and rain, leaves flying. She was fairly sure that "like a dancing daughter" in the last line was not a good idea and she was already thinking about what she could write instead.

Her father studied the poem with his eyebrows scrunched together in concentration and his lips pursed. He marked some of the words with his pencil. Marjorie thought his students at Corpus must feel like this when he was reading their work, excited and a bit scared. She badly wanted him to like it.

Daddy closed the notebook and tapped her on the head with it. "Not bad," he said, handing it back to her. "Some work to do."

Marjorie said thank you and let out a breath. She opened the notebook and peeked at the page—he'd crossed out some words and written in the proper spelling, or a better word. There were circles around some of the punctuation. He had underlined "dancing daughter" and put an exclamation point beside it, which was embarrassing, as though he was making fun of her. Marjorie was cross with herself about the punctuation mistakes.

"May I—may I—" she said, "may I bring it back when I've worked on it more?"

Daddy glanced at his watch. "I'll be downstairs in a little while, dear."

She made herself leave.

19

Der Zauberberg
1925

Translating *Buddenbrooks* had been like building the London Bridge, a task so huge and daunting as to seem impossible, now completed for crowds to pour across and marvel at. Gilbert Brooks wrote as soon as it was out, congratulating her with proprietary pride, congratulating himself on being the one who brought her to Knopf's attention. He hoped Helen would bring some of her brilliance, as he put it, to another German novel that he planned to publish. She agreed, though reluctantly—she was longing to get back to her own neglected writing, which seemed to retreat further and further into the background. She hadn't so much as opened her bottom drawer for weeks.

And she had been spoiled, translating the master. Other writers, by comparison, were merely competent, at best. She had developed an appetite for this Mann, who, to her great relief, praised her translation when it was finally completed: "Extraordinarily accomplished and sensitive," he'd written. "*Wie geboren*—as if you were born to it." His words rested on her shoulders like a cloak of feathers. Mann's letters had become more personal since their meeting in Oxford. Helen knew that she'd fulfilled the task well, in spite of Mann's fears and her own. She had proven herself. And now she was eager for a second book, like a mountaineer ready for a yet higher alp, muscles toned and limber.

Knopf wrote too: "Thanks to your enormous efforts as well as of course to Mann's matchless work, I believe we have succeeded in introducing a novelist of the very first rank to the English-speaking literary world," he said with uncharacteristic effusiveness. Helen read Knopf's letter in the kitchen over her morning tea. It was early autumn and the house was quiet, with Marjorie at school and Elias lecturing. She was expanded with pleasure and a rare, precious sense of achievement. The critics had been kind, though the sales, especially in England, were not impressive, which made no difference to her since their agreement was a flat fee—750 American dollars for the two volumes.

The next translation would be his new novel, the monumental *Der Zauberberg*—an even greater task for a translator than *Buddenbrooks* but one that she was ready to embrace. Mann had written a massive, profound narrative reflecting on physical disease and a diseased society, on time and space, on the struggle between humanism and totalitarianism. In Germany it was acknowledged as a masterpiece that left the reader—if he or she had the stamina to reach the last of nearly a thousand pages—with an altered comprehension of humanity. There was no higher function of literature, she believed.

Knopf wrote a few weeks later, offering her a contract. "We will call it *The Magic Mountain*," he said. And then, chagrined, even angry, though not at her, he wrote again to say that there was a problem: Herr Mann preferred his friend Conrad Schmidt, an American of German origin who had done some earlier translation for him, we are so very, very sorry, Mrs. Lowe, we hope to resolve this issue soon. Blanche Knopf wrote a note with her own regrets and determination on Helen's behalf. She expressed her admiration for the first translation, adding: "I do hope we have an opportunity to meet some day." Helen was briefly pleased by this but did not write back, unsure if there was any future with Knopf or not.

Mann's attitude shocked Helen. The blow felt physical, as though she had been punched in the chest. Had she not proven her skills? Was Mann not delighted with *Buddenbrooks*? The publication of his work in English had led to renewed speculation about the Nobel Prize. Wasn't it her labors that enabled such recognition? She knew Schmidt's translation of one of Mann's short stories—competent but lacking elegance, in her view. How could Mann possibly prefer him?

Thomas Mann wrote to her directly, trying, it seemed, to be diplomatic and failing badly. He was indeed grateful and respectful, he said. But a male sensibility was needed for this new novel of difficult ideas, "deeply intellectual and symbolic." He doubted that she or any female translator could grasp the novel's central parable. A woman of her intelligence, he pointed out, must surely know her own limitations. "I would suggest that if any scruples or doubts concerning the task have occurred to you, you do not hide them from Mr. Knopf." He raised the vague possibility of working together for less demanding novels in the future, making it worse, as far as Helen was concerned.

She read Mann's letter in the kitchen, hands shaking. Holding the letter, she strode out to the backyard. Up and down the small wet lawn she paced, ignoring her damp shoes and stockings, trying to calm herself. She wanted to rip up the letter and stuff it into the incinerator at the bottom of the garden. No, Thomas Mann, this is neither grateful nor respectful. You seem to have no idea of what a translator does, of the skills and commitment it took to bring your eight hundred pages into effective English. Which thousands of people are now eagerly paying good money to read. *A male sensibility!* The translator's mind has no sex! You might find a man to do this book, Herr Mann, but I promise he will not be better than me. "He will not be better than me!" she repeated aloud, her voice rising. Not masculine enough for Mann. Not feminine enough for Elias, who called her by a man's name and seemed to require other women's bodies while still desiring her own. *Cannot a person just be a person?*

She grabbed the old wooden swing that no one had used since Marjorie grew too big for it and let it fly in a wild arc. It swung back to her and she gave it a vicious sideways push so that it hit the frame with a thump, its chain clanking.

I will not accept this, she thought.

Elias was in Munich. She sent him Mann's letter with her own comments written hastily on the back: "I need not say to you, for you know me, that *just* that '*männliche Konstitution*' which is the fibre of the book, and *just* those speculations on relativity, and *just* those searching parallels between flesh and spirit, are what I should enjoy worming my way into."

Elias knew her capacities. She wanted his reaction. She said, trying to be reasonable, that she would do as Mann asked and honestly assess whether her skill was up to it or not, though her gorge rose at the idea of submitting to his condescension.

She wanted to do the book!

She wished she could talk to Pauline, whose outrage on her behalf she could count on. But Pauline was in Leeds, now the headmistress of a grammar school. "Sod him!" she heard Pauline say. "Who does he bloody well think he is?" Helen herself was not capable of vulgarity, but (she mused wryly) she was certainly capable of putting it someone else's mouth.

Elias's letter arrived a week later: "I have no doubt *whatsoever* of your capacity to accomplish this task, and brilliantly," he wrote. "Mann's position is absurd. Stick to your guns, Hal." She nodded, appreciating his encouragement. But by then, needing to deliver herself from an intolerable uncertainty, she had already written to Knopf: "I respect of course the right of the author to choose his translator, and will be content to abide by whatever decision you and he might make." "Content to abide" was a polite prevarication. If Mann prevailed she would be crushed.

Knopf wrote back by return mail, evidently as perturbed as she was: he and Blanche were in agreement that Helen was the best possible translator for *Der Zauberberg*, as well as anything else that Mann wrote. And there would be much more to come. They had contracted with his German publishers to translate one book each year, previously published novels as well as whatever Mann was yet to write. Please be patient, Knopf advised.

Eventually Mann surrendered, with considerable resentment, to the Knopfs' pressure. Readers and critics had embraced Helen's flowing and dignified translation, Knopf reminded him. He implied, but did not spell out, that Mann's income from the published translations might be adversely affected if he changed horses in midstream. This was a clever tactic, since Mann, despite his success and his wife's inherited wealth, was perennially concerned about having enough money to finance their grand houses and lengthy vacations with entourages of children and servants.

Helen plunged in to her first full reading of the book, her victory tainted by the knowledge that Mann did not want her. Page after page was filled with the tubercular characters' philosophical disquisitions in sentences as grand, complex, shapely, and elegant as a forest of massive oak trees, interspersed with comic-satiric scenes of life in a mountaintop sanatorium where men and women were exiled for years before being released to death or back to the bourgeois existences they had been compelled to leave.

After three solid days of reading, she sat back in her chair, exhausted and exhilarated as though she'd run a race. She still had many pages to go.

"So?" asked Elias. "Is it a work of manly genius, as Mann seems to think?"

"Utterly brilliant, certainly. Like nothing I've read before. *Buddenbrooks* was a country stroll in comparison. Manly? Yes, I suppose so, in the sense that no woman writer would have the gall to presume the reader's devotion the way Mann does."

"But do you like it?"

"I'm not sure yet." She leafed through the pages, trying to pin down her ambivalence. "I'm not fond of these profound philosophical debates cheek by jowl with descriptions of decay and grief. But the characters are striking. He does make me want to know what happens to them."

When she wrote to Mann to ask him to shed light on a particularly obdurate passage he couldn't resist responding, "I warned you, did I not?" The hated doubt came up in her—is he right? Am I inadequate to this task, because I am female? Do I lack the necessary mental equipment? The thought made her desperate. If the difficulties she encountered were simply because of her sex there was no way to transcend them.

In her mind she summoned a little tribunal of women: Aunt Charlotte, Pauline, and Ruth the imaginary artist. The three of them stood up, one by one and then all together: No, Helen, he is not right! You are in command of these languages. Your mind has all the muscle it needs. You will do justice to this great work.

20

The wooden doll
1925

I am a liar.

To Knopf, to Mann, to anyone who asks, I deprecate my work as minor, trivial in comparison to that of the creator. I have used the word lazy. I say that the novelist is the visionary, I merely the functionary following his lead with no need of invention or inspiration. Translation is mechanical, a matter of searching my memory or the dictionary for the English equivalent of a German word, then a bit of polishing, and it's done. It may be laborious, but it's the labor of the drudge, not the artist.

No. No, it is not. I lie.

It's the labor of the researcher, the linguist, the archaeologist, the scholar, the historian, the geographer. And yes, the artist too.

They ask me to translate a book. I say yes. The book, whatever it is, arrives on my doorstep. I pick it up, feel its weight, glance at the final page number. I read it from start to finish, committing all my time. I fall asleep with it heavy on my chest, its images and locutions permeating my dreams.

And then I get to work. I put on my metaphorical boots and my rucksack, I go exploring the world in which the story takes place, I breathe the air, I smell the vegetation, I walk the furrows, I shade my eyes and gaze at the surrounding hills. I float over farms and cities, I sit in town squares, I eavesdrop on conversations, I observe the clothes and gestures of the book's characters as they argue and conspire, as they love and hate one another.

I comb the libraries for books that can tell me the history and geography I will need to know. I seek the writings of experts to fill in the gaps in my own knowledge—the mythologists, the historians, the musicologists, the scholars of archaic Bible translations or mediaeval German. The pile of reference books grows and grows.

And then, finally, I am ready. I pile a stack of paper on my desk. I take up my pen. Word by word, sentence by sentence, paragraph by paragraph, page by page, chapter by chapter, a novel in English takes form alongside its German brother.

And then, inevitably, I see that this new work is hideous. Clumsy and unreadable. It makes me ill to look at it.

I have snatched a living child out of its cradle and left a crude wooden doll in its place.

Then comes the alchemy.

I must use my dark arts, my art, to breathe life into the doll. I whisper my incantations over it. The air fills with words, German and English words, idioms, words that are obvious and surprising, beautiful and grotesque, words no longer used, words not yet born, words that fly like birds, sometimes in formation, sometimes in a crazy scatter.

The words settle around the wooden doll, they warm it, caress it, clothe it. Slowly, slowly, the limbs move, the heart beats, eyes flutter open. There is new life, with its own new grace. I rejoice in its birth. I send it out into the world. A gift given.

21

Anticipation
1926

The older girls were home from boarding school and had condescended to play anagrams with nine-year-old Marjorie, who was surprisingly good at them. Phoebe, Rosalind's friend since they were babes in arms, sprawled on the floor with the others. A little Celtic beauty, thought Helen, admiring Phoebe's red-gold hair and shapely body, far more womanly than Rosalind, who was still physically childish at fifteen. Alice, a year younger, was catching up with her. "Alice is the pretty one!" people always said, contemplating the three girls, each so different. Alice was kind and witty as well as beautiful, always mad about collecting something. These days it was wildflowers that she gathered and pressed. No longer teeth, thank goodness—tiny yellowing baby teeth cadged from her sisters and displayed on velvet. Helen had tender hopes for all of her girls, even funny little Marjorie with her hedgehog hair. They'll be a credit to me, she thought. They'll be well educated and do something in the world. Rosalind was a gifted young artist. Helen envisioned her fulfilling that promise, attending an art academy, developing herself as a professional painter. Alice had a flair for languages. Marjorie was already an inventive and committed little writer. Whatever they did, her daughters would not be confined to motherhood and wifehood. Though she wished that sweetness for them too.

All day she had been shut in her study with *Zauberberg*, bushwhacking through its thickets of prose. And then to emerge at five, the day's work done, and make supper for these dear girls, who hugged her and made her laugh. A lucky woman am I, she thought. Marjorie jumped up to stir the chocolate fudge cooking over a chafing dish. "When is Daddy coming?" she asked her mother for the tenth time.

"Soon!" Helen answered yet again. Elias was on his way home from France on this rainy Saturday evening. They wouldn't know exactly what time until he burst through the door and shook his umbrella and beamed at his family arrayed in front of him.

"It's your turn, Mummy."

Helen leaned down and chose twelve cardboard letters. "Here's a word for you, Marjorie," she said, holding them out.

Marjorie arranged the letters on the floor this way and that.

"Here, try this," said Rosalind.

"An-tici-pation," Marjorie sounded out. "What does that mean?"

"Oh," said her mother, "it means waiting for something that you're excited about."

Marjorie looked at her closely. "Why are you smiling, Mummy?"

"I'm smiling because you're such a funny girl!" she said. But she was smiling because she could not help it. Elias was coming home to her. She could sense his longing as palpably as she felt her own.

Outside the door someone whistled "Yankee Doodle." Helen whistled back—their special signal. In another moment he was in the hallway. He sent his hat spinning like a flying saucer, landing it deftly on top of the newel post. The girls jumped up and ran into his embrace. Phoebe hung back, shy, and he reached out to include her. Helen stood and watched, holding her soft bright-colored shawl around her.

Elias extricated himself and opened his arms to her.

"Ooh ooh ooh!" sang Marjorie. "Kissy kissy!"

"Shut up," said Alice.

They were adept at making love with no sound, so as not to wake sleeping children. "I have missed you so," he breathed. They traced the beloved contours of each other's body. It had been four weeks. Afterwards they lay silent and entwined. Let me fall asleep without hearing who you bedded in Paris, she begged him silently. Without thanking me for my broadmindedness. The thud of his heart under her cheek slowed as he rested. Careful not to wake him, she slid out of his arms and lay on her back, savoring the sense of her domestic world re-balancing itself, a wife with her husband beside her once more, the children asleep with both mother and father under the same roof again.

22

In Brittany
1927

Helen and Elias were woken by Marjorie's jubilant shout: "Swimming day!" The skies had been disappointingly overcast since they'd arrived in France for their summer holiday. The girls' enthusiasm for brisk hikes through dairy farms and woodlands was wearing thin, despite frequent stops to sample Breton cheeses and apple cider. But now the sun was high in a cloudless sky at eight in the morning.

"Soon, dear! We have to have our breakfast. And the girls aren't even up yet."

Rosalind, Alice, and Phoebe asserted the right to sleep as late as they wanted in their attic room at the top of the tall, higgledy-piggledy old house. Stretching and yawning, they filed into the kitchen just as Elias returned with croissants.

"Chop chop!" said Marjorie. "We're going to the beach!"

Helen lounged back on her elbows, smiling as she watched. The four girls held hands, jumping over small waves and shrieking at the unexpected chill of the water—the older three completely abandoning their dignity as young ladies. There were a few other beachgoers around, and a pleasing murmur of French and English against the sibilance of the sea. Helen wasn't ready to swim. Not just yet. She'd wait for the warmth of the sun to overcome the cool Channel breeze and propel her to her feet. Then she'd throw off her wrap and run barefoot and whooping down to the water, startling the girls. Elias was a speck in the distance, striding toward the cliffs at the far end of the cove. The pleasure of sitting still on warm sand, lulled by light and heat, the cry of seagulls, the rhythm of the waves, was incomprehensible to him.

The sun made a thousand flickering diamonds in the blue water. She lay back on the sand and closed her eyes, her mind blessedly empty of Mann's erudite phrases.

After lunch they rested in the cool house. Elias disappeared upstairs to the little room he'd claimed as a study. Helen stayed in the living room with the children, too overcome with lassitude to open the notebook on her lap.

"Look what I found!" said Marjorie, who'd been rummaging in the bookshelf for children's books. "*Contes du Petit-Château,*" she read aloud with a terrible accent. "It's stories. With pictures."

"Let me see," said Alice. She was the best at French.

"Can you read one to me, Alice?" said Marjorie.

"If you're a good girl." Alice leafed through the book. "What about this one?" She began reading aloud, a sentence in French and then a translation. Helen listened, impressed. The girl seemed to do it effortlessly.

The story was both foolish and moralistic—a quarreling sister and brother punished by a fairy who, preposterously, turned them into each other. But Marjorie was intrigued.

"Could that really happen, Mummy? Could a girl turn into a boy and a boy into a girl by magic?"

"Magic isn't real, dear."

"But what if they could?"

"Well. I suppose they'd have to think quite hard about what it really means to be a girl or a boy."

"Would I be different if I was a boy?"

Helen looked fondly at her youngest daughter with her rumpled hair and grimy shorts. "Probably not very different."

"Good, because I like being a girl." She ran halfway up the wooden stairs and jumped down with a thump that shook the floor.

"*Marjorie!*"

"Six steps, Mummy! Yesterday I could only do five."

As darkness fell they walked down the cobbled street to the village square, hungry for dinner. "Well, Goldilocks?" said Elias. "What shall we drink tonight?" Every night he had been coaching Phoebe on how to choose wine. His own daughters had no interest at all.

Phoebe took his arm in her confident way. Helen watched, amused at the child's grown-up airs.

"A light red, I'm thinking," said Phoebe. "Pinot noir? After that big Bordeaux last night."

"They're too young," Helen admonished Elias privately. "I don't think they should be drinking wine at all."

"Nonsense. Sixteen is not too young to develop a palate." He stood behind her, looking at her in the clouded mirror of the dresser as she took pins out of her hair. "Wine is one of the great comforts of life." She leaned back against him and yawned. Experimentally he gathered her long brown hair into his hands and piled it in a coil on top of her head, grinning at her in the mirror. "What do you think?"

She laughed and pushed his hand away, then held it to her cheek. "It's so good to be here, isn't it? Just us and the sea."

23

The bottom drawer
1927

Mountain is at last on its on its way to Knopf, thank god. A mountain of a job, and it's done. Gilbert has nothing for me at the moment.

Elias is in Germany.

The girls are at school.

The house is tidy. Tidy enough.

No one is expecting me for tea. Or a meeting.

I have only myself to conjure a meal for. Soup will do, with a nice glass of wine.

There is nothing and no one between me and my writer self. At least for today.

Helen sat down at her desk, the door to her study open since no one was there to disturb her. She unlocked the bottom drawer, pulled out her notebooks, and leafed through the most recent one, stopping at an unfinished poem:

> *Have I any tool at all to write a poem with?*
> *For sharp it must be, and all I have are rusty;*
> *And bright it must be, not long laid by and dusty.*

She murmured her lines aloud. The self-deprecation pleased her, and the recursiveness, a poem about writing a poem. *Ars poetica*, of a humble sort. Her mind shook open. The next words came into focus. She wrote until the poem was finished, at least for now.

Then she turned to her long-accumulated notes for new stories, some so old or so cryptic that she no longer remembered what was in her mind when she made the note. "*Elinor Horsefield's stale sponge cake.*" She had no idea. "*The Calvados man sans teeth.*" This one was more recent.

She stepped outside to pace up and down the quiet cobbled street, letting herself re-enter that moment in France with the girls and the toothless man, recalling what struck her at the time, until the sliver of an idea started to gather substance and complexity, then she hurried inside and wrote.

Hidden at the very bottom of the drawer was *The Artist,* her unfinished novel. Seventeen chapters completed, but she hadn't added to them for a long time. Poor Ruth's life was arrested on the edge of whatever triumphs or catastrophes awaited her. With sorrow and shame Helen admitted now that the novel would never be finished. There was a point when lack of momentum spelled death.

Why did she give up? It was not only her failure to claim the time that she needed. It was also the story itself. Ruth was to become a full-fledged artist, recognized and honored. But her path had to be convincing. She would have to wrestle with the obstacles that any woman would face—the distraction of motherhood or the choice to live alone, perhaps in poverty. The condescension, or worse, of her male peers. But how would she overcome these impediments? Every plotline seemed unconvincing.

She recalled Elias's comments at an exhibit of Impressionists in London. "Competent and charming," he'd said as they stood in front of a work by Mary Cassatt. "But not of the first rank, you must admit."

Helen started to demur. She thought the painting was marvelous, capturing the sensuous, mystical bond between a mother and child.

"Women's great talent is to nurture, not to create," Elias continued. "That's why Cassatt paints motherhood. A decorative substitute for a family of her own."

"But—her work is extraordinary!" argued Helen. "Are you saying that women's domestic experience is not a fit topic for art?"

Elias looked at her fondly. "Of course it is. But its audience will be other women. No, Hal, I'm afraid genius is the province of men. It's self-evident. Where are the female Shakespeares and Miltons? The female Rembrandts?"

Helen knew there was something very wrong with this argument but she could not put her finger on it.

What about me, she wanted to say, but didn't dare. She could already hear his answer: "Translation is the kind of thing where a woman can truly excel, as you have, Hal. Whereas your own writing..." His imaginary voice did not need to finish.

Sometimes she dared to send something out to a publisher or a journal, typing the final draft with care and writing a cover letter with as much skill as she could summon, crafting it, reaching for that pivot point between modesty and bragging. She knew better than to mention her translation, which she was sure would get her ejected immediately from the world of fiction where she yearned to be recognized.

Then she would walk the fat envelope, camouflaged between bills and family correspondence, to the post office. Her face betrayed nothing as the clerk weighed and stamped it but she was thrumming with an addict's eagerness for this periodic infusion of hope, this surge of excitement in the veins.

The foreordained rejection would arrive soon enough. But her disappointment could not suppress the stubbornness that prompted her, a few days or weeks later, to try again. She could see it so clearly— her full name on a beautiful book cover, a legion of readers ready to leap with her into an imagined world, respectful reviews mentioning translation only to wonder at the writer's versatility, her own originality of language.

24

Glory
1929

Because of the time difference between New York and England Helen saw the London *Times* headline before Knopf's telegram arrived: "Nobel Prize for Literature Awarded to German Novelist," followed by columns of praise for Thomas Mann's work. She stood arrested in the hallway with the newspaper in her hand, devouring the article with its large studio photo of Mann looking handsome and severe. Paragraph after paragraph about his accomplishment. The Nobel committee, apparently, singled out *Buddenbrooks*—"the first great novel of the twentieth century"—rather than *The Magic Mountain,* which she thought was the greater achievement, though more controversial. Knopf had been sure that publication in English would tip the prize to Mann, after years of rumors that he was being considered. He was compared floridly to Goethe, to André Gide, to Thomas Hardy. She nodded, yes, he was all of that, he was indeed Germany's most illustrious living writer, possibly the most important twentieth century novelist in any language.

Elias came downstairs for his morning tea and saw her standing by the front door with the paper. She held it out to him, eyes shining. "What do you think of this!"

He read the headline and the opening lines. "Well, well!" he said. "We knew it was going to happen, didn't we?" He scanned the article. Helen knew what he was looking for. She had searched for it too, in spite of herself—her own name, some tiny mention of her role in making Mann's work known outside the German-speaking realm. But the long article made no mention of herself nor of Knopf, none whatsoever. The book titles were given in English—this was the London *Times*, after all—but the translator and publisher themselves were invisible. As we should be, she reproved herself.

The telegram arrived at one in the afternoon, and there she was acknowledged by Knopf and Blanche. "Mann wins the Nobel. Glory all round. We hope you will take pride in your share of Mann's great recognition. A. and B. Knopf."

Helen wrote a warm letter to Mann, made a little shy by the man's new public stature. Her personal congratulations could not mean much to him when he was being celebrated by the grandest names in literature and society.

Knopf sent her another lengthy article from the *New York Times*, this time a personal portrait by a German writer whom Helen knew—she'd translated two of his own novels for Quest. The article was full of affectionate respect for Mann, the writer's pride in his personal friendship with the great man leaking out of every line. The minor business of how Mann's novels came to appear in English was not touched upon. Helen shrugged, trying to ignore the peevish voice that said "But he *knows* me! He knows what I did for Mann, not to mention for himself!"

But still she felt a little spray of glory, inadvertent though it might be. *Her* hard work, *her* carefully crafted sentences and imaginative transformations helped to bring Mann's novels to this summit of recognition, whether anyone acknowledged it or not.

A few months later Elias rushed out to meet her as she came home from shopping on the High Street, a heavy basket over her arm. He was percolating with some kind of excitement.

"Hal, dear, don't take off your coat," he said. "I'm taking you for lunch!"

"Are you now!" said Helen. "Come inside and help me put these groceries away." He flew around the kitchen in her wake. "Not in the cupboard, silly," she said, taking the Cheshire cheese from his hand and putting in the cold safe. The moment they'd finished he grasped her arm and steered her back to the street. It was a windy winter day and he clutched his hat to stop it flying away. Helen, good-humored, decided to go along with this mysterious adventure.

They walked towards Cornmarket, talking about the girls' recent amusing letters from boarding school, about Mrs. Woolf's new novel that Helen was reading in which a man becomes a woman and lives for three hundred years, about anything but the secret he was about to reveal. She let herself enjoy the suspense.

In the restaurant Elias asked for a table by the window and ordered champagne. A significant triumph of some kind, apparently.

He reached into the inside pocket of his jacket and drew out an envelope.

"You're not going to believe this." He studied the envelope as though he was seeing it for the first time and shook his head, incredulous.

"*What*, Elias? You have to tell me!" She reached for the envelope and he held it above his head.

He was suddenly serious. "I've got it, Hal."

"Got...?"

"The Rockefeller grant."

She leaned back. "The whole thing?"

He nodded. "The whole thing."

Her hand flew to her mouth and she gazed at him, trying take in the scope of this news. It's the magic fertilizer at last, she thought. Elias could finally grow his giant beanstalk, the major research project that he had dreamed of for fifteen years. Helen was intimately familiar with the proposal, having read and critiqued each iteration of it. The research would lead to a work of many volumes—he thought at least ten, perhaps twelve—its scale unprecedented in his field. His standing, now and for posterity, was assured.

The amount of money was enormous in relation to the income they were used to.

"Of course, it has to last a long time—this will take the rest of my life, I imagine. But now—Hal, I can do it! I can hardly believe it."

She stood up and walked around the table to embrace him. "Darlingest!"

The waiter opened the bottle of champagne with a flourish and a satisfying pop and poured two glasses.

"To my brilliant husband!" she said. "To your now and future success!"

"Thank you, dearest!"

They clinked the glasses and sipped. The wine was like cool nectar. Elias and Helen were as buoyant as the bubbles breaking its surface.

"Too bad there isn't a Nobel for paleography," he said. They both laughed.

"What Olympian company I travel in!" said Helen. "What a pair of immortals!"

"We couldn't do it without you, Hal," said Elias generously. "Neither of us could possibly do it without you."

She knew it was true. "It's my pleasure, dearest," she said, meaning it. "But today is your triumph. I salute you with all my heart!" and she raised her glass again.

25

At Merton Chapel
1929

Marjorie's parents were arguing about Miss Pauline Mackie, who was coming to visit. Marjorie had invented a private color system for her parents' quarrels. Yellows were minor, and likely to end with teasing each other or hugging. Oranges were unpleasant to listen to. Mean things were said. After an Orange her parents didn't talk to each other for a few hours and then they pretended they'd forgotten. A Red, which didn't happen often, was the worst and led to tears (Mummy) and shouting (Daddy). Marjorie escaped upstairs or outside when there was a Red going on. Sometimes her mother apologized to her after a Red. Her father did not seem to notice that Marjorie was upset.

The quarrel at the breakfast table was an Orange. No one was shouting or crying but there was a scratchy, unpleasant feeling in the air. Daddy called Miss Mackie "your feminist friend" and said he did not want to have dinner with her. She was coming up to Oxford for a special poetry and music recital at the Merton chapel. He didn't want to go to the recital either. He said that he feared it could only be sentimental. Mummy said that sentiment, also known as emotion, was not inappropriate for people who had been shell-shocked, which Elias had not. He asked if she would have preferred him to endure shell shock. She said, "Don't be ridiculous, you are deliberately misinterpreting what I said."

This was all part of the Orange.

Marjorie was to go with Mummy and Miss Mackie to the recital. She was excited about it. She liked Miss Mackie, who had visited them a couple of times before. Marjorie felt a little shy of her, since she was a headmistress at a school in London. It seemed very peculiar to have a headmistress at the dinner table, eating like anyone else, in fact more than anyone else. She always said yes to a second helping and sometimes to a third. But Miss Mackie always asked her so many questions about what she was doing, what she was reading, what she thought about her school and her friends, that Marjorie's shyness disappeared and she found herself chatting as though Miss Mackie were twelve years old too.

"Please yourself, Elias," said her mother when her father said he'd stay at Corpus for dinner and the women could discuss feminist rabble-rousing without a male of the species to inhibit them. "We are content for you to eat with us, or not, as you wish." Her voice was deliberately calm, as though Elias were a sulky child. "Pauline's going to take the early train back to London, so you won't have to face her over breakfast."

Marjorie was delighted to hear that Miss Mackie would stay overnight. "I'll help you tidy up Rosalind's room!" she said. Her parents both looked at her in surprise, as though they'd forgotten that she was there.

They walked over to the recital at Merton in the dusk. "Sorry to disrupt your domestic bliss," she heard Miss Mackie say. "Oh, he'll recover," her mother answered. The two women talked in low voices, turning to include Marjorie from time to time, but then going back to their own things. Marjorie didn't mind. It felt very grown-up to be going out in the evening with Miss Mackie and her mother and she hoped that other girls from school would see her.

The performance they were going to see was unusual.

"It's poetry with specially composed music," her mother had told her. "Poetry by a famous poet. It's not meant for children but I think you'll like it." The poet had been killed in action at the very end of the war. "Just a year after you were born,

Marjorie," she said. His fellow-soldiers had brought his notebook of poems back to England, and got them published, and everyone read them because they described so well what it was like to be at the front. And now a composer had written music to go with the poems. At the concert the poems would be read by other men who who'd been in the war, while musicians played the music. Marjorie had never been to anything like this. As a poet herself, it interested her.

"Pauline knew him," her mother told her. "The poet. She looked after him in Serbia. That's why she's coming with us."

On the clipped grass courtyard outside the chapel people were clustered in small groups, some in uniform, smoking cigarettes while they waited to go in. "Returned servicemen," said Miss Mackie with a sigh. "This won't be easy for them." A man broke off from one of the groups and walked toward her with his hands outstretched. She took his hands and they stood there for a moment looking at each other but not speaking.

The dim-lit chapel smelled of stone and wood and incense. It was already full of people. They found seats on a back pew facing across the nave. Marjorie could not see any other children. A piano was set up on the chancel. There were three chairs, two music stands with music on them, and a collection of bells and chimes and a xylophone. Lulled by the whisper of voices around her, Marjorie gazed up at the huge rose window. A tall, thin man with an eye-patch walked out in front of the audience, a book in his hand. He was followed by three young people, a girl and two boys, one of them carrying a cello. "Students," whispered her mother. The girl sat down at the piano. One of the young men positioned himself behind the percussion instruments. The cellist had longish fair hair and was rather handsome—Russian-looking, Marjorie thought.

The musicians started playing. The music was unlike any other music that Marjorie had heard. Sometimes there was air between the notes. Sometimes they clashed with each other, but in a way that was beautiful, not ugly.

The music paused and the reader began reading the poems. Quiet notes from the instruments wove with his voice, making the poetry sink in deeper, Marjorie thought, as though the music was a sort of funnel into her heart.

She didn't understand what all the words meant but they made images in her mind—mud, a high blue sky, gunfire, wounds, birdsong, men who were hurt or dead. The images were so sad and the music so lovely. The long tones of the cello tore into her. Some people were crying, even men. Her mother held Miss Mackie's hand.

The first reader sat down and a different man got up, leaning on a walking stick though he was not old. He waited while the musicians played again. Marjorie watched them, the girl bending over the piano keys, the boy with the chimes and bells, the young cellist with his eyes closed as he dug his bow into the strings. He seemed almost crying himself, his face contorted, his hair flopping as he tossed his head. Something rose in Marjorie as she gazed at him, not sadness exactly but a passion of some kind. She wanted to talk to him. She imagined them together after the concert, drifting away from the others, walking slowly on the dark lawn. He might put his arm around her shoulders. She would tell him about her own poems. It occurred to her that they would also go very well with music, particularly the cello. He would understand that although she was only twelve years old she was not just a child.

26

The fireplace
1930

In her study on a cold February morning, a shawl wrapped around her shoulders and a cup of tea to warm her hands until the fire asserted itself, Helen was summoned to the front door by Mr. Barwick the postman. He touched his cap and handed her a manuscript-shaped package. It was not from Knopf, nor from Brooks. She knew immediately what it was. For a mad moment she considered saying, "I'm sorry, Mr. Barwick, I can't accept it. Please return it to the sender"—putting the poor man into consternation. Instead she thanked him, closed the door, and carried the package like an undetonated bomb into her study.

It was one time too many.

She tore it open and took out a brief letter. "Thank you for letting us consider your collection of short stories, which we herewith return. We regret to say that it does not meet our needs at this time."

Neither critique nor praise, just this pro forma dismissal, signed by someone whose name she did not know.

Then the penciled note at the bottom, the humiliating coup de grâce: "We do wish to convey our admiration for your fine work as Thomas Mann's translator."

Her pathetic ambitions exposed—the translator who did not know her place and dared to aspire to a higher order of literary creation. Why on earth hadn't she used a pseudonym?

She dropped the letter onto the carpet and leafed through the disgraced pages, some slightly dog-eared—perhaps they had actually read them? The title, crafted with such care for its allusions, its economy and style, now seemed pretentious.

Beneath it was her full name, not just the androgynous initials. Her full name as author, not translator, standing proudly, foolishly alone.

Helen steeled herself for the familiar ritual: enter the rejection in her notebook so that she did not forget and embarrass herself further by sending the same work to the publisher in a year or two, after it had been rejected a few more times by others. File the letter. Leaf through the manuscript to see if any of it can be salvaged for another submission, to save her from typing the whole thing again. Discard the worst of the dog-eared pages. Permit herself one rueful sigh or a muttered curse. Tell herself not to give up.

But the bile was rising in her throat.

She crumpled the title page of the manuscript into a ball. A missile. She threw it across the room, then retrieved it and hurled it again, this time into the fireplace where the coal fire was starting to catch. After a moment the paper flared brightly. The flames snaked across the page, leaving a black-edged gash. Her typed words shriveled and the page subsided into ash. She crushed the next page, then the next and the next until the pile of pages was gone. All her words, thousands of them, vanished up the chimney. The stories no longer existed. Poof! Expunged from the record. As though she never wrote them, never welcomed the gift of fresh ideas, never spent hours clothing them in the most vivid and precise words she could find. As though she'd never spent hours—and days, and weeks—writing, revising, revising again, then submitting to one indifferent editor after another. *An expense of spirit in a waste of shame.* Shakespeare was talking about lust but the words fit exactly.

Helen unlocked the large bottom drawer of her desk. Folders, notebooks, manila envelopes, manuscript boxes full of her efforts of the past—what?—thirty-five years. Since her hopeful girlhood. Bundles of rejection letters held by rubber bands. She yanked the drawer out all the way and emptied it onto the floor, creating a disheveled pile. A vast, useless mess of pages mixed with dust, rusted paper clips and curled postage stamps, long obsolete.

Handful by handful, Helen incinerated her pages. Flames leapt dangerously in the small fireplace. No one was home to wonder about the conflagration going on in her study. She grabbed one of her poetry notebooks to fling onto the flames, then stopped. I wrote them only for myself, she pleaded. And for the children. And Elias. They weren't rejected because they never went anywhere. They don't deserve to die. She scrabbled through the heap, rescuing three more notebooks of poems.

The rest of it burned. She pushed at the singed fragments to keep them inside the grate, holding them down with the poker until they disappeared.

The novel took the longest. Nearly two hundred pages. Ruth's frantic voice rose in her mind—don't do it, Helen! It's not too late! Don't destroy us! But Helen ignored her. Why have I even kept these pages, she thought. Some unreasonable loyalty to Ruth and Nellie, long after even they themselves must have concluded that their story would not be completed, would never reach the eyes of readers. Ruth's ten-year deadline had come and gone came years ago.

Helen got tired of burning the pages one by one and thrust a thick wedge of paper onto the blaze, almost smothering it. She pulled the wedge apart with the fire tongs and let oxygen do its work.

Nothing was left but the bundles of letters from editors who declined to publish her work, each letter closing a small, secret arc of hopefulness. A few leaving it open just a crack: "Please do not hesitate to send us further work in the future." But the subsequent submissions fared no better.

She pulled off the decaying rubber bands, ripped the letters in half in their envelopes, and fed them to the fire.

The pile was gone, the drawer empty except for the notebooks of poetry. With her hands she swept up the remaining detritus from the floor and dumped it into the wastebasket. She sat on the floor, purged, stunned, and gazed at the flames until they died.

27

On the river
1930

Marjorie and Phoebe's friend Walter each took an oar—
Marjorie looking like Walter's younger brother with her trousers
and cropped hair—while Helen leaned on a cushion in the bow
and Phoebe lounged hatless and barefoot in the stern, calling out
instructions like a coxswain. The river was glassy, the water
almost warm to the touch of Helen's trailing fingers. How
delightful to spend a summer afternoon with these lively young
souls, who seemed to enjoy her company as much as she enjoyed
theirs. Recently emancipated from childhood themselves,
Phoebe and Walter were quizzing Marjorie with evident relish.
The girl preened in their attention.

"What is your best subject at school?" asked Phoebe.

"English, of course," said Marjorie. "I'm also rather good at
Latin." She had her father's lack of false modesty.

"English *and* Latin," said Phoebe then interrupted herself—
"hold on, left!" and they veered left to avoid a low willow branch.

"And what are you going to be when you grow up,
Marjorie?" asked Walter. In Helen's youth only boys were asked
this annoying question, the future of girls being self-evident.

"A writer," said Marjorie without hesitation. "A novelist. Or
I might be a paleographer and work with my father."

"A novelist, by George. Like our Phoebe here," said Walter.

"Well, not yet," said Phoebe. "One day, though."

"Who's your literary model, Marjorie?" Walter asked. He
was reading English at Trinity himself.

"Oh, I read very widely," said Marjorie. "I've read Dickens
and Austen and all that. I plan to do something rather different."

"Something modern?" said Phoebe, shifting in the stern and causing the rowboat to wobble. Helen gripped the sides, suppressing a squawk. "Like Mrs. Woolf, perhaps? Like James Joyce?"

"Like myself!" Marjorie retorted. "I'm trying out some interesting ideas right now, in fact."

Helen listened, amused and impressed as well. Why shouldn't this girl succeed, with ambition as defined as this at the age of thirteen? Marjorie already spent hours at her desk or on the floor of the living room, chewing her pencil and then scratching furiously at her notebook. Sometimes she showed her parents a new poem. Elias would critique the grammar and metaphors, leaving Marjorie crestfallen. But Helen found the poems genuinely promising and told her so. The girl had an eye, an ear. A sense of language.

"Well, you're lucky then to have a literary mother," Phoebe said. "I wish I did. Mrs. Lowe, would you—I was wondering if you would read my stories sometime? And tell me what you think?"

"Oh—certainly, dear," said Helen. She might have abandoned her own work but she could still help a young writer, surely.

"That's so kind!" said Phoebe. "Oops—boat on your right!"

Marjorie and Walter steered out of the way. The other boat glided upstream, packed with sweating young men in bathing suits.

"Avert your eyes, Marjorie!" ordered Phoebe. Marjorie giggled. "No, really," Phoebe went on, "your mother knows a lot."

Marjorie did not turn to look at Helen behind her. "Mother is a translator," she said to Phoebe. "That's not the same as being a writer. *I'm* going to write novels and poems and short stories."

"And so you will, dear," Helen said. "And I'll be very proud of you." She tried to ignore the little bruise to her heart. Marjorie had never seen her mother's original work and now never would.

Helen pushed away the thought of the flames in her fireplace and instead pictured Marjorie at twenty-five or thirty, a published writer, recognized and respected, still boyish but now elegant as well.

"I've been thinking about it," Marjorie continued. "Most likely I will not get married. I'll need to devote all my time to my work."

"Oh, come on, that's not fair," said Walter, pushing his hair out of his eyes. "What about the poor chaps who're going to want to marry you?"

Marjorie splashed him with her oar and he squealed. "They'll just have to understand," she said severely.

Helen watched her young daughter's slender back, her easy, strong movements as she wielded the oar. Only months ago women had finally won full voting rights, finally on the same basis as men's rights. But otherwise nothing had changed. There was still no accommodation for a young woman who wanted to write—who wanted a profession of any kind—if she also embraced conjugal love and family responsibility.

Marjorie had no inkling that her own innocent advent into the world, and her sisters', had fatally sabotaged a writer's work. And that is as it should be, Helen thought. They must never know. It was not their fault. Was she deceiving herself? Yes, there was resentment. But not towards her beloved girls. Towards Elias, towards Mann, towards all the men who could not conceive of a woman possessing the same ability, the same drive as themselves. And towards herself, for failing to exorcise that narrow belief.

Phoebe arrived on her bicycle two weeks later. "My two best short stories. I hope you enjoy them, Mrs. Lowe!"

Helen read the stories that evening. They were clearly the work of a very young writer—Phoebe was barely nineteen. The writing was energetic and assured. The stories, about young people like herself, were full of the novelty of college life and the dawning of sexuality. Helen could discern little capacity for insight, no depth or original perspective—qualities that Marjorie as a writer already possessed at thirteen. But Phoebe deserved encouragement, Helen thought—a female writer who would no doubt face the implacable literary order that she herself had struggled with and lost.

She gathered the pages together, sighing.

"Something wrong, Hal?" asked Elias. "What are you reading?"

"It's our young Phoebe," said Helen. "She wants me to tell her what I think of her stories and I'm afraid I might not have much good to say."

"Well, tell her the truth. May I read them, do you think? Would she mind?" He reached out his hand.

Helen gave him the pages. "I'm surprised you're interested."

Elias raised his eyebrows as he read. "Rather racy, don't you think? 'Nila's body ached with wanting Gordon's strong chest against hers.' I suppose this is what undergraduates get up to these days."

"Yes, but that's not the problem. I don't mind the raciness. I want to push her a bit, help her look more deeply into human experience. I'm not sure I can, though."

He handed the pages back. "You'll find a way. Anyway, the fact is she could do very well if she keeps writing like this. The hoi polloi love this sort of breathless stuff. She'll get snapped up by the publishers."

Helen made a face. "Doing very well is not the point. Deepening her readers' understanding of the human condition is the point."

"That's very high-falutin', my dear." He stood up and stretched, then squeezed her neck. "I'll see you upstairs. Don't be long."

Phoebe came three days later as planned, bringing a posy of sweet peas and phlox. Helen greeted her with a kiss. She could see that the girl was jumping out of her skin with eagerness. She sympathized—she knew all too well how much a writer wants her words to be read and admired.

"Sit down, Phoebe dear. May I give you a piece of gingerbread with your tea?"

Phoebe was disciplined enough to sip her tea and nibble at the gingerbread, waiting for Helen to start the conversation.

"Well, I read your stories," Helen began.

"Yes?" said Phoebe, leaning forward.

"Well done, very well done indeed. I—"

Phoebe cut in, smiling broadly. "Oh, Mrs. Lowe, thank you! That means so much, coming from you."

"But I do think you need to look more honestly and carefully at yourself, at your friends, at the themes that interest you. Don't be too easily satisfied, Phoebe. When our writing comes too fluently it can result in a kind of superficialness." She paused.

Phoebe's smile was gone. "You think my writing is superficial?"

Helen tried to soften her comment. "You're a good storyteller, Phoebe. You make the reader keep turning the pages. But literature can do more than that. It can make us question ourselves. It can make us see our world with new eyes."

Phoebe's own eyes were filling up. She shook her head. "I don't understand. Isn't that what we want, for readers to keep turning the pages? Isn't it a good thing for stories to be entertaining?"

Oh no, Helen thought, I've hurt the poor girl. But— entertaining? Is that all she's aiming for? She put her hand over Phoebe's. "I'm so sorry. I do see promise here. I just wonder if you've really fulfilled what you intended." Helen picked up a page where she'd made notes in the margin. "Here, for example: you say that Nila was disliked by the other girls. The reader doesn't know why, nor whether you like her yourself."

Phoebe took the page from Helen and stared at it. "I worked very hard on these stories. I really thought they were finished. I thought perhaps you might…"

At that moment Elias appeared.

"Good afternoon, ladies!" he said, doffing his panama hat. "How are you, Goldilocks? And you, Hal?" He leant over his wife and kissed the top of her head. "Do continue with your literary discussion." He cut himself a piece of gingerbread and disappeared upstairs with a jaunty wave. Helen was sorry to see him go. The conversation was not easy.

"Go on, Phoebe. What did you think I might do?"

Elias's brief interruption seemed to have restored Phoebe's spirits. "I hope this isn't too much to ask, Mrs. Lowe. If I work on them a little more, might you suggest a publisher I could send them to? Someone you know, perhaps?"

Helen was almost speechless at this self-confidence. Or naïveté, more likely. Was Phoebe really thinking about publication already? Did she imagine that Helen was on friendly terms with editors who would oblige her by reading a beginning writer? I can't tell her, she thought. I can't tell her that I have tried and utterly failed to get my own work into print. That I've given up.

She tried to demur. "Let me think—I'll let you know if there's anyone…" The conversation had become painful for her. She stood up to signal that it was over. "Phoebe, you are a gifted young writer. You'll do well." And she meant it. Phoebe would not allow criticism to hold her back. She was far more likely to find success than Helen would ever be.

28

Tonight
1932

It was the subtlest of signals—a certain warmth between them, a different quality of attention. Passing each other in the hallway closely enough to touch, as if by accident. During the busy day, beneath the reading of the newspaper, beneath her toil in the study, the shopping for meat and vegetables, the annoyance at forgetting to buy rice and having to cook some wrinkled potatoes instead, beneath it all there was a pinpoint glow: tonight. They had learned that in their middle age it no longer worked to be carelessly spontaneous. They needed time, both of them. But his physical self was still magnetic for her and hers for him. And perhaps, at last, they were equal in desire. His vaunted life force had abated with age, though hers had not, even after the change of life.

She was aware that this sturdy attraction was a kind of touchstone, bringing them back to the love that lay between them over and over again despite their mutual irritations, her own disappointments and resentments. She was grateful for it. Did other couples have this endlessly renewed passion? She had no idea. It was not something that one talked about. Nor wrote about.

There had not been a tryst to report for quite some time—not, she thought, since the South American scholar in Rome, alluring though not beautiful, he'd told her, as if she cared to know—and that was at least two years ago, possibly three. The years passed so quickly now. With the children grown, their ages no longer providing milestones, she often placed a remembered event in the much more recent past than it belonged. But nothing had happened for a long time, of that she was sure. Perhaps it's over, she thought as she waited for him to emerge from the bathroom in his navy silk robe. Perhaps it's just the two of us at last, sufficient to each other.

He turned off the light and climbed in beside her and into her arms. She could not see his face. His skin felt smooth, his limbs muscular and strong. Under his hands she felt her own shape delineated, her breasts, the indentation of her waist, the slenderness of her neck. She had the illusion that he was young, that they both were young, though their lovemaking was gentler now. She marveled yet again at the joy that their bodies engendered together—physical or spiritual, she could not distinguish.

They lay resting with fingers interlaced, her leg across his. Motionless as they were, a palpable energy flowed between them wherever their skin touched.

"Either we're degenerate or it's just a pernicious myth about sex being extinct after the age of fifty," she whispered, though there was no one else in the house and no need, these days, to be quiet.

"Degenerate, definitely," he whispered back and turned to kiss her shoulder. "My degenerate doxy."

After a while she said, "Do you think we'll still be doing this in our sixties? Our seventies?" But he was asleep.

29

The happiest day
1963

The dinner bell jolted her. She must have dozed off again, sitting there on the floor with the sherry glass in her hand. Darkness had fallen. The glass was empty, fortunately. Helen twisted up to place it on the windowsill behind her, grimacing at her stiff neck. Someone knocked on the door to call her for dinner and she sent them away. She was not the least hungry. I must have eaten lunch, she thought—yes, and something quite substantial. Quite enough for one day. She hoisted herself to her feet with a grunt and switched on the light. The window was a square of cold blackness and seemed menacing. An abyss, which she could topple into if she wasn't careful. She drew the heavy curtain. Pulling a shawl around her shoulders, she went to the bookshelf and took down her book, her own book, her darling play: the only one of her writings to find a real audience. She studied the photo on the cover. Yes, she remembered that actor, with his eyebrows like patches of fur and his voice like a bassoon, filling the theatre effortlessly. His name came into her mind. MacLiammoir. Yes. And that lovely grey-eyed woman. The silk and velvet Elizabethan costumes and the elaborate stage set, so beautifully lit. She pressed the book to her chest.

Warm now in her quiet room, Helen closed her eyes and summoned the sound of her iambic pentameter declaimed on that distant Irish stage:

> *Why, even a beast hath leave to choose his mate*
> *And shall a king in his desire be balked?*

The audience sighs and settles into the worn plush seats, ready to be stirred and shocked and entertained. Helen perches with family members in her special author's box. Had she traveled all the way from New York? With Elias? No, Elias was not there on opening night. He came later, from Rome or Paris, reserved but civil, and happy for her.

She remembers sitting pink-cheeked with pleasure, watching the story unfold on the stage as if she herself had not written it. She is wearing an evening gown and feels secretly lovely, not seventy-two years old—her back feels straighter, her knees less stiff, her smile wide and easy. At the end the warm applause ascends to her like a thermal current, faces are upturned and happy, the actors gesture toward her magnificently from in front of the maroon velvet curtain, someone behind her—Rosalind?—pushes her to stand and bow, which she does with embarrassed delight. A blond child is there beside her, Kate, it must have been—an excited little girl in her best dress and a blue ribbon in her hair. The child holds her hand tightly. "Grandma!" she whispers, tugging so that Helen bends down to listen. "Look at that man!" and she points to a stout young man in the crowd below them casting extravagant kisses up to her, one after another, with both hands. Laughing, Helen blows a kiss back to him and Kate does too.

Afterwards there is a reception with champagne and fruit salad, flouting rationing—it's only three years since the war's end. (Which war, she asked herself, suddenly unsure. The second war, it must have been. I was an elderly woman.) The actors and actresses circulate with their made-up faces, clownish at close quarters. The lead actor kisses her hand. She finds suddenly that she knows quite well how to be the illustrious playwright, a literary personage, as though she has rehearsed this role for a long time. It feels fitting. She makes a joke to two of the actresses—a risqué joke. They laugh, and she laughs with them. She drinks another glass of champagne.

"This is the happiest day of my life!" she bursts out to the son-in-law who has accompanied her. He looks down at her and she sees that he is taken aback by her exuberant remark, even disapproving. To him she is not the author covered with glory but his wife's mother, his children's grandmother. She realizes what he is thinking: the happiest day of your life, Helen? What about your wedding? What about the births of your children and your grandchildren?

And then the reviews the next day, the critics generous with their praise, though with a note of condescension—"the diminutive authoress." Exultant, she clips the reviews and sends them to the Knopfs. A few days later they send adulatory reviews from the *New York Times*—"a riot of gorgeous, colorful splendor" —and the *Christian Science Monitor*. It is simply beyond her dreams, this recognition. She feels like a comet in unstoppable orbit. *Now*, she thinks, *now* it will start, the writer's life that I have awaited for so long. Already she is flooded by ideas for stories, more plays, perhaps even another novel. To the voice that whines "But Helen, you are already so old!" she says "Age means nothing! Look at what I've done, and how they love it!"

Helen sat on the bed holding her book. She was tired now and tempted to lie down. She had no idea what time it was. Once it was dark it made no difference to her.

She turned on the bedside lamp and opened the small book again. What a good job Alfred Knopf had done, in spite of his reluctance. But not Alfred himself, of course. It would have been his designers who rendered it so beautifully. Helen admired again the generous margins, the dignified typefaces, the many photos from the production, the way the book fell open and flat as it should. She avoided the back flap where she was described as a housewife who assisted her distinguished husband and found time to do translation on the side.

She read aloud:

Ah, gentle friend, betwixt that would and could
Stretcheth a flinty waste, where nothing grows
To keep such hope from starving overnight.

She stopped, listening to her voice hanging in the still night. A sense of fullness and repose sweetened her. I wrote this. I, Helen.

Part Two

Lilacs

30

The refugee
1934

The Women's Cooperative Guild Hall was stark and poorly lit. Rows of rickety chairs faced a dais with a lectern. Someone had thought to stand a vase of lilac and apple blossom on the dais. Helen and Pauline sat near the front. The empty chairs around them soon filled with women mostly like themselves, middle-aged or older, respectably but not elegantly dressed. A sprinkling of men. Many of the women had marched for suffrage in their youth and now, like herself, were searching for a more equitable world order. The last meeting had been about the Soviet Union—the great new Communist experiment. Pauline was eager to visit Russia and wanted Helen to come with her.

But tonight was to be the opposite, a firsthand report on the alarming rise of National Socialism in Germany. Why, then, am I sitting here with a sense of wellbeing, Helen asked herself. Because of her meeting in the afternoon with Gilbert Brooks, she decided. It had gone well, with Gilbert's usual flattering praise— "Mrs. Lowe, you know that your work with Dr. Mann has set a standard for translation that will prevail throughout this century and beyond." They'd worked together for a long time now, she and Brooks, even longer than with the Knopfs and Mann. Aging has its satisfactions, she thought, these long friendships built on fruitful effort. She was aware too of a sense of pleasurable freedom being away from Oxford and her overflowing desk, in the company of her dear comrade. She would spend the night in Pauline's flat, making up a bed on the sofa in the small front room, talking together, no doubt, late into the night. In her Gladstone bag she had a seed cake that she'd made before leaving

Oxford in the morning. They would eat slices of the cake and drink Pauline's smoky Chinese tea. Perhaps Elias would take Rosalind to dinner at Corpus, a treat that all the girls enjoyed when they were home.

The speaker, when he at last appeared, extinguished all thoughts of pleasure. Everyone in the room knew of him, a German conductor famous throughout Europe and Great Britain for his gramophone recordings of the nine Beethoven symphonies. Herr Blau had no words of greeting or thanks. He dismissed the lectern with an impatient gesture—"I have nothing to read! I am telling you what happened to me!" He was a short, square man with disheveled hair and trousers that were too long for him. "You are expecting the great conductor? Well, I do not apologize for this—" he gestured to his person. "I am a refugee. I have no home. I have nothing." He seemed unable to decide where to start his story.

Helen found herself leaning forward, wanting and dreading to be open to his words. Herr Blau spoke of such terrible things, of betrayal and hatred, of friends and colleagues silenced or arrested, books and music banned, the ceaseless marching in the streets accompanied by pounding military music and screaming speeches. He spoke of his own opportunities as a musician truncated until the scope in which he could work shrank to nothing. Because he was a Jew.

"I will never go back. I can never go back. And you must listen to me, ladies and gentlemen, and prepare, because this horror may engulf you all as it has engulfed us. Herr Hitler intends it. I am here to warn you!" He rubbed his left hand vigorously with the other fist as though trying to clean it. "It is a poison. I am poisoned by it, I tell you!"

And indeed he looked ill and damaged. The picture he painted was appalling.

Helen thought about Mann, who had agonized about criticizing Hitler's horrifying regime, afraid that the publication of his new novel would be threatened if he spoke out. His cautiousness had not saved him from vicious slander and threats. He and Katia, an assimilated Jew, were holidaying in Switzerland when they were warned abruptly not to return to Germany: they were in danger of arrest. Their robust bank accounts and international supporters assured them a comfortable exile in Zurich. Unlike poor Blau.

Elias, too, was reluctant to publicly condemn the developments in Germany, which indeed seemed remote from the peaceful sanity of Oxford. Helen wished he could bring himself to say something, to identify himself as a Jew and use his privileged position to warn of the dangers of anti-Semitism.

Without turning, Pauline put her broad, gloved hand on Helen's. Helen looked at her friend's grim profile and read her thoughts. War. This was going to lead to another war, with the wounds still unhealed from the last one. After fifteen years Pauline had still said little about what she had witnessed in Serbia.

And if there's another war with Germany what will that mean for my work, Helen thought. Will English and American readers turn away in revulsion from German writers? From Mann, who refuses to use the full strength of his stature to oppose Hitler's fascism?

Herr Blau finished speaking and sank into silence. The president of the Women's Cooperative invited questions from the audience but Herr Blau seemed too spent to respond. He sat down heavily on the edge of the dais as audience members left the hall, silent or talking together in subdued voices. A few approached him to offer a brief word, which he acknowledged with a perfunctory nod. He did not look at their faces. Helen considered asking him about Mann, whom he surely knew. But Mann's political timidity would be anathema to this man, who had suffered far more. She decided not to take the risk. She pitied him, the refugee, sitting there in his ill-fitting trousers, exiled from a country that in its honorable past had given birth to the music that was his life's mission.

Pauline slipped her arm through Helen's as they walked. "We must do what we can," she said. Yes. There was always something to be done. "I will write a letter to the editor tomorrow." Pauline's occasional letters to the *Times* were always published, riveting a reader's attention in ten trenchant lines.

"If there is another war..." Helen began to say, and then stopped. We will simply have to leave, she thought, but did not say aloud. Helen and Elias had another country to escape to. Pauline did not.

The June night was mild and the streets quiet. Helen felt her wellbeing return as they walked, relishing the slight exertion as they climbed the hill to Pauline's street. She felt alive and ageless, glad to be awake in this vast pulsing city. Pauline unlocked the heavy front door and they climbed shallow marble steps to the second-floor landing. Helen was taken by the familiar charm of entering Pauline's little flat, snug as a ship's captain's quarters, if there were ever a ship's captain with such bold female taste. Cushions in purple, yellow, and orange velvet covers were piled on the sofa. One of Pauline's own paintings, bright and abstract, hung over the mantelpiece above a small fireplace where no coal had burned since the house was divided into flats and the legions of coal-scuttle-carrying maids departed.

"Make yourself at home," said Pauline. "I'll put the kettle on."

Helen unwrapped the seed cake and brought it into the windowless kitchen to find a plate and knife. "Naughty lass," said Pauline, pleased at the cake. Helen cut it in slices, then stood for a minute at the living room window looking down. The window of the tearoom across the road was lit by a streetlamp, showing neat cloth-covered trays awaiting Saturday morning's buns and sausage rolls. A man strolled by whistling, his face invisible under the peak of his cap. She drew the curtains and sat down with a sigh, thinking again of Germany and its monstrous Führer. When she returned home she'd have to make Elias listen.

With his wife on her way to London Elias indulged in a long morning bath with elderflower bath salts. Afterwards, naked and warm, he performed calisthenics in front of the window, breathing deeply, being careful with his back which had developed a tendency to ache. The lilac in the back garden was in bloom and its voluptuous scent drifted up to the bedroom. Rosalind was out until supper or later. Until his lunch guest arrived he was alone. He hummed a drinking song from his student days in Munich and took a few dance steps with an imaginary partner. Still humming, he chose a cream-colored linen shirt and looked for a tie to complement it.

He heard a knock, then the front door opening. "Hello?" called Phoebe's voice. "It's me!"

Elias broke off his song. From the top of the stairs he called to her. "Goldilocks! Do come in!" He knotted his aubergine silk tie hastily and skipped down two flights.

Phoebe held out a basket covered with a red and white checked cloth. "New potatoes and carrots from Mother's garden. And some mint."

"Rosalind's not here after all, I'm afraid," he said. "And Helen had to go to town, until tomorrow. But we'll have a little salad and some cheese, shall we?" He took the basket. "How very kind. Nature's bounty. Your dear mother's bounty." He looked again at Phoebe, fresh-faced from her walk, her light dress skimming bare knees. A tennis dress, Rosalind would have called it. "A small glass of Sancerre?"

Phoebe had a bit of a palate, unlike his daughters. On holiday with the family in France when Phoebe and Rosalind were in their teens, it had been a ritual—Elias would invite Phoebe to choose a bottle for the evening meal, then wait for her verdict on the first sip, coaching her wine-lover's vocabulary.

"Sancerre would be lovely!" She followed him to the living room where the scent of lilac was even stronger—Helen had put a vase of purple and white blooms on the mantelpiece. Elias touched the bottle: cold, though not chilled. It was opened last night but was still fresh. He poured two crystal glasses of the faintly golden wine. Phoebe sat on the edge of the couch. I must put her at her ease, he thought. He knew she'd enjoyed their lunches and walks but they hadn't been alone together in the house before.

Elias pulled a footstool near to her and perched on it, looking up at her. The leaves of the ficus by the window cast a patterned shadow on her arm. "My dear…" he began.

But Phoebe was shaking her head with a smile. "My goodness, your tie, Dr. Lowe!" He glanced down and saw the knot askew. "Shall I fix it?" She dropped onto her knees for a moment and retied it for him. "There!"

"Ah yes, thank you," he said. He raised his glass to clink hers, looking at her with plain admiration. "Here's to you!" Phoebe flushed charmingly. "And to you!" she said. They drank, suddenly silent, glancing at each other and smiling. He was engulfed again by the surge of desire which Phoebe aroused in him—this girl whom he'd known since she was in pinafores. He was reasonably sure by now that it was reciprocated.

They both spoke at once—"How was the rest of your time in Paris?" "What did you think of the Evelyn Waugh?"—and then laughed together.

"You first," Phoebe said.

He asked again about the book he'd lent her, watching her mouth and the animation of her eyes as she answered. She was wearing lipstick but no other make-up, an attractively healthy girl with the breath of the outdoors on her.

"Excuse me," Elias said and reached up to pick a hair off her dress. He held it up to glint in the light. It was like a strand of twisted gold wire. She looked at him, eyes wide. She *sees* me, he thought. My age doesn't matter.

Elias put his glass down on the carved sandalwood cake stand and sat down beside her on the couch. He turned to her, lifting the cloud of hair that lay on her neck.

"Beautiful girl." He took the wineglass gently out of Phoebe's hand, then stood and drew her to her feet. "Beautiful girl," he said again, softly. His arms encircled her. She was his height, slim where he was broad and sturdy. Their bodies fit together. Elias inclined his head and looked at her, a question in his eyes. Phoebe's eyelids closed and her body pressed into his. He kissed her neck and felt her tremble.

"Dr. Lowe!" she whispered. "Is this…"

"Don't worry," he murmured. "Don't worry." Her mouth was as delicious as he'd dreamed it would be, her arms around him a blessing.

The house was silent. Rosalind would not be home for several hours, Helen not until the morning. Alice and Marjorie were far away. He led Phoebe upstairs, with a great flare of gratitude to his beloved Helen for understanding that these encounters were necessary for him, that they had nothing at all to do with the enduring love between them. What a truly extraordinary woman I am married to, he thought.

He walked past their bedroom, instead taking Phoebe into Marjorie's room, empty and tidy now that she was at boarding school. The bed was narrow, the gingham-covered pillow crowded with the stuffed animals that Marjorie insisted on keeping, to Helen's annoyance. Elias gathered them up and piled them on the scratched-up desk by the window. He closed the curtains and did not look at the framed photo of the family, ten years ago at the beach in Dorset.

Phoebe unbuttoned her dress and let him draw her down onto the little bed. Elias proceeded with practiced skill, savoring the firm youthful flesh. The girl was worldly, he knew that, but perhaps had not yet experienced the full joys of lovemaking. But after a few minutes she paused and put a hand on his chest. "I'm not a…" she whispered. "We don't need to go so slowly." He understood, and was relieved, though with a tinge of disappointment. This young lady knows what she wants, he thought, pounding into her without reserve.

31

Meeting Helen's train
1934

Early morning light awakened her, in spite of the curtains, and for a moment she had no idea where she was. Helen coasted pleasurably on this momentary disorientation—where was she? *who* was she?—and then recalled that she was in London, and would go home soon. She was immediately wide awake, eager to tell Elias about the refugee conductor, how he spoke of feeling poisoned and frightened. Elias, who once saw Herr Blau conducting in Berlin, would be disturbed. Helen wanted him to be disturbed. She believed he was too complacent, too quick to dismiss the growing anti-Semitism in Europe as a passing idiocy. He certainly felt no threat to himself. Sometimes Helen suspected that he'd forgotten he was a Jew. He never talked about it, barely mentioned his Russian émigré family in New York, did not note the Jewish holidays. "A Jewish don at Oxford!" Elias had exulted when he was offered the position, but since then he had not wanted to think of himself in these terms. He was Professor Lowe now, not Professor Loew.

The girls didn't think about religion at all. They were Anglicans by default, like all their friends, attending church occasionally, taking for granted the marking of the year with Easter and Christmas.

But now, with prominent Jews in Germany being shut out of their professional circles, arrested, disappeared, and worse— would not Elias feel a chill of foreboding? They must talk about contingencies, plans.

Helen tiptoed to the window and opened the curtains. The street was empty except for a black and white terrier trotting purposefully along the pavement as though to an appointment. The tearoom was still closed but she could see someone bustling in the shadows.

She put on the kettle, trying not to wake Pauline, and carried the teapot back to the front room. Pauline appeared after a few minutes with a dressing gown over her red flannel nightgown.

"How nice to find you in my living room!" said Pauline. She went into the kitchen and returned in a few minutes with a rack of toast along with butter and marmalade. On her armchair in the sunlight, a plate of toast on her lap, she preened like a cat. Pauline does look rather like a large and well-fed feline, thought Helen, appreciating her friend's broad, contented face and orange-grey short-cropped hair. She lacked only whiskers.

"Do you think I'm mad to keep translating German writers?" asked Helen, buttering her toast.

"Mad because no one will read them? Or because you find it morally equivocal?" Outside there was the percussion of horse's hooves and a rattle of bottles. "Behold the milkman cometh," said Pauline.

"Both, I suppose," Helen responded. "Losing readers and possibly supporting this dreadful regime. Not Mann, of course, now that he's finally burnt his bridges with the Nazis. But I don't know about this fellow." She leafed through the book of short stories that Brooks had given her. "I should investigate his political views."

"Translate Mann and the other good Germans, love. They deserve our solidarity. But you're right, we might decline to buy their books, if war starts to loom." Pauline sighed through her nose and shook her head. "Excuse me a moment," she said, slipping out the front door still in her dressing gown and slippers. She came back upstairs, slightly out of breath, with a pint of milk. "He brings me a bottle every other day but I can barely finish it before it goes off," she said. Pauline did not complain about her solitary life and claimed to prefer it to family cacophony. "I get quite enough of the noisy young every day from nine to four, thank you very much," she'd said once. "I'm quite happy to come home to Mr. Nobody."

Helen admired her. If Pauline had been forced into a single woman's life by the Great War, like thousands of other girls, she did not claim this as her story. There were compensations, Helen could see: Pauline was a well-respected headmistress in a good London school instead of a rank-and-file teacher in Leeds, as she would have been if half the men of her generation were not moldering under the killing fields of France. And she'd created this cozy little nest without having to accommodate anyone else's taste or needs.

"I must go," Helen said after breakfast had stretched into morning tea. They had consumed all of Helen's cake. There was always so much to talk about. "I promised Elias I would be on the 12:10."

"Oh well, and who am I to compete with your lord and master?"

The women laughed and embraced quickly as they said goodbye. "Come back soon," said Pauline. "Stay with me whenever you want."

Elias woke early as well. At breakfast with Rosalind they chatted about her classes, the weather, her imminent trip to France to visit Alice, who was taking classes at the Sorbonne. He was suffused by the wellbeing of yesterday, at the edges of which lurked an uneasiness that he did not want to explore.

"Where did these lovely things come from?" asked Rosalind, noticing the basket of vegetables. She brandished a carrot with a luxuriant green top, then rinsed it under the tap and took a bite.

"Oh!" said Elias. "I meant to put them away. Phoebe brought them by yesterday, from her mother's garden," he said casually. He watched to see if she reacted to Phoebe's name but there was nothing. "You look rather like Peter Rabbit, dear." He piled the carrots and potatoes into the hanging wire baskets that Helen used.

"Very nice of Phoebe and her ma. I'm sorry I wasn't here." She bent to tie her shoe. "I'm off to play tennis, Daddy, then the library. Home tonight."

Elias found his panama hat and took his work out to the ironwork table on the back porch. The weather was heavenly, almost Mediterranean. After a while he looked at his watch. I'll surprise Helen, he thought. And take her for lunch.

Helen's compartment was empty except for a plump woman softly snoring in the corner with her hat pulled down over her eyes. The countryside clicked by, tranquil waterways, green and yellow fields, all benign in hazy sunlight. Helen took out the story collection by a man who might or might not be a Nazi sympathizer. It occurred to her that she had never once been asked to translate a woman writer. She was struck with wonder that this was so, and that she had never realized it before. There were plenty of contemporary women writers in English, formidable authors like Mrs. Woolf and her daring friend Mrs. Sackville-West. They must have counterparts in German, and other languages. Why did their works not appear in translation? Why should those voices be known only to their compatriots? The male stranglehold again, she supposed. I must take this up with the Knopfs, she thought. Blanche, particularly, will be interested. Perhaps we can start a small revolution. The idea excited her. She'd ask Mann to suggest works by women that merited publication in English. Why on earth had she not thought of it before?

Helen was thinking about this new frontier when the train pulled into the station and stopped with a jolt. The idea had put her in excellent spirits, in spite of Herr Blau. She quickly stuffed her books and papers into her bag and climbed down.

Elias was waiting on the platform. He smiled at her pleased surprise and kissed her cheek. He was dapper in summer linen and a panama hat, and looked at peace with the world—the opposite of the unkempt and unhappy Blau.

"A beautiful day to meet the London train!" he said, taking her bag from her. "Have you lunched? I thought we might find something on the way back." They walked together along busy George Street. On the bridge over the tree-lined canal the air was sweet with the scents of June, a green smell, Marjorie always said. It was not just the lilacs in fragrant bloom. It was the smell of leaves, of running sap, breathing bark, growing grass. Helen longed to talk about her idea of translating female German writers but decided to wait until she'd taken the first steps on her own, knowing from past experience that Elias was likely to smother her excitement with either skepticism or his own enthusiastic suggestions.

"Elias, I must tell you what Dieter Blau said about Germany." She repeated what the conductor told them, how he frantically scrubbed his hand and spoke of poison. She tried to describe the man's urgency, unmediated by diplomacy or caution.

As she expected, Elias demurred. "The poor man. I don't doubt his suffering. But his story can hardly be common, surely."

Helen turned to look at him. "Elias—that's the point. That's what he's telling us. It's happening to Jews all over Germany and Austria and Poland. He says Hitler plans to destroy them all. 'Liquidate' is the charming word he uses, apparently. *Liquidieren.*"

Elias was shaking his head. "The Jews have a very nice line in martyrdom, after two thousand years," he said, as if he was not one of them and would not be rounded up by Hitler's thugs without a second thought. "Anyway, let's not spoil a lovely day with such dire thoughts." He chuckled, as though he'd just thought of something amusing. "Hal, you'll never guess—may I change the subject?—you'll never guess what happened yesterday."

Helen pulled herself away from the outrages of the Third Reich. He heard me, she thought. He'll let it sink in when he's ready. Or when there is no longer any choice. "What happened yesterday?"

"I was upstairs getting ready to go over to college and young Phoebe came by, looking for Rosalind, I suppose, or you. Bearing a cornucopia from her mother's garden. Really, it was like Persephone at the front door."

Helen waited.

"But, of course, neither of you were there," continued Elias. "She's grown into rather a lusty young wench, you know—have you ever seen that in her?"

She didn't speak. Yes, of course, how could one not see that in her?

"She joined me in a glass of wine, and then she wanted to tie my tie for me, since I had done a poor job of it, and before you know it, we were simply swept off our feet. I mean literally horizontal." He chuckled again. "Not at all what I was expecting on my quiet Friday. I have a feeling she came with seduction in mind."

Helen was fighting a sense of unreality. The world seemed quite preposterous all of a sudden. She stopped in the middle of the sidewalk, oblivious to the passersby who had to step around her and Elias.

"You slept with Phoebe Hadley."

He glanced at her. "Yes, that's what I said."

"You slept with Rosalind's friend."

"Hal..."

"In our house." Her voice was trembling. "*In our bedroom, Elias?*"

"No, no, Hal, not in our bedroom, of course not," he said hastily. "Dear, it was just one of those moments. A life force moment of tidal wave proportions. It would have been a violation to say no."

Helen was afraid she might lose her balance and fall to the ground. She grabbed Elias's arm to steady herself, for a second comforted by the familiar feel of it, then repelled. She let go and pushed him away from her.

"Elias!" she cried.

He seemed shocked at her anguish. "Hal—I don't understand. You've always been so wonderful about this."

Words had fled. She snatched her Gladstone bag from him and walked on at a furious pace. All she wanted was to get home and lock herself in her bedroom. To put a solid door between her and this man who had stabbed her in the heart and didn't have the wit to realize it.

Elias tried to overtake her but she would not look at him or speak to him. The fifteen-minute walk seemed endless. Would Rosalind be there? She hoped desperately not. She could not bear to see her daughter at this moment, though it wasn't the poor girl's fault that her father had seduced her friend. Did she even know? Most likely not.

At least Alice was in France and Marjorie away at school. At least that.

Helen was aware of drawing curious looks as she rushed down Cornmarket at breakneck speed with her face set in misery. She must not collapse, she must not cry, until she was safe in her room.

Elias followed her home, walking like an automaton along the familiar streets. He couldn't finish a thought. "I would never—never—" he said to Helen in his mind. "Hal, please try to—" "It meant nothing—" "I was taken by surprise—"

He went straight up to their room but the door was locked. He knocked and called out: "Please, Helen! Please!" She did not reply. After a while Elias gave up trying to talk to her, instead leaving a tray of tea and bread and butter outside the door.

He sat in the kitchen, an untouched cup in front of him. She is a reasonable person, he said to himself, an exceptional woman. We adore each other. She'll calm down soon and then she will understand that I meant her no harm in succumbing to that damned girl—that it had nothing to do with her at all. He longed for the moment when Helen came back to herself and forgave him and they returned to their pleasant way of being together. It would simply take patience.

32

Montmartre
1934

She did not have a map for this new territory, the bleak country of the betrayed wife. Elias's sexual encounters in Rome or Berlin or New York had been painful but shallow wounds that healed eventually, leaving scars that she could ignore once the hurt subsided. Though she had wished often that she could annul the stupid promise made when she did not know any better. She was Elias's wife and his lover and she did not accept that he needed more than they had together.

This was different. A body blow, a cruel treachery not only from her husband but from a girl she'd looked after and loved along with her own daughters. Every day Helen was forced to anticipate where she might encounter Phoebe and plan her movements so that she did not. Oxford was so small. Phoebe, she presumed, was just as anxious to avoid her. She tried to suppress her reflexive concern for the girl herself, who must have been suffering her own torments. She did not believe for a moment that it was Phoebe who was the seducer.

The raw pain abated intermittently, from sheer exhaustion, and then she found herself viewing the whole thing as a very bad novel, the kind of rubbish that she would never read. How distasteful, how mortifying, to be thrust into this mess.

The strain of living alongside Elias was all but unbearable. She tried to work on the translation waiting on her desk but her mind refused to focus, imprisoned instead in obsessive thoughts that she knew, with a small sane part of her, could lead nowhere. I'll get another scolding from Alfred, she thought, and this time his impatience will be justified. But there was nothing she could do about it, not yet.

She and Elias tried to talk but each attempt collapsed in anger and accusation. In their sleepless nights they passed each other in the hallway like ghosts. In August Elias escaped to Paris with open relief, shared by Helen. But after a week he begged her to come and visit for a few days.

"Please, Helen," he wrote. "It would be salutary for both of us to see each other here instead of Oxford. We must give ourselves a chance to find peace together again."

Reluctantly she agreed to come, though she feared that the precious thing between them had been irrevocably lost. Elias found a room for her at his pension near the Bibliothèque Nationale. The room under the mansard roof with its sloping ceiling, its chaste white-covered single bed, the sanded floorboards reminded her of Munich. She glanced at Elias and knew that he was remembering too.

Could he be right, wondered Helen. Perhaps, here in Paris, away from Oxford, we'll be able to talk more openly and calmly. Perhaps we can find each other again. She let herself harbor a small hope.

Paris in high summer was perfumed with blooming lilies and roses, festive with high-spirited visitors. They decided to visit Montmartre, like people at leisure. Then she learned, to her annoyance, that he had invited two of his French colleagues to join them, young men who were assisting in his research. "I thought—" she began to say, then stopped herself.

They climbed cobbled streets with the white dome of the Basilica soaring against blue sky like an Utrillo painting. The day was hot and they paused to drink water from a canteen that Elias produced from his satchel. Helen was caught again by memory, this time of the Bavarian woods. A lifetime ago, when they were falling in love.

Elias's friends were waiting for them on the steps of Sacré Coeur, well-combed young men who clearly looked up to Elias, as other paleographers always did. They greeted her with small bows and kisses on each cheek.

"*Enchanté*, Madame Lowe," said one of them. "We had the pleasure of meeting your daughter in May."

"Oh, you met Alice!" said Helen, pleased that Elias would think to introduce them.

"I think your other daughter. A lovely name—Phoebe."

Helen felt her lips grow white. Elias's hand tightened on her arm. He chatted to his friends as they walked on. Helen could not speak. Phoebe was here, with Elias, in Paris. Three months ago—a month before the supposed *coup de foudre* in Oxford.

"Do forgive me," she interrupted. "I must sit for a minute." Elias waved the others ahead. He and Helen faced each other.

"Well?" she hissed. "Well?" Tears threatened and she willed them away.

"Helen. She wasn't—we didn't—"

"You always swore you would not lie to me!"

"And I haven't! Helen, please believe me. Yes, Phoebe happened to be here in May, and we had a drink together. That's all. At the Café Paix."

"I don't care which damn café!"

Elias glanced at his friends who were still in earshot. "Let's not shout, for god's sake."

She wanted to scream but did not.

"I didn't lie to you," he said. "I didn't think I had to report to you every time I see a friend at a café."

Helen forced her voice to be quiet and steady, though she permitted herself sarcasm, since he had.

"So, may I ask, have there been other times that you and Phoebe have just *happened* to cross paths?"

"No! Well, perhaps once or twice in Oxford, I really don't remember exactly. We might have bumped into each other. Honestly, Helen, do you really want to submit me to an interrogation? This is demeaning to both of us. Here, why don't you examine my diary?" and he pulled out his pocket diary, where meetings with Phoebe were cryptically noted, and offered it to her. She pushed it away, as he knew she would.

Helen strode ahead and he had to trot to catch up with her. The French men chatted with an artist in front of his display of paintings. Elias ventured an arm around her waist but she flung it off. He saw that she was in distress and felt stricken himself.

"I have not lied to you," he said again.

She turned to look at him with scorn. "There are different ways of lying, Elias. As you know."

They said little to each other for the rest of the day. During their silent dinner Helen stopped drinking her glass of wine when she realized that she was in danger of losing her composure. Or, worse, reaching for his hand. She couldn't quell her yearning for the touch of him. At the pension they retired to their rooms with a curt good night.

The curtains were open. Helen gazed unseeing at the moonlit Paris rooftops. Church bells rang the half hour, the hour, and the next. Every nerve was attuned to Elias in the next room. At midnight she got up, opened his door quietly and tiptoed to his bed. He opened his arms to her without a word. They held each other, both weeping.

When he woke in the morning she was not beside him. Her own bedroom was empty. He found her in the breakfast room downstairs, pale but composed. She told him that she was leaving him. Their marriage is over, she said, though for everyone's sake they would not publicly announce a separation. "I will live in London," she said. "With Pauline, I hope."

"Helen—no—please," he stammered. He wanted to remonstrate with her, to tell her how foolish this is, what an absurd overreaction, but knew these were not the right words.

33

Who am I?
1936

Riddle:
I have a home but I do not live in it
I have found refuge but I am displaced
I am a wife but I have no husband
I am a mother but my children do not need me
I am a writer but my work is smoke
I fight for justice but I am oppressed
I am read by thousands but no one knows my name
Who am I?

Elias is invited to go to America, to a newly founded enclave of scholars. It is a great honor, he says. He asks me to come with him. He wants me to have forgotten his betrayal. Two years apart is long enough, he says.

No. Not long enough for me.

I will never share a home with him again. He squandered my devotion and trust. Thirty years' worth. I'd rather be a wanderer forever, making my bed where I can find it. Like here, on this brown couch, folding up my sheets and blankets each morning and tucking them out of sight.

He reminds me that he's been endowed with good fortune all his life, which is true. He says he would like to share it with me. He points out that, unfair as it is, I myself am not so endowed. Which is also true. I deserve better. So he says.

He reminds me that I could go to the island in the summers, if I lived in America again. Charlotte's island, the house in the spruces, now mine, waiting for me. An inducement, I admit.

But I am not ready.

He warns me that another war is likely, and I should get to safety while I can.

I am not ready.

Let him go to his Institute. Let him make a new life.

Meanwhile all I can do is keep my feet on the ground. Like Pauline. She knows how to do it. One foot in front of the other until you turn around and realize that the past is far behind you. She says I should start writing again, my own work. That it would help me. But I cannot.

There was yet another Mann manuscript on Helen's desk, the third of his *Joseph* tetralogy. Mann was writing steadily, never a pause in his daily output despite being displaced himself. It helped, she thought sourly, to be living in Swiss luxury. Mann's study was now reconstituted exactly as it was in Munich, he'd told her with complacency—whereas her territory had shrunk to whatever corner she could claim at Pauline's. And her lap desk, a board slung across the arms of her chair. On the worst days, when she hardly knew where or who she was, she was grateful for the work—the descent into the depths of Mann's German, emerging with a frail English sentence and holding it up to the light, breathing strength and vigor into it until it could stand on its own. Over and over, thousands of times. It kept the blood moving through her veins and her mind turned away from her fate.

Helen envied Mann's momentum and his absolute belief in the worth of what he was doing. How on earth does he do it, she wondered. Well, there's a foolish question. Genius, to start with, and adulation, and money, none of which I have.

Pauline nodded when Helen told her about the bonfire in her study. "You know," she said, "in Cumberland the farmers burn the fields on purpose. We all go out and watch. It's quite a sight, acres of flames leaping to the sky. They have to do it every now and then, to bring back the fertility."

Helen looked at her. She had no hope or expectation that her own conflagration would lead to fertility. So far she had written not a word.

"I'm afraid I've come to the valley of never," she said.

Pauline raised her eyebrows.

"Do you remember that banner, at the suffragist rally ages ago, when we met?" said Helen. "'Over the pass of by-and-by, You go to the valley of never.' They had drawn the letters so beautifully. It's always stayed in my mind. They meant the vote, of course. But now, for me..." She stopped. A quicksand of misery lay in front of her.

"Oh, dear one," said Pauline. "You're thinking about your writing."

"I tried for so long, Pauline! It was what I've wanted more than anything. And now..."

Pauline heaved herself out of her chair and came to sit next to Helen on the couch.

"Tell me," she said. "Tell me why you haven't done what you hoped."

Helen frowned. "What do you mean? You know perfectly well."

144

"I want you to put it into words for me." There was a touch of headmistressly authority in her voice.

Helen nodded. "Well then." She took a deep breath and exhaled sharply. "I disobeyed Aunt Charlotte. I married and had children. My children needed mothering. My husband needed moral and secretarial support. That's part of it. And the other part..."

"Yes?"

"The other part is my profession. Pauline, it's such a paradox. I do relish translating, it stretches me, I am constantly gratified to engage with Mann's writing. And I believe I'm competent at it. There is happiness in doing work that one does well, isn't there? Not to mention earning an income, humble as it is."

"All of that, yes," said Pauline. "But the fact is it's not enough. Why?"

"Is this how you quiz your sixth formers?" asked Helen wryly. She sat in silence for a moment. "All right. Let me ask you a question. What about your own work? Do you feel—what's the word—*aligned*—with it? Would you say that education is your calling?"

"It is. And I do. There's nothing else I'd rather be doing."

"See, Pauline, that's what's different for me. You're aligned with your work, Elias is aligned with his, Mann with his, god knows. Both of them are completely single-minded. They're not plagued by the suspicion that there's something else they should be doing. But me—committed as I am to translation, it's *not* my deepest calling. Being a writer, being an artist is my calling. And I've betrayed it." She was alarmed to hear a sob in her voice and tried to summon control. "I feel it as a sin. A grave sin that I am guilty of. And I see no way to change course. So here I am, you see, stuck in the valley of never."

Pauline reached an arm around her. "But listen, we did get the vote eventually, didn't we? Persistence pays off."

But Helen shook her head, despairing.

34

A college girl
1936

It was her father's decampment to the Institute for Advanced Study that put the idea into Marjorie's head. They all expected her to follow her sisters to Oxford University once she left boarding school, but with her mother now in London and her father in America, how perfect to go to college instead in the land of her birth, sidestepping the likely shame of being turned down by Oxford. She wasn't a brill like Rosalind and Alice.

And then she had a further inspiration—her mother's alma mater! Wells College was Great-Aunt Charlotte's alma mater as well, so it was a family tradition. And a small American women's college in rural New York would surely be easier than Oxford.

Marjorie was eager to tell her mother about her idea. They met occasionally in a tearoom or a park, avoiding both the soon-to-be-sold Oxford house and Miss Mackie's flat. Her parents' vague explanations about their new living arrangements had left Marjorie and her sisters mystified. Until her father's decision to leave the country Marjorie had hoped that they would think the better of their incomprehensible separation. She looked forward to everything returning to normal. But now...

"Mother, I've been thinking about something. I want to tell you," she said as they carried their trays of tea and scones to a table by the window. "Since Daddy's going to live in America, I'd like to go to college there. Instead of here."

Helen, walking in front, didn't react. Marjorie waited impatiently until they were seated in front of their cups and saucers.

"Mother? What do you think?"

Helen looked blank.

Marjorie repeated her suggestion. "I've been thinking a lot about it," she went on. She leaned forward. "And—guess what! I've decided to go to Wells College! Following in your footsteps!"

But Helen did not light up as Marjorie had imagined. "Oh— no, dear, I don't think so," she said, stirring her tea. "That wouldn't be a good idea."

"But why not? I don't understand!" She forced herself not to pout like a disappointed child.

"They know who we are," was all Helen would say, leaving Marjorie to conclude that her mother thought she would not be a credit to herself or to Aunt Charlotte. "There are plenty of other colleges, Marjorie, if you really want to go to America."

But Marjorie couldn't give up her vision of Wells College. It was so clear in her mind from her mother's stories—the rose-wallpapered parlor where Helen and her friends had read Shelley and Wordsworth aloud together for fun, the blue lake where they dipped their toes on hot afternoons.

Her mother was not the arguer she used to be. She seemed unsure of herself and lacking stamina. Her work was not going smoothly, she told Marjorie. In the end Helen shrugged, and said, well, go ahead then, and your father can be responsible for you.

Marjorie applied to the college, emphasizing her distinguished forebears in hopes of compensating for her academic record. She was accepted and wrote to Elias, who was at first taken aback. He hadn't expected to have a daughter nearby, in his new life. But he rather liked the idea, once he got used to it.

She landed in New York and, following her father's instructions, found the bus that would take her to Princeton, then a taxi to his home at the Institute. At his front door he greeted her with arms wide. "Welcome, dear!"

She stepped into his embrace. "Daddy!" Here we are, she thought, just us, in a new country.

It was jarring to find her father in this unfamiliar place with its endless green lawns, towering trees and imitation-old buildings, like a college campus in an American movie, though unlike the movie-set campuses there were no clean-cut young American students strolling around the Institute with striped scarves and books under their arms. Marjorie saw only old men and one or two old women, all of them famous scholars, Elias explained. They were there to do their research and writing, enriched by proximity to other extraordinary minds. No one was expected to teach.

Her father seemed different from his Oxford self, more casual, friendlier, in his open-collared shirt and slipper-like shoes with no laces.

"I must say, it's very nice to have a daughter around," he said, sitting down to a lunch that she had prepared. "I'm not cut out to be a bachelor."

It seemed impossible to ask him what she really wanted to know: why are you here? Why is Mother not with you? She could not get used to the idea that her parents were on different continents instead of in their cozy house with bedrooms for all their children, and the books and paintings and tablecloths and plates that she'd lived with all her life. Marjorie and her sisters, in their worried speculation, had concluded that the separation was their mother's doing since it was she who'd left. Helen, in her new remoteness, had offered them no explanation. "It's as though she left us, too," Marjorie had complained.

Marjorie was both eager and scared to get to Wells College. "Oh, you'll be fine," her father reassured her, patting her knee as he drove her back to the bus station after a few days. "Just keep your head down and do the work. And come and visit me."

Marjorie was used to her English schoolmates being impressed when she told them she was born in America. So it was a surprise to discover that now she apparently had cachet for

148

being English. "You sound just like Merle Oberon!" the other girls exclaimed admiringly. Marjorie knew she did not sound like Merle Oberon or any of those pretentious British actresses. No one talked like that in real life. But the attention pleased her. She wanted the American girls to like her. In this bewildering new environment she tried once or twice to raise her stock by mentioning Oxford or Thomas Mann. But her new friends knew little about either.

Their voices seemed over-loud and effusive to her own ear, not at all like her mother's mild, refined way of speaking. Two months after arriving she was still pricked by homesickness for England's narrow streets and terraced houses and polite people. She missed Yorkshire pudding and the toffee that she would stockpile in her drawer, to her mother's exasperation.

Her roommate Susan told her that her boyfriend from the men's college a couple of hours away was coming to visit for the weekend. "And he's bringing his friend Ken to meet you," she said. "Ken's cute!"

Marjorie reminded herself that in America "cute" meant sexy, rather than small and dimpled.

"He's going to love your accent."

Marjorie wondered how much time she'd have to spend with them. The assignments from her classes were harder than she'd expected and she was alarmingly behind in her reading. But having friends was important too. She was determined to succeed at Wells, to fit in and pass her exams and prove to her parents that coming here was indeed the right thing to do.

35

This upstart crow
1936

For months the London newspapers had been full of royal upheavals—the death of the beloved king, the succession of his popular son, the new king's refusal to rule without the woman he loved and wished to marry, the church's refusal to accept a queen who was foreign and divorced, therefore immoral; the surprising protests from commoners who thought a king should be allowed to choose his mate.

"Spoiled, self-important idiots, the lot of them," said Pauline, looking at a photo of the assembled royal family in their finery. "What they need is a revolution. Where are the Bolsheviks when you need them?"

Helen agreed, in principle. The monarchy was an anachronism, a feudal system that should have no place in the modern world. Hereditary privilege should be banished, as in the Soviet Union, letting equality reign in its stead—"'From each according to his ability, to each according to his needs,'" quoted Pauline if given a chance. She was still determined to visit Moscow. Helen shared her idealism but expressed caution. There had been disturbing rumors of brutality in Stalin's utopia. "Well, we should go and see for ourselves!" Pauline had said. "Well, maybe we shall!" responded Helen.

The current chaos in the British establishment seemed to offer up the possibility of something new—not communism, but a departure from the old ways.

"He's not like the others," protested Helen. "He's almost a socialist. Look at his solidarity with the Welsh miners!"

"Don't be taken in, dear," said Pauline. "He has no more political analysis than my old tabby cat. It's sentimentality at best, if not cynical posturing. He's a solid right-winger at heart, like the rest of them. You'll see."

"Good heavens," said Pauline a week later, slapping the evening paper then holding it up so Helen could see the huge headlines. "He's going to do it—he's going to abdicate! How very Shakespearian it all is."

The word pulled a switch for Helen. Shakespearian indeed. A situation worthy of a Shakespearian play, or at least an ersatz Shakespearian play: royalty, succession, defiant love. She was seized with the old desire to write, to create—an almost erotic desire that she thought had gone forever, suddenly back full force. The play demanded to be written. She would call it "Abdication, or All is True"—stealing *Henry VIII*'s original name for her subtitle.

It was a perfect moment. Her most recent translation was on its way to Knopf. Before long the next one would land on her desk with a thump. But now a little gap, a hiatus, enough to get started, at least.

Helen leapt in with the ghost of Aunt Charlotte cheering her on. Blank verse flowed like a native language. She knew, even as she wrote, that it was the most dreadful nerve to adopt this archaic style. But it so accommodated the story, and her own passion and humor—the pleasure was exhilarating. She sat down at Pauline's little dinner table each evening tired but energized and merry, drinking her glass of red wine with a sense of well-deserved reward.

It had been years since she'd been filled with this particular happiness.

The play found its shape with relative ease. Her characters took on their own fictional lives—they were and were not the real-life royal characters now riveting the attention of the country. Her abdicating king was not Pauline's self-indulgent ignoramus but a noble idealist who'd earned the support of the common man. He adored the woman he wanted to marry with a passion and loyalty that stirred yearning in his creator—what must that be like, to love someone enough to defy the demands of history? To be loved like that? She turned away from the thought before it pushed her into sadness again.

Helen stilled herself to hear her characters' voices, crafting their words, choreographing their encounters on the stage. The work elated her. She felt at last the sense of alignment that had been so elusive—each facet of her life at last in its rightful proportion. In the mornings she sprang out of bed before it was fully light, eager to return to the page she had left the night before. The inevitable artistic obstacles left her undaunted. After four weeks she had a draft. She gathered the manuscript together and sat down to read, pencil in hand. Again she had a sense of surprise, as though these words and characters were not her own creation. She found herself entertained by their earthy wit, their pathos.

The final pages made her chortle aloud.

"What's funny, love?" Pauline asked, looking up.

"Sorry!" Helen said. "I didn't mean to interrupt you." It was a fading, drizzly Sunday and they were at their usual stations in the living room, Pauline reading on the sofa with her slippers on the wrong feet, for comfort, as she explained, and Helen in her armchair with her writing board. A platter of asparagus rolls from the tearoom across the street sat on the coffee table between them, so far untouched.

"May I read you a few lines, Pauline? It's the epilogue—I've enlisted the Bard himself to do it."

"Have you now!" Pauline put down her book and took off her glasses. "I'm listening."

Helen stood up with her pages and struck a bard-like pose, a theatrical sneer on her face: "'This upstart crow hath thought to beautify herself with my feathers, and hath bombasted out some lines of blank verse—as cometh pat to my tongue, since it hath in my time been said of me too, though truly the wench doth not merit the coupling.' Et cetera et cetera. He goes on for a page or so, craving the audience's indulgence on my behalf."

Pauline clapped her hands and whistled. "You are indeed a wicked wench, Helen," she said. "Very wicked and very clever. Didn't Shakespeare get called an upstart crow by one of his rivals?"

"Yes, I stole it, magpie that I am."

"And why not. Helen—this play is going to be a great success. I do believe that it will."

Helen stared at her. She felt a sense of confidence and accomplishment that had never accompanied her own writing before. The Mann translations brought a kind of stolid satisfaction, a journeyman's pride in a difficult job well done. The artistry of it was covert. Not like this—not this headiness of pure creation, this mysterious sense of aesthetic rightness; the right word, the right dramatic interaction to embody the meanings and turnings and archetypal echoes of the story.

Was it possible that Pauline's words were prophetic—that at last she'd written something that was going to succeed?

But no one in England would touch it. The manuscript traveled the desks of editors and theatre directors who told her with regret that although they admired the play, the libel laws made it impossible to produce. "It's not simply that they're living people," they explained. "They're royalty." She scolded herself for her naïveté—but how could she have resisted? Shakespeare himself would have seized on it, libel laws or not. Of that she was certain.

"You mustn't give up," said Pauline, patting Helen's arm as she opened another letter with yet another apologetic two-sentence rejection.

"I won't," she answered.

Taking trouble
1937

Dear Helen,

It is awkward to pass this information along to you, but I have heard from Mann who is increasingly perplexed—and, dare I say, displeased—at your slow rate of progress with the translation. I must ask you to do all you can to work more quickly, without compromising the high standard of your work.

I have, for now, discouraged Mann from complaining directly to you, but if you are unable to provide us with the finished work in a timely manner I cannot continue to protect you from his full expression of disappointment.

Yours,
Alfred

Dear Alfred,

I appreciate your position, which is uncomfortable; at the same time you will recall that when you were here in London early in the year we discussed all this and came to the conclusion that Mann was unreasonable. He did not give me the German book until November; if he thinks that eight months is an unreasonable time in which to translate a work of that size and difficulty I can only say that I disagree with him profoundly and so did you. If he wants to complain let him write to me. I will not do this book under pressure. If he wants to take it away from me he is at liberty to do so. As for the little play which has evidently disturbed you, I took between three and four weeks, part time, to write it.

One other point I must cover. I did receive ms copy, irregularly and with gaps during the summer and even spring. (Mann has a feeling that his translator must sit waiting and doing nothing else in order to devote him or herself entirely to the task.) I translated a good deal of it. But it was just as I thought, more or less time wasted, for there <u>are</u> alterations, omissions etc., that is to say difference between it and the printed text. It had of course all to be carefully compared.

Yours,
Helen

Dear Helen,

My position is indeed uncomfortable, poised as I am between an annoyed author and an annoyed translator. I trust we will all soon return to our more amicable communications. I remind you, as I reminded Mann, that we are in this together for the foreseeable future. There is no question of replacing you as his translator.

Thank you for reminding me about our earlier discussion. If you have had the book only since November then I agree that it is reasonable for you still to be working on it. However, you must admit that your progress has a tendency to slowness, and I urge you to move along to the very best of your ability. I will try to reassure

Mann that we will have the finished work in good time. I will also discourage him from sending you manuscript sections that are likely to be further revised.

Yours,
Alfred

Dear Alfred,

I am reasonably certain T.M. and Katia both would rather take a chance of a bad translation, if it could only be done more quickly—both of them having a pretty slight regard for translations in general and mine in particular. I doubt if he understands that his books would not have made money in English translation if they had not—out of my profound respect for the English tongue—been "easily readable".

And what do I mean by "easily readable"? My aim, always, is to get Mann's words into my ear and feeling, and then create as meticulous, supple, and intuitive a rendering of the original as I possibly can. (I think there might easily be a difference of opinion about the result.)

I am surprised that after more than ten years of my translations you do not seem to fully understand what the work entails. Since you see only my finished text, perhaps a brief example will help to show you the evolution from literal to literary translation.

Here is my literal translation of a sentence from Joseph in Egypt:

"And in a later time which enters sympathetically into man's beginnings, we find ourselves in the sign of unity still drawn to that ancient partaking."

And now my rendition:

"And in a late age, which is aware of its affinity with human beginnings, we find ourselves still united with them in that bond of sympathy."

Of course a single sentence does not convey the effect of the whole. I would be happy to send a longer sample to you, if you would like to see it.

Yours,
Helen

The exchange left her irritated. Why should she have to point out to Mann and Knopf the accomplishment of her translation? Here I am, she thought, putting my lifeblood into Mann's work instead of my own, and all they can do is scold me for being slow. She promised herself the comfort of complaining to loyal Pauline when her friend returned from Moscow, though she suspected Pauline might be need some comfort herself. Her letters, cautiously worded as they were, hinted at dismay and disillusionment along with due praise of the Communist emancipation of women and workers. Perhaps the rumors are true, thought Helen, perhaps all that progress comes at terrible cost.

37

Sustenance
1963

"Hell-o!" sang a young voice. "Just me!" The door opened and in pranced curly-headed Barbara, carrying a tray covered by an embroidered linen cloth. Helen was immediately cheered, as though a sprightly parakeet had alighted on the windowsill. Laying the tray down on the little table, Barbara sent a quick, expert look around the room. She put an arm around Helen, the only person at Mrs. D's who would dare. "How are we doing today, Mrs. Lowe?"

"We're quite all right," said Helen, more humorous than sarcastic, or so she hoped. Let's not be sloppy with our pronouns, she wanted to say.

"Did you have a nice visit this morning?"

This morning? It must have been Marjorie. Or Nicky.

"Did my grandson come?"

Barbara smiled reassuringly. "Your daughter, Mrs. Lowe. I'm sure your grandson will visit soon." She took Helen's wrist and felt her pulse while looking at her watch. "I brought you a little snack since you missed dinner."

Helen started to demur. Barbara lifted the cloth, revealing a small plate of sliced pear, blue cheese, crackers, one foil-wrapped chocolate, and her evening pills with a glass of water. Helen realized that she was exactly hungry enough for this particular snack.

"Thank you, dear," she said, meaning it.

"Oh look," said Barbara, picking up the book that lay on the bed. "You wrote this one yourself! You never showed it to me!" On other occasions she'd professed interest in the translations, which Helen had reluctantly taken off the shelf for her. "May I, Mrs. Lowe?" She leafed through the play, making little noises of admiration. "My goodness, it's like Shakespeare!"

Helen could not help feeling gratified.

"Is there a photo of you?" asked Barbara, turning to the back cover and then the back flap. "There should be a photo. I've never seen a picture of you when you were young."

"I was already old when that was published."

Barbara skimmed the short biography.

"Don't read that," said Helen.

"Well, whoever wrote it didn't do a very good job, in my opinion," said Barbara, closing the book. "You weren't exactly a housewife." She reached into her apron pocket and drew out a folded piece of paper. "I brought you this. Just in case." It was the crossword from the afternoon activity session.

Helen glanced at it. 2 across, 9 letters: Bulbs for Wordsworth. The answer presented itself instantly. Well, the puzzle would while away fifteen minutes of the evening. "Thank you, Barbara."

"Shall I come back and help you into bed?"

"No, no, I'm perfectly all right."

"Well then, I'll say good night. Don't forget to do your routines, will you?"

Did Barbara think that at eighty-six years of age she had forgotten how to brush her teeth and wash her face before bed?

The girl paused at the door. "It must be such a comfort to look back at all you've achieved in life," she said, indicating *Abdication* and the empty shelf where the Mann books used to be.

"Oh yes," agreed Helen to humor the girl, who meant well. "A great comfort."

38

Snowstorm
1938

Marjorie shifted in her seat. The large dozing man beside her grunted but did not wake up. She checked her watch yet again. It was 9:15pm. The bus was already more than an hour late. It crawled along the northbound turnpike, the wipers laboring to clear a trapezoid against the heavy snow. The headlights picked out dim white mounds at the side of the road: cars whose drivers had decided to wait until the snow stopped. There was nothing to be done. She hoped Irving would figure out where she was and why she was so late. Whether he would wait for her was another matter. She tried to resign herself to soup alone in her room instead of dinner downtown with an attentive, amorous, worldly man.

But the satisfaction of the afternoon with her father remained with her despite the snow and the spoiled plans. Marjorie had not hesitated when he'd called asking for her help. After her shameful failure at her college her father's need for her felt like a reprieve—a way to justify her existence, since she so clearly was never going to follow in the accomplished footsteps of every other member of her family. Elias explained: irreplaceable papers and books had to be shipped in preparation for his February sojourn in Key West, where he intended to finish Volume III of his magnum opus. He was leaving in a couple of weeks.

"I can't trust a paid minion to do it without mislaying or jumbling things," he'd said on the phone. "But I know I can trust you, dear."

Marjorie persuaded her boss to let her leave at noon to catch the bus to Princeton, promising to make up time on the weekend. It was a perk of her poorly paid editing job that she could do some of it outside of conventional working hours, if she wanted, allowing her to persevere with her own writing. She'd started submitting short stories to magazines for other lowly assistant editors to look over. She hoped they at least enjoyed them.

Elias's desk was invisible under stacks of books and folders, handwritten index cards sticking out of them. More piles lay on the floor. Elias in his reading chair gestured to it all with a comically helpless shrug. Marjorie assessed the situation and took command, selecting similar-sized books and tucking them into boxes, making lists of which books were stowed where, carefully immobilizing everything with balled-up newspaper pages before sealing and addressing the cartons.

"You're very good at this, Marjorie," Elias said, watching her. "You've inherited your mother's practical skills."

"Where are your scissors?" she said, straightening up and stretching her back, not letting him see how his compliment warmed her. When she was a little girl in Oxford he sometimes appointed her "Junior Fellow," with the solemn task of handing out the after-dinner nuts and dried fruit—his approval, when she did so without spilling, as sweet as any dessert.

"Scissors, hmm." He thought and then pointed to a drawer. "I'm trying to persuade her come here, you know. Your mother."

"Really?" She paused with the scissors in her hand and looked at him in surprise. She'd come to accept that her parents would never reconcile. "Well...that would be very nice, wouldn't it? To have her here." She tried to imagine them sharing a house again, being a regular married couple again, and was puzzled by a slight sense of disappointment.

"We don't want her stuck in Britain in the middle of a war," he said. "War is coming, sooner or later. I am still responsible for her. She should be here." He made a vague gesture that took in the bright room and the leafless trees visible through the window in fading winter light.

The newspapers reported every day on the rising tensions in Europe. Marjorie read the headlines, hoping to see that the efforts to avert war were gaining strength. Here in America it didn't seem of immediate concern. She had plenty of other things to think about—her job at the publishing house, the exciting promise of her own writing. And Irving, ten years older, formerly married, who seemed to have claimed her. She was still trying to sort out her own feelings. She was a little shocked to find herself thrilled by Irving's loud bossiness, though at times it stifled her. He took her to the opera and to art galleries. He bought her expensive jewelry and even clothes. They were not to her taste, though perhaps her taste was changing. Irving was a self-educated man, not ignorant but with rough patches in his mind. He was impressed by the idea of Marjorie's distinguished parents. Sooner or later he would have to meet them, her mother as well as Elias, if her father succeeded in persuading Helen to come. She did not look forward to the encounter. Her mother despised people like Irving, wealthy men who fawned over "intellectuals" while convinced of their own worldly superiority. It was a relief to be able to tell him, at least for now, that Helen lived in London.

Marjorie knelt in front of the last box and wrote her father's Key West address in careful capitals. "Of course Mother should be here with us," she said. "I hope you can persuade her."

Elias surveyed the neatly stacked boxes and his cleared desk. "Ah, wonderful," he said. "Thank you for coming, Marjorie." He glanced outside, where flakes of snow now floated in the dusk. "And now we'd better get you to the bus station."

Enveloped in the darkness and the engine's loud vibration, she let herself hover over that flicker of disappointment at the idea of her mother coming to Princeton. Was it about Irving?

Was it about sharing her father's attention—was she as selfish as that? She admitted to herself, sternly honest, that she liked being her father's only nearby family member. They'd become close— far closer than he'd ever been to her older sisters, a secret source of pride and pleasure for her. It would change, with Helen there.

But there was more. What was it?

She'd seen her mother for the last time shortly before she herself had left for the States. They'd gone for a walk and then returned to Miss Mackie's flat, which Marjorie had visited only once before.

And now Marjorie remembered. The room full of papers, books and magazines, a drawing pad and pencils, a set of dominos—yet somehow serene. The resplendent vase of roses and lilies, a few dropped petals allowed to rest on the table like a still life. Her mother's attractive things sitting comfortably among Miss Mackie's worn and practical furnishings. Helen's inlaid card box on top of the bookshelf—Marjorie had an urge to empty out all the picture postcards and sort them, as she did when she was a child. Paintings covered the walls, dissonant in their colors and styles. Helen sat down on the couch with a sigh of contentment, slipping off her shoes and wiggling stockinged toes. "Home!" she said, and held her arm out to her daughter. She looked different, Marjorie realized, quite bohemian, in her paisley fur-cuffed jacket and a beaded comb in her grey hair. This room with its art and clutter was exactly the right setting for H. Lowe-Porter, the famous translator and writer. A woman unto herself. Marjorie had a sudden longing to live in a place like that herself one day. She sat down next to her mother and rested her head on her shoulder.

If she comes back to Daddy she won't be bohemian any more, Marjorie thought now. He would never put up with that. She'll have to be a well-behaved Institute wife, with a tidy house and shoes on her feet at all times.

39

Reunion
1938

When Helen's ship docked in New York he was there to meet her. For a moment they did not know each other, each seeing an old stranger, small and grey. Then he grasped her hand and the touch became an embrace. They disengaged and stepped back. "Welcome, my dear," he said.

It took them both by surprise, the happiness that suffused them after the initial awkwardness. Several times one caught the other staring, and they laughed. Elias had hoped at best for a conciliatory and polite Helen. She had anticipated a brisk, busy Elias offering statutory kindness.

But here they were, lingering over toast and a second pot of tea, he unwilling to go to his study, she content to sit as long as he was there. Her suitcase held another book to be translated, of course, but she was ignoring its summons. They talked about the eminent neighbors she would meet at the Institute, the colloquium he was planning, the complex plot of Mann's four-volume novel. Her attention was on Elias's face, so deeply familiar, like a childhood landscape rediscovered after years.

Neither was inclined to put this state of being into words. It was enough to be aware of it and to know that they both shared it. They had arrived at the age where joy was inward and did not demand expression: a kind of nectar in the marrow as intense, or more, as the exuberant happiness of youth; an acceptance that by its nature it will not last.

Before Helen left England she had viewed the Institute's comfort and safety with mild scorn. Elias and the other scholars seemed to her a little effete in their protected haven, in comparison to the stoic British bracing for war. But now the Institute appeared in a different light. She was grateful for Elias's large, comfortable house, despite its prosaic décor, so bland after Pauline's colorful flat.

Her skin seemed to soften in the quiet air. A pressure lifted and she could breathe.

Slowly, Helen established herself in this new home. The kitchen, bigger than the sitting room in Oxford, was equipped with unfamiliar luxuries—a stand mixer, an enormous refrigerator—but lacked basics like an electric kettle and wooden spoons. She was thankful that there were enough rooms for each of them to have a bedroom and a study. Sharing a bed was unthinkable in this new era, despite the tenderness of their reunion. And that happiness was fading, as of course it had to. A brief delusion. Or just a passing relic of their long life together. She tried to appreciate the sense of physical security and concentrate on translating Mann's new novel, *Lotte in Weimar*. The story intrigued her, with its mirroring of historical fact and literary fiction, past and present. Mann's characters were Goethe and his lover Lotte. The story evoked Goethe's own 150-year-old novel about their love affair, and the real-life Lotte's anger at being exposed in his pages.

A passage in chapter seven gave Helen pause.

"Listen to this," she said to Elias. "Does it say what I think it says?" She pointed to the German paragraph.

He read it and laughed. "Very bold of him! I mean Mann, not his character. Yes, you're correct. Goethe wakes up aroused, as men often do, and sets about to pleasure himself. A bit oblique, but I'm sure that's what's happening. Playing on his magic flute, indeed!"

"Well…" said Helen, looking dubiously at the German lines. "I'm not sure I can get away with it for our puritan American readers. I'll have to be even more oblique."

With the war in Europe now underway it was bizarre, Helen thought, to be immersed in German polysyllables when the language itself was now an object of hatred and mockery—Hollywood disgorging film after film with monocled brutes in polished boots decreeing torture and murder in staccato German-accented English. Mann, by now a revered spokesman for the German community in exile, was gloomy about the prospects of ever being published in his native language again. "These English editions are my one and only standby," he wrote to Helen, hinting that she should hurry.

Her dreams were filled with fear. In one, Alice's house crumbled slowly to dust, crushing everyone in it. In another, a tiny baby lay alone crying on the street as the Luftwaffe roared through the bright moonlit sky. She ran to rescue the child but rough hands pulled her back. Helen had come to dread the full moon, when London would be attacked, though here in Princeton it sailed through the night sky as benign and majestic as ever.

Helen woke in panic and tried to calm herself with her obsessive mental rollcall of the family: Alice and her husband did not live in London anymore, they were in Cambridgeshire, unlikely to be hit. And Rosalind, newly pregnant, would give birth in the safety of her parents-in-law's village in Scotland. Her husband was in the navy. Helen canceled out her fearful images of where Douglas might be and what might happen to him with a deliberate fantasy of his joyful homecoming, Rosalind running to the gate with the bonny baby on her hip, stepping into her husband's arms. Marjorie, thank god, was out of harm's way in her New York rooming house—not only safe but thriving, with her first short story soon to appear in print. She had sent it to her mother, with shy satisfaction and a request for critique. Helen found the story astonishingly accomplished, and told her so, though with a few suggestions for polishing. She's going to do it, thought Helen—my daughter will be the writer I wanted to be myself. Her pride in Marjorie was entirely free of envy, she was relieved to find, though the pain of her own failure remained raw. The exhilaration of writing *Abdication* had long evaporated and new ideas no longer visited her.

Helen chided herself for singling out her own precious family for protection. We all want our own beloveds to survive, she thought, but every soul who's lost is someone's beloved. "A plane is over the house now, so near it shakes the night," Pauline had written just a few days ago, "—one of ours, and in it a dear English boy. In another, a dear German boy. Heroism in them both."

Helen did not dream about Pauline herself, but it was Pauline who was in the most danger. Pauline had tried to volunteer again, as Helen knew she would. They refused her— we are sorry, Miss Mackie, but we need younger women, and besides, we consider that your patriotic service is to stay here and do your job. The children who were not evacuated needed to go to school. So Pauline still lived and worked in the middle of London, detouring around debris-blocked streets, conveying to her teachers and pupils with her stolid demeanor that, despite appearances, life was normal. When word reached her that a child or a staff member had been killed in an air raid she closed her office door and sat alone for a few minutes. She wanted to rest her head on the desk but she did not. "Come on, girl," she whispered. "Where's your Cumbrian backbone?" She walked down to the assembly hall but did not speak until after the first hymn. Then "Children," she said, "I have some sad news."

"Don't be daft," she wrote to Helen. "What earthly good would it do anyone if you came back? I'm perfectly all right, don't you worry about me. That little goose-stepping gauleiter isn't going to get all of us, I can assure you. Carry on with your work. We're going to need some good books by good Germans when this insanity is over, to counteract the propaganda."

Helen did not confide in her friend about the precarious state of affairs at the Institute. The short-lived rapprochement with Elias had collapsed decisively. We used to be the best of friends, she reminded herself. Companions, compadres for such a long time. Why can't we summon friendship back, if not love? Why can't we find the courage to reflect together on what has happened between us? But it seemed beyond them. Instead, like statesmen sidestepping confrontation, they mapped a careful pattern of co-existence, avoiding each other where possible and attempting to rein in the mutual irritation that flared up at the slightest misunderstanding.

40

The Mann dinner
1940

In the Institute's oak-paneled dining room the long table was set with white linen and galaxies of flower-patterned plates, gleaming silverware, crystal glasses, opened bottles of Chablis and Bordeaux clustered at intervals, bowls of small fragrant roses echoing the plates. The scholars were in dinner jackets dug out from the backs of closets, their wives in cocktail dresses. The Knopfs, visitors from a more glamorous world, orbited smoothly among them—Blanche with her sleek hair and thin bare shoulders, Alfred with his lovingly groomed moustache which always made Helen think of a show pony. Helen was in dark blue velvet, a color that flattered her eyes, her daughters had told her. She stood at Mann's shoulder, introducing guests, murmuring translation when he needed it, relieved not to have to make cocktail chatter herself. Such occasions intimidated her—she disliked the feeling of awkwardness and was glad of her role as Thomas's intermediary and interpreter.

Mann looked every inch the celebrated author with his well-cut jacket and bow tie, his straight-backed stance. His collar was so stiffly starched that it dug into his neck. He did not seem to notice. He and Katia were the Institute's guests of honor—double exiles, since after an uneasy sojourn in Switzerland they were now seeking refuge in the United States. They were displaced and sad, haunted by the nightmare taking place in their homeland. But tonight they radiated wellbeing. Everyone in the room was a friend, a reader, an admirer, a like-minded opponent of Hitler who respected their courage in leaving. They were safe, they were embraced and adored.

Dr. Milstein summoned them all to the table.

"You must sit beside me, Helen," whispered Thomas, taking her arm. "I will need your help."

"A toast!" proclaimed Dr. Milstein when everyone was seated. "To our honored guest, the greatest living German novelist and a courageous opponent of fascism." Vigorous nods around the table. "To Dr. Mann and his wife!"

"Hear, *hear*!" chorused the scholars. Glasses were raised and sipped. The Manns smiled graciously. "'His wife'," thought Helen as she clinked glasses with her neighbor. Does Milstein not know her name? But Katia Mann did not seem affronted— no doubt used to being subsumed in Mann's persona, no more expecting specific mention than would his ear or his thumb. Helen admired the woman's apparent equanimity as she blinked in acknowledgment. The perfect wifely companion, according to Elias's theory of men and women, she thought. Happy to abandon her own ambitions in favor of her husband's.

Mann raised his wine glass and waited. The cheering table quieted down instantly.

"It is my turn to propose a toast," he said in German. He paused for Helen to translate, not looking at her. "To Mr. and Mrs. Knopf, my visionary publishers!" said Mann. He gestured grandly to them. "They have done me the great honor of introducing my work to the English-speaking public. My wife and I thank you both!"

The German-speakers at the table applauded when he paused, joined by the others as soon as Helen translated. "Hear, hear!" they all cried. "To Mr. and Mrs. Knopf!"

Mann lifted his hand and again there was a hush. "And above all," he continued, now in rehearsed English, "I must thank my dear Mrs. Lowe, my devoted and brilliant translator! If you know my work it is because she is working so very, very hard. Without Mrs. Lowe I am an unknown German only." He smiled down at her. "To Helen Lowe-Porter!"

And they all drank to her, looking at her with admiration and pride—our Mrs. Lowe, our own Mrs. Lowe. Elias, across the table, joined in the chorus of "Brava!" with gusto.

Helen hardly knew what to do with Mann's praise, so rarely had she received it in any form. "Thank you, Dr. Mann," she said, trying to summon an articulate response. "May I say that it is the greatest privilege and pleasure to spend my days immersed in the works of a master." For a fleeting moment she and Thomas held each other's gaze. No one else could possibly know what it meant to dwell inside his invented worlds, to take account of every word, every subtle connotation. No one else, not even Katia, shared their partnership, invisible to others and never before acknowledged even to each other. An unfamiliar sweetness permeated her.

The moment passed.

"Dr. Mann," said Professor Berenson, one of the younger scholars, "may I ask, what is it like for a native of Germany to be in the United States at this moment?"

Mann looked at Helen, eyebrows raised. She murmured the question in German, trying to warn him with her choice of words that diplomacy was needed here.

"Ah," he said, bowing slightly to the questioner. "We are filled with gratitude. My wife and I find here an indescribable sense of freedom." Helen translated faithfully, though irritated by his sentiment, which she'd heard before. She did not share Mann's idealism about America, as naïve as her own misplaced idealism about Communist Russia, for which she had not forgiven herself.

Mann went on: "And may I add that we are confident in America's ability to defend this precious freedom."

Berenson raised his eyebrows and glanced around the table. "Do you mean that you believe we should enter the war?"

Helen held her breath. In their private communications Mann was scornful about the United States' isolation. "Is it not time," he'd said, "for your countrymen to share the sacrifices that

171

your allies are making every day? On America's behalf?" She could not disagree, much as she loathed the fact of war. But it was not an acceptable position for a recently arrived refugee, no matter how elevated his status.

Now Mann responded to Berenson: "I mean only that your magnificent country embodies the future towards which we can all work together." With relief Helen rendered this into courteous English and Berenson nodded.

There was another star at the table, of even greater magnitude than Mann: the Institute's legendary physicist and another exile from the Third Reich. Professor Einstein was the only man not wearing a tie, his gesture to the occasion an attempt at smoothing his white mane and a tweed jacket instead of his usual unraveling sweater. He said: "And Helen, what about you? How do you find your native land these days?" They were friends, he and Helen. She sometimes translated his papers and speeches. They wrote affectionate doggerel for each other's birthdays.

Helen's thoughts flew at the speed of light. She was a refugee herself, of a sort, and almost as constrained by her outsider position as Mann was. "I am happy to be here again," she said carefully. "We are a fortunate country. But I believe that what happened in Germany warns us to be vigilant. No country, including ours, is immune to political madness."

Einstein nodded. She knew that he shared her skepticism about American moral pride.

The conversation flowed in braided streams of penetrating observations about war and politics, literature and science: the cleverest people in the world exercising their minds over a feast that defied wartime austerity, all in honor of Thomas Mann, the great novelist and heroic symbol of resistance, and his esteemed wife.

Helen, now at her ease, found herself enjoying the conviviality, switching smoothly from English to German and back. She even ventured an amusing story, about the time she and Alice, visiting Berlin in 1933, tried to hex Hitler by setting fire to a tiny Hitler doll—"with a movable right arm for heiling," she said. But thanks to clever German engineering the doll was made of asbestos and wouldn't burn. Enough wine had been drunk by now that a couple of the scholars banged on the table to punctuate their laughter, rattling the knives and forks.

"I am happy to see this recognition of *ein prachtwoller Mensch*," said Professor Einstein as they said goodbye. "A beautiful person. And I mean you, Helen. Not him, though he impresses, certainly. Come to me tomorrow, if you can, please. I need your help."

"I will, gladly," Helen said, kissing him on both cheeks. She enjoyed sitting with the professor at his table piled with mysteries and miracles, tackling whatever new letter or article needed her linguistic lift, with pleasurable detours into political conversation or whimsy. It was the opposite of her collaboration with Mann. Albert did not stint on gratitude. After his last thank-you gift— a vase of white peonies—she'd responded in verse:

To A. Einstein

The record of this partnership unequal
Shall now be duly banked;
Yet not before in fit and proper sequel
The gentle donor's thanked.

Sweet unction to the Lowely accessary
This piece of paper lays;
In gratitude wherefore she would not tarry,
And in requital prays:

If it be not too willfully aspiring
That she such hope espouse—
Then, lion, roar, when next you are requiring
And she will be your mouse.

173

Apple trees
1942

Searching for a postage stamp in Elias's desk, Helen came across a miniature card in her own handwriting, dated 1928. With the card in her hand she looked out the window, seeing not the Institute's magnificent maples but the pocket-handkerchief backyard of the house in Oxford with its one lilac bush and the children's swing. She had no idea, in 1928, what was to come.

She'd written to Elias in Rome, where he had another stint at the Vatican library. He'd been gone for two weeks and would not return for another two. His birthday would fall while he was away. She had an inspired idea for a gift for him—how lavish! Feeling bold and sophisticated, Helen went to some trouble to order it and have it delivered to his hostel, along with the little card.

She had crafted her words as though writing a poem. A pause here, an allusion there. Echoes subtly invoked. After she'd sent it she felt as uncertain as a young girl instead of a woman in her fifties writing to her husband. What if her words were not welcome? What if he was not thinking of her on his birthday, so far away? What if he was with someone else?

But he'd written back lovingly. And had kept her card.

> My dear (*she had written, sitting on the long-ago back porch in Oxford*),
> With my love and best wishes for your birthday I send you this plate of fruit. To us both, fruit means something more fitly expressed in poetry than in prose: it means

consummation. And, especially, figs. So let these figs express both their sensuous and their spiritual symbolism; express it to the full, and blend one with the other until you are utterly conscious of the ultimate identity of these two.

Thy H

The signature made her wince. *Thy H.* The tenderness of it, the trust. She had always signed her letters to him in this way, had always begun them with *My dear* or *My dearest* or *My darlingest.* Until Phoebe.

Since then, only the businesslike "Dear Elias," and her bald initials at the end.

"I've ordered a new car," Elias informed her one day as they waited for the coffee to percolate after lunch. "A Buick. More comfortable and reliable. In dark red." Complacently he listed the desirable features of the new vehicle: the six-cylinder engine, the moleskin leather seats, a heater, even a radio.

Helen had no idea he'd been contemplating this major purchase. "But—what's wrong with this one?" She pointed to the serviceable black Packard sitting in the driveway. "It runs perfectly well. We don't need a new car!"

"In my opinion we do," he said. "And it will be here in two weeks."

"Couldn't we have discussed this, Elias?" she said. "Isn't it rather distasteful to be so extravagant, at this particular moment? In the middle of a war!"

She couldn't help arguing, though she knew there was no point. The money was Elias's.

"As I said, Helen, I considered it necessary. You must admit I know more about cars than you do. And about our finances." He shot her a look of annoyance and went back to his newspaper.

But Helen was not ready to give in. She leant across the table and pushed the paper down so he was forced to look at her, irritation plain on his face.

"Do you realize what you're saying?" she said.

He got up from the table, abandoning the paper and his half-finished coffee. Helen followed him into the hallway. She was not able to stop herself. "You're saying 'Let us not discuss, let me make all the choices, I will act with benevolence.'" Her voice shook. "No free person and no free nation can accept this kind of dictatorship!"

Elias was pulling on his overcoat and hat. "For god's sake," he said coldly. "You are indulging in melodramatic exaggeration. And I have to be in the library in five minutes." He closed the front door behind him without saying goodbye.

She stood in the hallway after he'd left, her heart racing. Why was it impossible to win an argument with Elias? In this new epoch of their marriage she had come to see that he exerted a kind of baronial authority over everyone around him, his students, his assistants, Marjorie, Teresa who cleaned the house and John who looked after the garden. And herself. His lordliness disturbed her not only because her life was shaped by his edicts, but on moral and political grounds as well. The whole world was in the midst of carnage and collapse because of the abuse of power. She found it unbearable that her own domestic life resembled political oppression in miniature—the antithesis of the emancipated marriage they'd both aspired to when they were young. She'd failed her own ideals, on this most intimate scale. What is wrong with me, she thought. How have I let this happen?

The beautiful car was delivered. Elias gloated like a boy with a new toy train. Helen admitted that the car was luxurious but could not bring herself to share his delight.

A few days later she woke to a terrible sound. She looked out the window in horror: a huge machine was gouging the lawn exactly where she had planned a little grove of apple trees. She had been dreaming about the trees, which would flourish here as they had in her Pennsylvania home.

She rushed to Elias's study in her dressing gown, her hair awry.

"What on earth are they doing?"

He seemed startled by her dismay. "It's going to be a garage, for the Buick. A car like this has to be protected from the weather. They're digging the foundation."

"But you didn't ask me! I was going to plant apple trees there! Couldn't they put a garage somewhere else?"

He frowned in puzzlement. "Apple trees? Why do you want apple trees? You can buy apples anywhere."

She stammered out her vision of a hammock slung between tree trunks, like in the orchard of her girlhood. Resting, reading there in the springtime, intoxicated by a soft perfumed breeze.

Elias interrupted, shaking his head. "Admittedly I don't know much about trees, Helen," he said, with the amused condescension that she could not stomach. "But don't they need to be mature to support a hammock? How many years do you think your putative apple trees would take to be strong enough?" He refrained from mentioning her advanced age relative to the growth rate of a tree.

A sturdy garage was built to house the handsome car. Helen acquiesced to being driven in it. After a while she learned to drive herself. She did not speak about the lost hammock, the lost clouds of pink-white apple blossoms with their cool, subtle, ephemeral scent.

Letters from Rosalind made their way each month across the mine-infested sea, bringing news and occasional photos of the baby, who was growing up plump and healthy in the Scottish countryside. Rosalind, clever with her pen, evoked the roly-poly, wispy-haired little Kate in a few sentences: the child's first enchanting smiles, the achievement, to be marveled at, of rolling over, the delicious feel of her little arms around her mother's neck. Helen yearned to feel those tiny silken arms herself and exulted and grieved in the same moment. The *minute* the war is over, she promises herself, the absolute minute. She taped the small scalloped-edged photos to the wall where she could glance at them as she worked.

Even without meeting baby Kate, something within her had transformed. She was a grandmother. A child had entered her life again, giving her a renewed stake in the future of the world. There is a force, she thought, some gravitational pull from the future, that makes women bear children in wartime. As she herself had, so many years ago. She was discovering now that the force swept in grandmothers as well, old and barren as they were, infused with vigor by the advent of a new child.

And now Marjorie was pregnant as well. Helen let herself dream about the coming baby—her American grandchild, a bus ride away instead of across the perilous ocean. She put aside the awareness that the baby was also Irving's and made plans instead for the room in her house that would be the baby's room, because of course he or she would visit often, perhaps stay with them by himself, once he's a little older, of course. Elias was pleased at the news as well, though it did not seem that grandparenthood had transformed him as it had her. She bought a white-painted crib, a rocking chair, and some toys and books, and commissioned Teresa to make new curtains with a pattern of bears. Elias, magnanimous, did not comment on the cost.

42

Mountain House
1945

It felt a little like running away from school, the spur-of-the-moment "Yes!" to Blanche's phone call with a last-minute invitation: "Helen, I know you're busy but it's hellish hot and I've got to get out of the city. The Manns are up in the Catskills, in some old hotel on a mountain. It sounds heavenly. Let's visit them!"

"Go! Go!" said Elias, gesticulating from his office when she consulted him. "I'd get away from this heatwave if I could. I don't suppose you want to take the car." She didn't. She was looking forward to the three-hour train journey north along the Hudson, reading and chatting with her friend.

They met at Grand Central under the starry ceiling, two ladies on an adventure, Blanche chic in a black and white sundress and jacket with white sandals. Helen briefly regretted her plain skirt and walking shoes.

"Tommy's pleased that we're coming," said Blanche. "He says they're in need of some amusement."

"That means you," said Helen. "He doesn't look to me for amusement. On the contrary." The war was now in its sixth terrible year. Mann was working on a new magnum opus, propelled by his despair over Germany and the horrors that it had inflicted on all of Europe, most dreadfully upon itself. "An irredeemable degradation," he had said in a letter. She knew he was in anguish.

"Do not try to translate this monster yet," Mann warned her when he sent her the new book's early chapters so that she could begin to make its acquaintance. "It cannot be finished until the war is over, and God only knows when that will be. I am not even sure that it will ever be published in German."

She was relieved that Mann was not, with this new book, demanding that she translate from the manuscript as he wrote it—an infuriating experience with the last of the tetralogy, which had led to weeks of wasted effort on her part. Perhaps he'd listened to her frustrated complaints.

"Have you seen any of this new work?" asked Blanche, fanning herself with the train schedule as they waited to buy their tickets.

Helen glanced at her—not a casual question, from Mann's publisher. "Yes—he's sent me some of the beginning section. Not to translate, just to let me see what he's up to."

"And?"

The opening chapters of the new novel perplexed her, with their dull, loquacious narrator who idolized but did not comprehend his friend, the reclusive, gifted musician who was the book's main character. After two hundred pages there was still little hint of the subject matter that she knew he was going to address—the fatal corruption of the German soul, embodied in the composer who makes a pact with the devil: his humanity traded for musical genius.

"This will be controversial," Mann warned her. "My fellow émigrés maintain a gratifying fiction that there are bad Germans and good Germans. I am saying there are not. I am saying we are all cursed."

"It's highly original," Helen said to Blanche. "Unlike anything else he's written. I'm longing to see where he'll take it. But it will be tough going, Blanche. He and I both know that."

The carriage was half empty. Helen and Blanche settled themselves into the worn red seats and watched the upper reaches of the city slide past. Blanche dug into her purse and pulled out her cigarettes, then a small silver flask. "It's run by

Quakers, you know. Mohonk Mountain House. Strictly no drinking. So I came equipped." She held the flask out to Helen, who shook her head.

"Perhaps later."

"Here's the river!" said Blanche. They leaned toward the window as the train tracks drew parallel to the wide Hudson. "Lovely, isn't it?" The water stretched out beside them, a mile to the opposite bank. On the far side the hills rose steep and forested.

Blanche delved in her bag again. "Here, Helen, I brought something for you to peruse." She drew out the new issue of the *Knopf Quarterly*, a glossy periodical that Alfred produced for their most devoted customers. "A dollop of publishing gossip, a soupçon of flattery, a dash of boasting for us. Keeps them loyal," he'd explained when Blanche had expressed concerns about the time and money that the newsletter required. She shrugged. Publicity was his forte, not hers. What she was good at was recruiting writers, nurturing trust and affection, editing their work, holding their hands through doubts and discouragement until a new, wonderful book was born.

Helen noted the large photo of Alfred on the newsletter's cover, chin on manicured hand, hooded eyes looking pensively into the distance. She turned to his opening piece, "Thirty Years of Publishing" where he congratulated himself on recognizing writers far ahead of their time. The problem with his discoveries, he wrote, was finding readers who were intelligent and intellectually curious enough to appreciate them.

"Ahem," said Helen, turning to Blanche with raised eyebrows. "'*My* discoveries'?"

"Keep going," said Blanche.

"I am proudest, perhaps," the article went on, "of publishing seven Nobel Prize winners." At that Helen slapped the newsletter in exasperation. "Oh, come on, now! What does he mean, '*I*'? You found at least half of those Nobel winners. Didn't you?"

Blanche nodded, narrowing her eyes against her cigarette smoke.

"Did he show you this before it was printed?"

"No, I had no idea what he was writing. Not that he'd have changed it if I'd objected."

"Well," said Helen. "I will say something to him. It really is not fair, Blanche. You shouldn't let him get away with it."

But she was remembering her own feebleness when Alfred, in an earlier newsletter, omitted her own name as the translator of one of Mann's novels. All she could manage was a coy objection: "I was so interested as not to notice for some time that I was not mentioned as the translator of DEATH IN VENICE," she wrote to him. "I make this little comment not very seriously, yet as a sort of protest in the name of the humble craft — people are always so ready to say that we do not get enough credit!"

Alfred had apologized for his mistake and promised to correct it if there was a reprinting—unlikely, as he acknowledged.

"It's a problem that men have," said Blanche. "As you've no doubt noticed."

The river narrowed, then widened again. Small waves broke on rocky beaches between headlands. They passed through riverfront towns either prosperous or forlorn. Helen thought she recognized the small city on the opposite bank where Elizabeth and her family had lived before moving to the Massachusetts coast. She remembered being there long ago in the first war, when the children were little. Before Mann, before Phoebe.

Helen shook off the past and unpacked the picnic supper that she'd brought to share with Blanche, hoping that her quiche Lorraine, light and tasty, would tempt her friend's elusive appetite.

"Beautiful!" said Blanche. "You made this yourself?" But she waved it away, nibbling a few walnuts instead.

At the station they were met by a polite elderly driver in green livery. "This way, ladies," he said, picking up their suitcases and bobbing his head toward the car. The riverside air felt cooler. "And even cooler up at Mohonk," the man said as they drove west across the tall bridge. "You'll see. Always a lovely breeze off the water up there."

Water? "Aren't we going to be on top of a mountain?" asked Helen.

"The lake, ma'am. The hotel is beside a lake, on top of a mountain."

It sounded like a fairytale. Helen settled back into the comfortable back seat. How luxurious, to be driven to a Mountain House by a lake, where the air was fresh and cool.

It was early evening by the time they arrived, after winding for what seemed like hours upward through dense woods. She thought she saw bushes with pale flowers amongst the trees—tomorrow she'd go and look. A massive four-story wooden building loomed ahead of them, with gables, wide porches and stone foundations—she immediately thought of *Magic Mountain*'s sanatorium, with a twinge of alarm. They followed the driver into the high-ceilinged lobby.

"*Herzlich willkommen, meine Damen!*" called a jovial voice. It was Thomas in pink shirtsleeves, waving his pipe at them. Helen had never seen him so informally dressed. "You've come to take the cure?" He laughed. "Don't worry! No illness here. We are on the porch. Do join us, when you have found your rooms."

The wide porch stretched along the side of the hotel. A row of rocking chairs faced a narrow lake reflecting the cliffs that rose above it. Thomas and Katia sat side by side, their greying heads recognizable from behind, hers almost hidden by the seatback. She shook hands with Helen and Blanche in her usual reserved way, barely a smile—why always so reserved, thought Helen as she sat down. Katia and I would have much to talk about. She knew how much Mann's wife did for him, everything from writing his letters to managing his business affairs and packing

183

his multiple suitcases. But there was no opening for sisterly confidences as there was with Blanche; not even a hairline crack in Katia's devoted loyalty.

They sat smoking in silence, the Manns, Blanche, and Helen, as the midsummer sun flared and sank above the hills. Faint fragrances wafted from the nearby gardens.

Mann reached past Katia and patted Helen's arm. "Tomorrow morning, after our breakfast," he said. "We shall talk, you and I. Are you ready to meet the Evil One?"

43

The island
1947

The granite mantelpiece was carved with a quote from *The Tempest*: "The air breathes upon us here most sweetly. Here is everything advantageous to life." Aunt Charlotte with her optimistic bent had omitted the sour rejoinder: "True; save means to live."

Helen remembered seeing the house for the first time as a young woman of twenty—the tall silvery-shingled cottage among dark spruces, the cold sparkling sea below, where Charlotte, her companion Helen Clarke, and their bluestocking friends came to read and write and act out scenes from Shakespeare in a clearing in the woods.

And now it was Helen's own refuge. The emptiness, the water, the trees nourished her spirit as the green lawns of the Institute never could. Thank you, dearest Aunt Charlotte, oh, thank you, she thought, as she did every time she unlocked the silent house for another blessed respite of summer weeks. She had come here every year for seven years, bringing Marjorie and little Nicky when she could. Rosalind promised to come next year, with Kate, whom Helen hadn't seen since her short visit after the war, and Kate's baby sister. She wanted the island to get into the children's blood, as it had hers.

Elias did not enjoy the island, with its complete absence of intellectual activity or culture. He had waved goodbye at the door with evident relief—relief not to be going, and relief, she was sure, that his increasingly eccentric and quasi-estranged wife would be out of his sight for two months. She was relieved as well. The jaggedness between them seemed impossible to anneal

185

and they'd both come to depend on the respite of Elias's trips to Europe or Key West. And now her own escape. She looked forward to weeks without fighting.

Marjorie and the little boy had come on the understanding that they'd give her uninterrupted mornings to work. Helen's private agenda was to prompt Marjorie to do some writing herself, in the island's fertile atmosphere. She had done nothing, as far as Helen knew, since Nicky was born, in spite of her early success, in spite of ample household help and no money worries. Here she'd be even freer, without her social life and the overbearing husband.

And perhaps I can pay some attention to my own writing too, thought Helen. Wisps of inspiration had once again been visiting her but she'd had little time to do more than scribble down her ideas. Her notebook waited on the desk in case she could release herself from the Evil One long enough to enter her own imaginative world.

She could hear them upstairs, Nicky's high-pitched prattle, Marjorie's sleepy voice reading to him. Helen listened for a minute, then turned back to her pages. After more than a year she was still working on Mann's enormous, daunting *Doctor Faustus*, about the composer and his pact with the devil—his spectacular success and ultimate catastrophe an elaborate metaphor for Germany's self-destruction. It made her think of Blau, the tormented conductor, who made no such pact.

Mann, an accomplished amateur musician himself, had acquired the knowledge of composition that he needed for the book—he had told her as they walked around the mountain lake in upstate New York—with the guidance of two German-Jewish composers, both of them neighbors in the California community where he and Katia had settled.

"One of them was delighted to help," he said. "The other..." He shrugged. "Let us just say he helped me in spite of himself. I have made his work my own."

Helen looked at him with a frown.

Mann smiled at her disapproval. "We writers must use whatever we can find."

Despite Mann's ethical lapses Helen believed that the novel was a masterpiece, with its shocking theme and its passages of archaic language that hypnotized the reader like an incantation. Helen was determined to do it the fullest justice that she could. Which meant that now she had to translate Mann's sophisticated musical references with the technical accuracy of the original as well as its complex connotations. Helen loved listening to the classical greats, to Bach and Mozart and Beethoven, and even the bold composers of her own century. But she'd never studied music.

Helen had brought with her some weighty musicology reference books, a gramophone, and a stack of recordings, along with a typewriter, food and other necessities. The mail boat captain's gawky young crewman carried all of it in relays up the steep gangway when they arrived, out of breath by the time he stowed the last box on the back of his uncle's ancient pickup truck. Four-year-old Nicky ricocheted around the pier, liberated after the two-day car journey and an hour on the boat. "Look, Mama!" he cried, pointing to lobster boats and buoys and the wheeling gulls. "Look, Grandma!" He was full of wonder but could not point to the most wonderful thing of all, the island air.

Helen climbed into the cab beside the taciturn uncle, tucking her legs to the side to avoid the jumble of oilcans and carpentry tools. Marjorie and Nicky perched behind on the truck bed, Marjorie already wearing the battered plaid sunhat that she wore only on the island, leaving fashion behind.

Nicky screamed with excitement as the truck swayed slowly along the bumpy roads and Marjorie turned to shake her head and grin at her mother through the window in the back of the cab. Nothing to be done! They were under the island's spell.

Helen slipped one of the records out of its sleeve and lowered the needle. It was Beethoven's last work for piano, the Sonata in C Minor, his opus 111. Mann devoted more than six dense pages to describing the piece when his composer-hero first listened to it. The devil himself discoursed about the somber opening dissonances now filling Helen's small high-ceilinged study. Marjorie and Nicky would be startled for a moment, but they knew she was working. She sat in the red armchair and closed her eyes. After ten minutes the first movement faded like a spent thunderstorm. The second and final movement, so lyrical and unpredictable, so extraordinarily long and abstract, carried her far away. Love was infused in these notes, love, sorrow, tenderness. The theme in its final, contemplative iteration echoed in her head as she went back to the typewriter and squinted at Mann's pages. She summoned her courage and determination—I *can* do this! Beyond the central task of rewriting this vast work in English were the usual pragmatic considerations. The English had to work equally well for American and British readers. She had to reject any idioms not familiar to both. Lucky for Mann, she thought, that his translator has spent half her life on each side of the Atlantic.

It was Mann's linguistic experiments that gave her the worst headache. He himself must have been possessed by the Devil, she thought sourly after wrestling with pages of a dreadful archaic German dialect. How am I going to find English equivalents for this?

For days she fought with a particularly obscure passage, finally writing to Mann, who, when the mail boat at last brought his response, instructed her to omit it. "Those pages are impossible in any language other than German, I quite agree," he wrote to her. "I struck them out for my French translator, after she refused to work on them. So I prefer now to leave them out in all translations."

There were more creative challenges—metaphors that no longer worked in their original position but were too beautiful, too apt, to discard, so she transplanted them into another sentence, even another page. A kind of sleight of hand, justified, Helen hoped.

At first she didn't hear Marjorie and Nicky in the kitchen. Then Marjorie's "Shhh!" She pictured Nicky earnestly mimicking Marjorie's gesture, finger laid across the lips, eyes wide. A ravishing smell infiltrated her study—fresh tomato soup? Helen realized that she was hungry. Starving! She stretched in her chair. Now she smelt bread toasting. Her mouth watered.

Another whisper: "Go and see if she is ready." Helen stayed bent over the typewriter, her back to the door, pretending to be lost in her work. She heard Nicky tiptoe into the room and felt a small hand on her arm. She started in surprise. Nicky laughed, throwing his head back. His little teeth were white and perfect.

"Grandma! We made lunch for you! Are you hungry?"

Helen closed her notebook and put a large pebble from the beach onto the stack of typed pages. Nicky climbed onto her lap and studied her face. With his finger he traced the deep lines in her cheeks, then her thin lips, and kissed them. She tried not to think of the doomed child in the novel, a tender portrait of Mann's own small, adored grandson. How could you do it, she addressed Mann in her mind—how could you decree such appalling suffering for a child, even in service to art? She tightened her arms around Nicky. If that kind of callousness was necessary for the greatest writing, well, she would never achieve greatness.

After lunch Helen took the little boy down to the pebbly beach, their ritual each afternoon except when the fog rolled in and turned to rain and they had to banish the chill with a log fire under the granite mantelpiece. Helen and Nicky picked their way down through the spruces, stopping to examine the blueberry bushes that crawled close to the ground, in case any berries were left. They clambered over the blowdowns, casualties of winter storms that uprooted trees from the island's thin topsoil.

Helen and Nicky emerged onto the small beach. He ran ahead of her. "I'm the king of the castle!" sang Nicky, scrambling up a large rock and standing with his arms outstretched. The sea wind caught his shirt like a sail and blew Helen's hair about her face. She started to tell him to be careful, the rock can be slippery, but stopped herself. He was agile and poised, an athletic little boy. No need to make him cautious. After a few minutes he scrambled down and squatted on the round pebbles, picking up one after another and examining them before throwing them into the sea. Now and then he looked up and beamed at Helen, who was sitting on a flat sun-warmed rock nearby. He had his grandfather's dark brown eyes.

"Let's take off our shoes!" he said, already discarding his.

Helen bent down to untie her shoelaces and roll up her trousers.

"Your feet are long and skinny!" the boy said.

Helen looked down at her crooked toes and yellowing toenails next to Nicky's shapely little feet. They held hands and stood together in the cold, lapping, seaweed-swirling Atlantic.

White elephant
1947

At last the work was done and *Doctor Faustus* sent to the Knopfs. But Helen was unable to emerge from its spell, instead seized by a passion to write about the revelatory masterwork that had dominated her time and her thoughts for nearly three years, even permeating her dreams. Ignoring Elias, ignoring everything, she spent weeks writing a lengthy literary exegesis— thirty typewritten pages, by the time she had finished. *Why* am I doing this, she asked herself repeatedly. No one has asked for it. No one wants it or needs it. But she knew this extraordinary novel more deeply than anyone except its author. It was of vital importance, a visionary, anguished, provocative work—not only a metaphor for Germany's tragedy, she realized, but also a cautionary tale for the United States, Mann's adopted country. "I feel there is a risk that many readers may take the novel as applicable merely to the German nation and people," she wrote in the essay. "I am concerned that the universality of the critique be pointed out; that we should be aware the bell tolls for us too." Mann's beloved bastion of freedom was now on the brink of selling its soul as Germany had, with the ominous emergence of widespread fearmongering and witch-hunting against supposed Communist infiltration.

Mann himself had become a target, unable to stay silent as he witnessed again the rise of hysteria. "I was too slow to speak up in Germany," he told her. "I will not make that mistake again." Helen applauded his courage and urged him to be careful. By now he had United States citizenship. But it would not protect him from persecution.

She sent him her *Doctor Faustus* essay. "I fear it's a white elephant," she said in her letter. "Far too big and of no use to anyone. With wrinkled hairy skin and flapping ears. I won't mention the steaming piles in its wake." But Mann did not agree. He seemed astonished and flattered by what she had done—"the comment of the most thorough and intimate connoisseur of the book," he wrote. "Every line bespeaks your loving absorption into this work." He urged her to publish it in England to build interest in the translated novel, soon to appear. She made a couple of attempts and gave up. As she expected, the piece was too scholarly and too long for a literary magazine, too personal and passionate for an academic journal.

Helen apologized to Mann. "It's my fate to evade publication, I'm sorry to say. Perhaps after I'm dead, but then again, probably not. In any case, it will not help your book."

She was left with a familiar sense of failure, even shame: such a major effort, followed by a complete absence of recognition, apart from Mann's. Was her essay worthwhile? Was any of her uncommissioned writing worthwhile? She suspected not. And yet I persist, she thought. I'm either deluded or heroic. Or simply pig-headed.

Helen was used to reviews that either ignored or criticized her translation. But after her strenuous efforts on a book that she loved more than any other she was wounded by the snarling comments of a prominent academic reviewer who understood some German and had spotted the omissions from the original. He accused the translator of laziness and incompetence. It did not occur to him that the discrepancies were not only approved but requested by Mann himself, pragmatic for once.

She wrote at length to Alfred and Blanche, who were afraid that the reviewer's influence would dampen sales. But there was simply no way to defend herself either to the reviewer or to the reading public without appearing ill-humored, ungracious, and downright pathetic. Only the author could have set the record straight, and he declined to do so, though he tried to console her in a private letter. "It is strange that Herr Professor should deplore this relatively small loss," he wrote to her. "Surely he ought to be glad that such a bad book is shortened by a few pages."

She wanted to protest, to demand that he speak up for her. But she knew it was useless. Mann was keenly attuned to what would or would not enhance his public image. Fairness to his translator did not enter the equation.

The praise from another well-known reviewer, referring to the "loving and extraordinarily proficient hands" of the translator, gave comfort. But the wound festered.

One day, she thought, one day I swear I'll liberate myself from this thankless business.

Famous artists
1948

Abdication was going to appear on stage at last. Helen could hardly believe it. Twelve years after she'd begun sending the play to producers and publishers it reached the celebrated Gate Theatre repertory company in Dublin, whose legendary actor-directors were eager to produce it. She'd opened the letter with her usual preparation for disappointment. But for once it was not a rejection.

"In Ireland we do not have to worry about English libel laws or the sensitivities of the British royal family," wrote the director. "We shall be delighted to produce your brilliant play and we do hope you'll allow us to honor you on opening night."

Helen read it again in disbelief, then gave an undignified yelp of delight.

"Are you all right, Helen?" called Elias from his study.

"Yes, I am!" She hesitated to interrupt him. But this was momentous. "Elias, come downstairs when you have a moment."

He appeared a minute later. Wordlessly she handed him the letter and watched him scan it quickly. For all Elias's lordly skepticism about her or any woman's artistic endeavors, she knew he understood very well what it meant to achieve a longed-for success.

He looked up, beaming. "But this is a remarkable triumph, Helen!" he said. "After all this time!"

And then, as if that weren't enough, Helen heard from a theatrical agency wanting to produce the play all over the world. After the stack of the rejections that *Abdication* had received—not to mention the categorical failure of everything else she'd ever written—she could hardly believe that she was being approached by an agency praising her work and offering money. And not just any agency—they called themselves FAMOUS ARTISTS, all in caps, and presented themselves as very important in the field, though she had never heard of them.

"So now you can call me FAMOUS PLAYWRIGHT," she wrote to Pauline.

Helen knew nothing about literary agencies and rights and money. She needed advice before replying to them. Elias's more worldly opinion would have been helpful but he had left for Europe yet again, and besides, he would have known little more, in this case, than she did. She spent nearly two hours composing a letter to Alfred, striving to calibrate the tone—excitement, but not too much; eagerness, but not too much; pride, but not too much. Surely it was not presumptuous to ask for Alfred's help. And she was eager for him to know of this new embrace of her play, since he himself had rejected it for publication years ago. "See?" she wanted to say to both Knopfs. "See? I'm not merely a translator. I'm a *writer* in my own right whose work is now recognized by the Gate Theatre and FAMOUS ARTISTS!"

The agency even mentioned film rights. And why not? It would make a stunning film. Who would play the abdicating king? It would need to be someone suitably handsome, but discreetly so, not the movie idol type. And a crisp, stylish actress for the king's lover, American, of course. But who were the prominent actors at the moment? Helen realized she hadn't seen a film for years. It called for some research, if Elias would agree to going to the cinema with her. Unlikely—he was spending more and more time abroad these days, and thoroughly occupied with Volume V when he was home.

Perhaps Alfred would be able to find a producer for the play in New York. He and Blanche socialized with such people. In her mind she choreographed a lunch with martinis, Alfred clapping his urbane theatrical friend on the back, the friend thanking him effusively for this opportunity to introduce something so original and striking to the American public. There was undoubtedly an audience for *Abdication* in the States. Americans, having rejected the monarchy for themselves, were infatuated by British royalty.

She debated whether to mention again the idea of Knopf publishing the play in print, and decided to risk it, bolstered by the enthusiasm from the Irish producers as well as the agent. Surely by now it was not presumptuous to consider Knopf her publisher, as well as Mann's. Was not their work a collaboration?

Feeling reckless, Helen wrote, "And of course if you and Blanche are interested in publishing *Abdication*, I would be happy to discuss an agreement."

There! She sent off the letter and was tormented for the rest of the day.

Husband of the playwright
1948

Lucie said she'd come with him to the airport. Elias knew he should demur—she was as busy with her research as he with his—but didn't. He held her arm as they navigated through the clusters of tourists and briefcase-brandishing businessmen. He held himself straight. She was taller than him, and much younger, though he believed no one would mistake them for father and daughter.

At the gate Elias resisted the impulse to kiss Lucie's pretty mouth, contenting himself with one smooth fresh cheek and then the other.

"Just a couple of days," he said. "I will telephone as soon as I'm back." He felt freer, these days, to enjoy a lovely creature like Lucie, now that he and Helen were no longer married in the usual sense.

"Je t'attendrai," she said with her calm smile. Lucie was far too self-possessed to express any anxiety about the purpose of his journey.

He walked across the tarmac to the plane, conscious that she was watching, but when he turned around for a last wave she was not there.

The stewardess showed him to his seat. "Anything I can bring you, sir? A cozy blanket around your knees, would you like?" He was mildly affronted—did she imagine he was an old man?

"Perhaps a whiskey when you have a chance, young lady," he said, though he did not normally drink mid-morning. She dimpled at him and promised to come back soon. Elias watched as she walked along the aisle, admiring the classical curve of her behind in her close-fitting emerald-green skirt.

The seat beside him remained empty, to his relief. No need for small talk with some Irish granny or a Frenchman with a head full of money.

The stewardess reappeared when the plane had taken off, bearing a glass on a tray. "Here you are, sir."

"Here's to you," he said, lifting the glass and looking into her eyes.

"And to you!" she replied. "Do I detect an American accent, sir?"

Elias admitted to being American.

"And what takes you to Dublin, if I might ask?"

He assumed that they were trained to chat with solo passengers, but he didn't really mind—the girl was delightful, with her brogue and her buck-toothed smile.

"My wife is there. She has written a play and I'm going to see it performed."

He saw her briefly grappling with the idea of an American traveling from Paris to see a presumably American wife in Dublin. "Oh, isn't that splendid, now, sir. And what is the play called? Perhaps I've heard of it."

Elias doubted that an air stewardess would have taken note of a play in blank verse about the British monarchy, but when he told her its name she clapped her hands.

"I've seen it! My friends and I went on our day off! It's brilliant! Really, your wife is the author? How wonderful!"

Elias stored the experience to tell Helen, who would be tickled.

A taxi took him straight from the airport to the theatre for a matinee performance, as planned. In the evening he would see the play again with Helen.

"Professor Lowe, we are honored that you could come," said the burly theatre manager with a warm handshake. "Please, this way," and he led him to a seat near the front.

Elias had not read the play, though he was familiar with its basic story. The grace and Shakespearean masterliness of the lines caught him by surprise. For twenty minutes he caught himself thinking with incredulity, "My Hal wrote this!" But then the narrative swept him away and he forgot about authorship. The drama unfolded, human nature playing itself out, venal, passionate, noble. He joined in the applause at the end with enthusiasm, even cheering aloud with the exuberant Irish audience.

Helen, when they met for dinner, greeted him with contained pleasure. She seemed different, neither angry nor self-deprecating. Still in the spell of the play, Elias found himself a little in awe of her. He praised her accomplishment effusively and she nodded but didn't respond. Did it please her that he was so impressed? He hoped so. He remembered with some regret his dismissal of her writing. Well, this is just one success, and belated at that, he thought. It doesn't change my point.

"Helen—the stewardess on the flight from Paris told me that she saw the play! And she loved it, she and her friends as well. They all thought it was wonderful."

At this she lit up. "Really?"

Her pleasure warmed him. There's still so much affection between us, he thought. He was glad he'd made the effort to come, to see the play's fulfillment, to see Helen in this new and surprising light.

Back at the theatre for the evening performance, Helen led him to her author's box where a few friends were waiting, writers and theatre people from Dublin who seemed to regard her with great admiration. "My husband, Dr. Elias Lowe," she said, telling him their names and who they were, which he promptly forgot.

"You must be very proud of your wife," said one bearded fellow. "Are you a writer yourself, Dr. Lowe?"

But when he mentioned paleography the man asked no more. I don't belong in a literary world, Elias reminded himself. Helen, on the other hand, seemed completely at home. She turned to him from time to time as if to include him, but he found he had little to say.

It is a new thing indeed, he thought, being the husband of the playwright Helen Lowe-Porter. I have to learn how to do it.

As the curtain rose he glanced at his watch. Lucie would soon be returning to her apartment after her day in the Bibliothèque Nationale followed by dinner with her parents. She would find his gift, a bowl of grapes and the most beautiful white peaches.

Back in Princeton, Helen wrote to Alfred Knopf again. Confidence was now in her bloodstream. This letter wrote itself quickly, no revisions, no regrets once she had sent it off.

> Dear Alfred,
>
> The Dublin season was great fun, the play ran twice as long as scheduled, which for a tiny public like Dublin was quite a triumph. The production was really brilliant—you may have seen in the papers. In New York many of the important producers are reading it and even Selznick has applied, showing that despite the difficult conditions it is not quite out of the question for film. We (the two Irish lads and myself) are pretty flexible as to conditions. I have given them an option. So now, dear Alfred, please, please find us an angel! The reason I did not go to Drake Desmond before is that some years back they turned it down — but now they are my agents, so-called "Famous Artists"

having fallen by the wayside. I have had a good
many applications over here for the published
text. I am probably not a good judge; but I think
it would sell well.

   Love to you and Blanche,
   HTLP

And then she had to wait while Alfred—she hoped—made
inquiries on her behalf about a possible New York production.
She tore open his next letter but there was no mention of any
conversations about the play. He did not refer to it in their next
few communications. Neither did he say anything about
publishing it in print. A familiar sourness began to replace her
dreams of a triumphant life for her play. She knew, of course,
that the historical moment had changed—people hardly
remembered the abdication any more. And if they did, they also
remembered that the former king, the outspoken supporter of
unemployed miners in his youth, was now reviled as a Nazi
sympathizer and a self-promoting member of decadent
European society.

 But none of that had deterred the Irish producers and the
Dublin audiences, she reminded herself. The abdication
remained a compelling story in itself. Her main character had
transcended history, no longer that disgraced flesh-and-blood
aristocrat but her own noble creation.

 She resolved to bring up the play the next time she visited
Alfred and Blanche in their grand offices on Madison Avenue. It
was late afternoon, rain beating on the windows and on the
pedestrians scurrying below. Alfred, busy with a telephone call,
waved her to one of the leather armchairs. I'll say something, she
thought, as soon as Blanche comes in and Alfred gets out the
cognac. But he raised the topic first.

"Helen, before I forget: I did speak to Arthur on your behalf, as I promised." His friend Arthur Hodge was a well-known critic, influential in the New York theatre. "He agreed to read your play. If he likes it"—"And he will!" chipped in Blanche—"there's a chance he could interest a producer."

"Thank you, Alfred," said Helen, careful not to show the excitement that quickly rose in her. She could almost hear Alfred's words to his friend: "I'd be grateful if you'd have a look at this. It's Mann's translator. We're considering publishing it as a favor to her, though not with great enthusiasm, I admit." He'd already said as much to her.

A month later Alfred sent her a clipping of the critic's newspaper column where he praised the text of the play—somewhat condescendingly, in her view—but implied that the subject matter was of little interest to Americans. Helen was annoyed and embarrassed at this public snub. Hadn't the play had already proven itself convincingly? It deserved better than this.

She braced herself for the crashing disappointment that now loomed. After her long, long, slow trajectory as a writer, leading miraculously to recognition and acclaim—could she bear it, if this triumph began and ended in Dublin?

"Dear Alfred," she wrote in haste that she later regretted, "thank you so much, and please thank Mr. Hodge, but I do feel that more could be done, and should be done. Did he actually speak to a producer, or did he just skim a few pages of the text and then whip off his comments? If he had read it more carefully he would surely have understood its appeal to a wide audience. Could you possibly approach him again?"

She knew her note was undiplomatic but she was a little desperate. Arthur Hodge was her only hope.

But her complaint made things worse. Hodge scrawled an offended note to Alfred, who forwarded it to Helen. The last sentence made her gasp aloud: "Women authors over the age of sixty-five should be handed over to the Ku Klux Klan."

The implicit violence sent a shock through her body. Why on earth did Alfred send this to her—could he have thought it witty?

And what would the Ku Klux Klan do with old women authors? Tie them to their flaming crosses? Oh, I'd give you all a bonfire you wouldn't forget.

Over sixty-five! Arthur Hodge himself was nearing seventy.

I will not give up, she thought. But something had drained from her, some essential energy that could no longer renew itself with ease. Is it old age, she wondered? Or just defeat.

Abdication did not appear on the stage again, in New York or anywhere, nor did it become a film. It lived only as a book, published by Knopf as a favor and soon out of print.

Kate polishes the shoes
1950

Kate was staying all by herself at Grandma and Grandpa's house in America, even though she was only eight years old. "Be a good girl," her mother had told her when she left for a few days with Aunt Marjorie in New York, taking Kate's two little sisters with her. "Help your grandma, won't you?"

"Of course I will!" said Kate.

She loved being in this big house with all the grass and trees around it, like a park. Grandma and Grandpa were so kind to her, and so were their friends, especially Dr. Einstein who liked her to visit and make up funny duets on the piano with him.

Kate did whatever chores her grandparents asked her to do, like clearing the table or bringing in the newspaper. "Really, darling?" Grandma had said when Kate offered to polish the shoes. "That would be wonderful!" It was her favorite chore at home in London and she was good at it. Grandma showed her the basket of shoe-cleaning supplies with brushes, soft cloths, and the little flat tins of lovely-smelling brown and black polish.

The porch was already warm from the early morning sun. All the shoes were lined up on sheets of newspaper just outside the kitchen door: four pairs of black shoes, two pairs of brown. Kate arranged them by owner: three pairs of Grandpa's, then three pairs of Grandma's. She slipped off her own brown Mary Janes and added them to the row. Hers were the dirtiest. The shoes reminded Kate of the three bears with their bowls of porridge, big, middle-sized, and little.

Kate decided to begin with her favorite pair, Grandma's lace-up boots. First of all she brushed them to get rid of dust and dirt—the tops, the heels, the soles, even around the little holes where the laces went in. Then she opened the tin of black polish and wiped a tiny dab all over the boots, making sure to spread it evenly.

Inside the kitchen someone opened a cupboard. She heard the rattle of plates. Grandma must be up. Kate was a little disappointed. She had wanted to surprise them at breakfast with the beautiful shiny shoes. She kept working, not making a sound, listening to Grandma set the table and fill the kettle.

A door slammed, startling her.

"Don't walk away from me." It was Grandpa's voice, but not his usual jokey voice.

Kate heard plates and cutlery again but Grandma didn't say anything.

"Answer me!"

"The conversation is fruitless, Elias," she heard Grandma say very quietly. Kate did not know what fruitless meant but thought it was not a good thing for a conversation to be. She knew it did not have anything to do with fruit.

She heard the faint jingle of knives and forks in the drawer.

Grandpa's voice got louder. "I think I deserve an explanation. Our guests arrive and you walk off and shut yourself in your study." Kate had heard the visitors' bright jabber at the front door after she'd gone to bed. "What kind of behavior is that? What the hell were you doing?"

"I told you—it wasn't a good night for me to entertain your friends. I have a deadline. And don't speak to me like this. I will not be bullied."

"I am not bullying you!"

Kate flinched and held her breath. Why was Grandpa being so mean? Usually he and Grandma were quite polite to each other.

He spoke again, not waiting for Grandma to answer. "Do I have to remind you what awaits you if this marriage breaks down yet again?"

Again a silence. Kate heard Grandpa sigh hard.

"I really can't do this anymore, Helen. It's taking a toll on my work. We've struggled long enough. It may be time to go our separate ways, once and for all."

"You seem to feel at liberty to go wherever you want," said Grandma, a sharp edge in her voice. "Off to Key West, off to Germany, off to France. Weeks at a time, leaving me stuck in this damned Shangri-La."

"I go because of my research and my writing, as you very well know." He paused and continued in a calmer voice. "Helen. I want you to think about going back to England and staying there. I think you'd be happier. This situation is untenable."

Silence. Then soft, awful crying. Tears sprang into Kate's own eyes.

"Weep if you want, but I'm not moved. Not any more."

Kate stayed still as a mouse.

"Where's the child?"

"Still asleep." Grandma's voice was choked.

Kate hardly breathed. What would happen if they knew she was listening? They must never know.

"Helen." Grandpa's voice was tiny bit kinder. "Talk to Rosalind when she comes back. She'd be delighted to have you in London for a while. It wouldn't have to be forever."

Kate almost called out "Yes! Please come, Grandma!" but stopped herself just in time. Grandma could have the spare room. They could play together after school every day. They'd been having so much fun together, making up stories, playing card games, dressing up. Grandpa was nice too, though very busy. But now she was cross with him for making Grandma cry. Oh, I do hope Grandma comes to London, she thought.

A distinguished alumna
1950

Seeing Elias every day, knowing he wanted her gone, was intolerable. She wasn't ready for the upheaval of moving across the Atlantic, yet again. But she had to get away.

Helen thought of her alma mater, Wells College. Surely they could provide a refuge for a distinguished alumna (as they'd described her in a recent *Alumnae News*, reporting on the Dublin production). She wrote hastily, afraid that her request would seem odd, her desperation too obvious. But they responded with enthusiasm, which might have simply been politeness—yes, please do come, we can certainly provide a room, and we would be very grateful if you could speak to our students about your work as a translator.

Elias's world receded behind her as she drove. Helen felt her spirits start to return and her body loosen. She wound down the window and cold fresh air swept into the car. I simply cannot be in that house anymore, she thought as she gained the outskirts of Princeton and turned onto the open road. Elias is right. We have become very bad for each other.

Could she possibly settle somewhere new, at her age? And where? If only they still had the little Oxford house on the cobbled Oxford street—now long gone, rented and then sold to strangers. There was the island house, of course, her summer refuge. But she couldn't live permanently in that remote spot, alone in an unheated cottage.

For a terrifying minute she felt unmoored, unconnected, suspended in airless space. She gripped the steering wheel so as not to drive off the road. No, she reminded herself, no, I am not a homeless supplicant, I have my daughters, I have my grandchildren, I have my dear old friend. They will welcome me. I can pick up my life in England again, if I want to.

She made herself breathe slowly until calmness returned.

The open road unfurled before her. Lunch—a thermos of coffee, a cheese sandwich, and an apple—waited beside her on the passenger seat. Helen drove three hours through small towns and villages into the greening countryside, pausing by a river to enjoy her solitary picnic. Spring was noticeably less advanced as she traveled northwest, the trees in their pale pointillist green, accented here and there by the off-white blossom of box trees. The beginning of the white tide after the yellow tide of daffodils and forsythia. Helen hadn't visited her old college in all the years since she graduated, though she would have come to see Marjorie if she had lasted there more than a few months.

At last the southern end of the lake came into view, sparkling blue. Helen had a sharp physical memory of the girl that she had been more than fifty years before, laughing with her friends as they stood with long skirts gathered up and water lapping their tender bare ankles. And now I'm a scarred old whale, she thought, encrusted with barnacles.

A small delegation of students and faculty greeted her with smiles and flowers at the entrance to the main building. She was evidently a personage, as far as they were concerned. Well, she was happy to play the part, a pleasant change from the role of Elias's annoying spouse.

Two of the girls led her to an attractively monastic little room, her home for the next month—a bed, a chair, a shelf, and a desk—and waited outside the door while she put away her things and combed her hair.

In the oak-paneled lecture hall, Helen looked up at the rows of young women with their glossy waved hair and neat blouses.

"It is a great pleasure and honor to be here at my alma mater again," she began, and indeed she felt enlivened to be away from home, to be speaking about her work to attentive ears. She talked to them about translation as an intriguing game—the conundrum of composing sentences to convey both the sense and style of the original, the exercise of inventing an idiom or a metaphor when an English parallel didn't exist. Her remarks were calibrated so as not to discourage those few of her listeners who might, perhaps, want to explore a career as a translator themselves. She did not mention the thanklessness of the translator's job, nor the literary critics who ignored or complained, the impatient publisher, the autocratic author and the moral burden of his dependence on her.

"I must say that literary translation holds deep satisfactions for us translators," she said. "For me, at least, it speaks to my love of language in general. And it is a great privilege to be so intimately involved with fiction writing in its noblest expression." Shall I divulge that I am a writer myself, she wondered. No. She did not want to answer the inevitable questions—what books have you written, are you famous, what are you working on now. She could tell them about *Abdication*. But that too would raise questions she did not want to answer.

Instead she told them that fitting her career as a translator into her family life was like a jigsaw puzzle. Sometimes it fell neatly into place; often it did not. "I'm afraid there were times that my family might have preferred me to be like other mothers, whipping up cakes instead of clacking away on my typewriter." There was polite laughter. "But I used to involve my small daughters when I could," she went on. "I'm quite unbiased when I say they were all very clever." She remembered Marjorie's ignominious failure here at Wells. But that had nothing to do with lack of cleverness, she reminded herself. "My children were good at languages, all three of them. Sometimes they helped me with bits of the translation, like the little poems that Dr. Mann sometimes writes or quotes in the text. It was fun for them."

It was not often that she had a chance to speak about her work to listeners who were both curious and respectful. One young woman with brown, intelligent eyes said she had been experimenting with translation already.

"I do so admire you, Mrs. Lowe-Porter," she said, blushing. "I would like nothing more than to follow in your footsteps."

Helen smiled at her warmly, accepting the girl's admiration. It's true that I've accomplished a lot, she thought. It was not a sentiment she allowed herself often.

The *Alumnae News* arrived a week after she'd returned to the Institute, with an article about her talk accompanied by a photo of Helen surrounded by cheerful young women. Helen sat down immediately to read it, already thinking she'd get extra copies to send to Rosalind, Alice, and Marjorie.

"Mrs. Lowe-Porter held her questioners spellbound while she told of the advantages of translating as a vocation and of the problems which occur in the work itself. She has found it to be an excellent profession for a woman since it can be pursued even in the nursery."

In the nursery!

"In fact," the article continued, "she doesn't look on it as a profession but as a relaxing occupation which can be picked up as one picks up sewing. It is like putting words into another dress."

Helen's pleasure curdled. It doesn't matter, she told herself. It does not matter. Why should I care whether they understand the scope of my work? But she could not convince herself. All she could do was wait for the sting to subside. At least she was old enough, and often enough stung, to know that it would subside. There were advantages to being an old whale with thickened skin.

She cut out the article and sent it to Blanche—she had no interest, now, in sharing it with her daughters. Blanche wrote back: "At least they didn't drool over your outfit. When you come to the city we'll drink our sorrows away." She enclosed a marked-up clipping of a recent newspaper interview where the reporter maintained that Blanche "married" the business despite her explanation that she had in fact cofounded it. Blanche had underlined the gushing comments about how feminine she appeared, how fashionably dressed. Even in the headline she was subordinated to Alfred, who was not present at the interview: "Man and His Wife Run Publishing Firm."

"Ha!" said Blanche's gloss in the margin.

Part Three

The Wanderer

49

Such human love as this
1953

In the London *Times*, carried upstairs to her each morning by Kate or one of the younger girls, Helen followed with dread the unfolding drama of the American Jewish couple accused of spying. It was the poisoned harvest of the American madness she had feared, the madness that had driven the Manns back to Switzerland. How far would it go, this anti-communist hysteria? Capital punishment, in her view, was barbaric even when guilt was proven. The death sentence for an innocent woman, guilty only of loyalty to her husband...they won't do it, she told herself. It's a civilized country. They can't. Even in these insane times.

But they did. Despair drove Helen to poetry once again. That tragic, martyred young woman, hardly more than Marjorie's age. Her brush of dark hair, her haunted eyes, her small taut mouth. Her stoicism in the face of preposterous accusations and the murderous power of the state. Her grief, unutterable and unuttered, at the loss of her two children and their loss of her. And then that extraordinary gesture of humanity in her last moment.

> *Before she sat in the chair*
> *She turned and kissed*
> *The wardress who had led her there.*
> *Then, thus sitting,*
> *She died.*
> *We can ill spare,*
> *And must not waste, such human love as this.*

50

The second wife
1954

I must practice patience, Helen thought. I can't expect Rosalind to look after me day and night just because I am a little unwell and unable to get out of bed. She'll trot up the stairs with some breakfast for me as soon as she can, as soon as the children are off to school and Douglas off to work. I know she has not forgotten about me—how could she, when I've tapped on the floor with my walking stick once or twice, just to be sure?

When Rosalind appeared with a pot of tea and some toast she brought the post as well. "Look at this, Mother!" It was a woman's magazine, such as Helen would never read. American. A well-endowed young woman smirked from the cover, her teeth fearfully white. There was a note clipped to the cover in Marjorie's handwriting: "Dear Mother and Rosalind, I hope you enjoy this little effort! Love, M."

Helen turned to the magazine's table of contents: effusive claims about hairstyles, five ways to get slim, family problems. Then she saw Marjorie's name, the author of something called "The Second Wife."

"How wonderful!" said Rosalind. "I'll read it after you." She scurried off to whatever she was occupied with. Sometimes she told Helen where she was going, sometimes not. She dabbled in a little editing for an art book publisher and performed various good works with charities, reading to needy children or serving soup. For someone who was unemployed, or under-employed, she was surprisingly busy. But never with painting.

Helen poured her tea and opened the magazine to Marjorie's article, fearing the worst. It did not disappoint her, in that regard. It was, if not the worst, pretty bad. She read as much as she could stomach. Marjorie knew her way around a sentence, without question. The writing itself had a distinction that she doubted the readers of the magazine would recognize, let alone savor. But the content...oh dear. Cloying and confessional, offering life lessons about marrying a divorced man and raising his child. Beside her byline was a nicely lit photo of Marjorie looking tastefully glamorous.

When Rosalind came back Helen handed her the magazine, open to the article.

"Did you read it?" Rosalind said. "I'm so happy that she's writing again. And getting published."

"Tell me what you think, once you've read it," said Helen. She raised her eyebrows but managed to resist rolling her eyes.

Rosalind looked at Helen with a tacit warning. "We should write and congratulate her," she said.

Helen shrugged and said nothing. I have to tell Marjorie what I think, she told herself. I owe it to her, as a fellow writer. She'll appreciate it.

Dear Marjorie (*wrote Helen a few days later*),

Thank you for sending us the magazine with your article, which I read with interest.

Darling, I must be honest. I don't think you would want me to be dishonest. The truth is that I found the article rather facile and shallow. Readers of this banal publication might like it but that means little. Their expectations are quite evidently not high.

The topic of your piece is not uninteresting. No topic is inherently uninteresting. A good

217

writer could write something worth reading about hair, for goodness's sake.

You are capable of so much more, Marjorie. A small suggestion from a fellow-writer: wouldn't it be more courageous and worthwhile to examine life through the prism of fiction, which allows one to tell a more resonant truth? I know you can do it. Your stories when you were young were very accomplished. Why did you stop?

And so on. She was writing out of concern, Helen reminded herself. She wanted her daughter to aim higher, because she believed that she could.

Helen did not hear from Marjorie for nearly two months. By the time her response came she'd already punished herself, lying awake with her own unkind words clanging in her skull. Hadn't she, decades ago, said something like this to that awful Phoebe? But this was far worse. She'd wounded her own daughter.

Dear Mother (*Marjorie finally wrote*),

I'm very sorry you were disappointed. I thought you'd be glad that I finally got something published again. I'm not a genius, like you and Daddy. I'm not an intellectual. This is the best I can do. I put a lot of work into it, believe it or not, though you find it so stupid and "facile," lovely word.

I know that Family Woman is not exactly the Paris Review but it's something. I've never said this to you but here goes, what do I have to lose at this point? You're a gifted and committed writer but, in my humble view, your own fiction and poetry would have actually benefited and

218

you might have sold more work if you'd ever condescended to write for a commercial publication like this, yes, even this "banal" publication. One learns a lot, writing to deadline, on a topic that one might not have chosen, for readers of all stripes.

And I've never said this to you either, but I'm going to say it now: do you have any idea what it's like to be the daughter of H. T. Lowe-Porter? And Professor Elias Lowe? To try to live up to parents like you? I've failed every step of the way and now I've failed again.

Helen sat with her hand pressed into her chest, the letter in her other hand. She knew Marjorie had wept, writing this. It was as clear to her as if there were tearstains on the paper.

Helen did not write this back to Marjorie:

Oh Marjorie. I am sorry. How can I explain. I always thought you would do more, as a writer. I've been waiting. I remember the poems you wrote when you were a young girl—real ability you had, and you knew it. You were so full of confidence and momentum. And then the stories in your early twenties: such original work, and it was not only your proud mama who thought so. At first I was afraid I might not be able to avoid envy, and how terrible that would have been, to envy my own daughter her success. But that didn't happen. Your achievement thrilled me, Marjorie, it really did.

I'm sure I told you so at the time, though no doubt I expressed myself with restraint as I generally did. I've never been in the habit of gushing.

And then you married, and the writing dried up, as far as I could see. I know you were immediately occupied with your stepson, and soon with your own child, but you had help, far more help than I ever did. You had money. You did not have a Mann breathing down your neck. You did not have a husband who skimmed off the cream of your brain to enrich his own work.

You have no idea how different it was for me. Do you know, Marjorie—no, you don't know, how could you know—that I spent every minute that I could spare producing poetry and prose, reams of it, dreaming about it, sending it out in dogged hopes of publication. All my life, Marjorie.

You won't remember but once when you were thirteen you dismissed me as a mere translator. Perhaps I was, but not for want of trying. You yourself could have been more.

So yes, I was disappointed. But I had no right to tell you so.

Marjorie did not write this back to Helen:

Well, Mother, it's not the end of the story, you know. Check back in a few decades if you're still around. You might be surprised.

In the corner
1954

Helen sat in the corner of Rosalind's living room with her faithful nomad's desk on her lap, taking up as little space as possible. She was not fond of her daughter's soft armchairs and couches with their big cabbage-rose pattern. But nomads did not choose. One of Rosalind's paintings hung on the wall above the piano, a watercolor portrait of her three children when small. The youngest had her back to the viewer but her mischievous green eyes were visible in the mirror she was holding. That was Rosalind's style, figurative but not trite. Helen liked it and wished that Rosalind, like Marjorie, had not abandoned her evident talent. "Oh, but there's no time for painting these days," Rosalind said. "Perhaps when the children are grown up." Be careful, her mother wanted to warn her. Wait long enough and it will be too late.

The life of the house clattered on around Helen, parents and children coming and going, guests for dinner, laughter, quarrels, Douglas practicing the piano, the phone ringing, the planning and making of meals that she did not have a hand in and did not always eat. At night their voices kept her awake and she would call out sharply when her patience ran out. Words had a way of leaping out of her mouth that she did not intend and quickly regretted.

"No, thank you," she said when Rosalind urged her to come downstairs and join them for dinner with friends. "I'd shrivel up with boredom." Rosalind's lips tightened and she left the room without a word. Helen immediately wished she could take back her rudeness. Her implicit criticism wasn't even fair. She had little in common with their friends but they were decent people—hardworking lawyers like Douglas and busy, cheerful women like Rosalind. It was just the pace and jabber of their dinner table conversation. Helen found it impossible to follow and would withdraw into frustrated silence, which no one seemed to notice.

A few weeks later Rosalind tried again. "Mother, Douglas's university friend Humphrey is in London and he's coming for dinner. Humphrey Cobb. You know who he is, don't you? He said he wants to meet you."

Helen did know who he was: a prolific author whose satiric novels were prominently reviewed. Not to her taste. But at least he was a fellow-writer. And he wanted to meet her.

"Is anyone else coming?"

"No, just Humphrey."

"Well yes, all right," she said. "What are you going to make?"

Rosalind laughed and hugged her. "What would you like?"

Humphrey Cobb was witty and garrulous, his voice tones as rotund as his well-fed self. If he was indeed pleased to meet her there was little sign of it. He seemed interested only in spinning his cruelly funny anecdotes, skewering leftwing idealists, poor people, and dark-skinned immigrants. Was he trying to provoke his old friend? Douglas, for all his mildness, was an outspoken defender of human rights, with Rosalind's keen support.

Helen grew indignant on their behalf as well as her own. Finally she hoisted herself up from the table. "That's quite enough for me, Mr. Cobb. Your Tory twaddle is ruining my digestion. Good night."

But when she reached her bedroom she was stricken to recall the discomfiture on Rosalind's and Douglas's kind faces. How could she have embarrassed them like that?

The next morning Rosalind was reserved when she brought breakfast.

"I'm sorry, Rosalind," Helen said in a small voice. "I behaved badly."

Rosalind picked up Helen's clothes from the floor and folded them. "He was dreadful, wasn't he? Douglas was quite upset with him." She sighed. "But he was a guest, Mother."

"I'm sorry," Helen said again. "I know I'm not an easy person to have around. You and Douglas must be ready to get rid of me."

"Don't be silly, Mother."

But Helen knew it was true. How long can they put up with me, she wondered. And where will they pack me off to this time? The question sometimes kept her from sleep. If only she could live with Pauline again. But poor Pauline was now mortally ill. Helen longed to take care of her, repaying her friend's kindness. But, to her shame and sorrow, helping Pauline, or anyone, was beyond her capacity.

Would Alice agree to have her in Cambridge again? Probably not. She'd found it even harder to harmonize with Alice's household than with Rosalind's, a gauge, no doubt, of how cranky and difficult she'd become. What had possessed her to mock Alice's china cat collection? She of all people should applaud eccentricity. And why hadn't she told her daughter how much she admired her good taste and her perfect, poetic French? Helen had observed how grateful those visiting professors were to have Alice at their side, how they relaxed and laughed and made sure that they stayed close to her. She was proud that Alice had inherited her mother's linguistic bent. Her spoken languages were far better than Helen's had ever been.

Alice's two young children were wary of their grandmother, ducking out of the word games she tried to amuse them with. She couldn't bring herself to engage in their own silly games. I'm too old for hide-and-seek, she argued to herself.

Eight-year-old Carrie reminded her of the pigeons who sat on the windowsill peering nervously into her room. Helen wrote a poem for the child and was rewarded with a smile. "May I— can I take it with me?" Carrie asked shyly with the page held to her chest. "May I show the others?"

I would repeat
That they are truly very sweet;
They do no harm,
Even charm, in their own way

And though belike you'd spurn the thought in dudgeon
I've often wished that you could be a pigeon,
So you could come,
And not almost but quite,
Into my room.

Among all the English granddaughters Rosalind's Kate was her only ally and co-conspirator, the only one in whom Helen confided about the stories that she was now writing. Kate was an able research assistant.

"I need to know," said Helen, "what a blind man sounds like running down the road with his stick."

Kate ran up and down the hallway with a yardstick in her hand and a blindfold around her eyes until they both collapsed in laughter. She would miss Kate terribly if she had to leave.

Rosalind had started making casual references to Elias's ample house, to the spectacular trees in the autumn. I know what she's doing, thought Helen. But I won't go back there. Ever.

Perhaps Marjorie would have her, if it came to that. She hoped that Marjorie had by now forgiven her ill-advised letter. Helen recalled Marjorie's apartment high above Central Park—spacious and comfortable, in her recollection, though reflecting Irving's taste more than Marjorie's with steel-framed furniture and stark modern paintings. I don't take up much room, she thought. You'd think they could fit me in somewhere. It would mean enduring the husband. Couldn't there be a détente where we simply ignored each other? She must write to Marjorie, before

Rosalind grew desperate and had to deport her. And meanwhile she must do her best to behave.

There were no more translations demanding her attention. Since the publication of *Faustus* a resolve had slowly grown within her: it was time to stop. She must, at last, come back to her own work, with full attention and creativity, without distraction.

Mann's new novella *Die Betrogene* had eased the decision. The story repelled her: a middle-aged woman obsessed by a young man and punished for her sexual passion by a fatal cancer of the womb—a sort of inferior, misogynist *Death in Venice*. The prospect of translating it was exhausting, short though it was. Like a revelation, the thought came to her: *I do not have to do it!* I have done enough. I will retire. They can find someone to replace me.

The idea of untrammeled access at last to her own writing, to crafting her own language instead of Mann's, was a liberation. The vision was strong enough to face the disappointment, possibly anger, of both Mann and the Knopfs.

"My dear Tommy," she wrote, summoning up her courage. "The time has come for me to retire as your translator, after all these years. The reason is perhaps silly: in the end of my life I have so many things in my head that I find I must get them down, whether they ever find a publisher or no." She said nothing about her dislike for the novella, though she wished, for his sake as well as hers, that *Doctor Faustus* had been his last work, as he himself had said he intended.

She sent off the letter, picturing Mann's raised eyebrows as he read it. "Our poor deluded Helen…" But perhaps he would understand, perhaps even accept her aspiration as a fellow-artist.

To her surprise and relief his response was kind. "Of course you must! You have served me so well and for so long. I am sure Alfred will provide me with another translator. Katia and I look forward to reading your new work. And we will always stay in touch, my dear Helen."

Of course they would stay in touch. Their friendship had been forged through so many years, so many struggles and triumphs.

She wrote to Alfred and Blanche as well, again resorting to exaggerated humility and scolding herself for it. Why did she have to cower like that? She referred to her desire as an infirmity, a weak craving, like a timid animal making itself appear as small and pitiable as possible to avert attack. But there was no attack. Alfred acknowledged her decision in a brief note, as if he'd been expecting it. "Bravo, Helen," wrote Blanche. "I applaud you and wish you all success!"

And now, she thought, suddenly panicked as well as elated—now there's no excuse for me! Can I, at seventy-eight, find my writer's spirit again?

Mann, even older than she, was uprooted yet again, pressured to leave the country of his citizenship for the second time in his life. Helen worried about him. He and Katia had thought they were safe in the mighty land of the free. But they were not. Exiles from exile, trying to rebuild a life in Switzerland.

Wealth and stature could not protect him from the vertiginous sense of displacement that she was all too familiar with. "My ending is despair," he wrote to her later, knowing that Shakespeare was her mother tongue. "Oh my dear Prospero," she wrote back. "Could it be time to abjure your magic?"

She pitied Mann. But the minute she shed her translator's role she felt so unburdened she could have flown. When had she ever felt such freedom? Not since her virgin days in Towanda, more than fifty years ago. She threw the windows open wide and said "Come on in!" and in swarmed ideas as though they'd been clustering outside for years, waiting. She welcomed them, she embraced them. In Rosalind's living room, or sitting up in bed, she wrote, wrote, wrote. Eleven short stories in four months—and then, to her own astonishment, a novel. The story burgeoned from a passing memory: a long-ago holiday in Brittany, a rainy summer day, Alice reading a moralistic French fairytale to Marjorie about naughty children punished by a magic spell that made the girl a boy and the boy a girl.

The idea took hold of her. The theme was not something she had ever considered. But the characters—her own characters, not the small children of that foolish fairytale—and their extraordinary predicament were palpable to her. They stood in front of her: a sister and brother, twins, sixteen years old, whose sexes are inexplicably switched on a beach in France.

A chorus of predictable and irritating inner voices sprang up: But this is bizarre! Perverse, even. Who would publish, or read, such an outlandish and scandalous story?

Helen ignored the voices. She was enraptured by the gentle, effeminate boy who becomes a girl and the rough girl who becomes a rough boy, forcing questions about being male or female. They hate each other, until there is a crisis of life and death. She drew the setting from the Brittany sojourn. The glittering sea with its mortal danger and its capacity to transmute. Of his bones are coral made.

It didn't worry her that the story might shock. What did she have to lose? The end of her life was approaching. She claimed the compounded freedom of age and dubious sanity. That inspiration could visit her again, after all those years, made her profoundly grateful. She worked hard, writing by hand. Her pages accumulated, her characters grew and developed. When she read over what she'd written it seemed to her that the work was good, perhaps the best of her life. Then a cloud would pass over the sun and it would seem worthless. Back and forth, impressive, worthless. Like Schroedinger's cat, dead and alive at the same time.

She typed up the novel surreptitiously, bit by bit, when no one was home, and had the nerve to send the finished manuscript to the Manns, both of them. A month later Thomas wrote back with sincere respect and detailed comments—he and Katia liked it very much, he said. But he was cautious about its chances and did not recommend approaching the Knopfs. Helen could not bring herself to ask him to explain. She knew why. It was not good enough, in his opinion, for the Knopf imprint.

And then—well, there was only one way this story could end. The novel got as far as an agent and no further. This time, though, she knew what to do. Oh yes. She was not going to let her precious work fester for decades this time. Out with the matches and up the chimney!

She waited until she was alone in the flat. Rosalind never knew about the novel's life, let alone its death. She asked once or twice about the bulging folder on the floor by her chair but Helen headed her off. "None of your business" was a succinct and useful phrase, she had found.

Helen was sitting spent and motionless when Kate came home from school. The girl came over to kiss her grandmother, as always, then lifted her head and sniffed. "Oh, Granny," she said, putting her arms around her. Helen had shoveled away the ashes but the smell of incineration was in the air.

It was a kind of annihilation. Her blood apparently still circulated, or she'd be dead in body as well as spirit. But nothing else flowed: no creative founts, no hope, no runnels of joy. Love had not entirely left her but it was passive and dull. I am in a wasteland, she thought. I *am* a wasteland, parched and barren. Dusty and dirty. She was comforted only by the thought that she was old and would not have to endure this wretchedness for long. To avoid inflicting her gloom on Rosalind and the family she quarantined herself in her bedroom. But they wouldn't leave her alone, forever knocking on the door and coming in with worried faces and offers of company, which she rejected. But she could not find the energy to care.

228

Bedlam

1954

A rest, Mother—
Just a little rest, Mrs. Lowe—
You'll feel better soon—
Where is this? Why am I here?
We'll look after you—
They'll look after you, Mother, it's the best place—
I don't need a rest—
The doctor thinks you need—
We're going to give you something to help you sleep, let me see
    your arm just a moment—
Don't touch me—
Mother, I'm so sorry, it's for the best—
Please don't leave me here—
I'll come back tomorrow, I promise—
Why are there bars on the window? Do you think Peter Pan's
    going to spirit me away?
Ha ha, Mrs. Lowe. We just want you to be safe—
Someone's screaming! What's going on—
Don't worry, dear, there's nothing to worry about—
This is Bedlam, isn't it?
No, no, Mother, it's St. Anne's Hospital, the best in London—
Why am I here?
It's just for a little while, you'll feel so much better after a little
    rest, things have been hard for you, so much disruption—
Don't leave me here—

The wanderer
1955

Oft must I, alone, the hour before dawn
lament my care.

And now he's dead, poor old Mann, dead at 80. Only a year older than me. Dead in Switzerland, another wanderer. At least he died a legend, receiving honor after honor until the day he died. Poor Katia, alone now. Whatever might have been missing, they had companionship together.

I, on the other hand. Especially after the extinction of my novel. I am evidently to die here in the valley of never. I have no spirit to start writing again. I have dried up like a raisin in the sun, like the American poet said. Festering, stinking, sagging. Perhaps exploding. What language he had. Not that I compare my feeble little dream with his.

It may be that I am losing ground, in my mind. I see how they look at me, wary and concerned. They're afraid I'll disintegrate again. Melancholia is always whimpering at the door. It's not my door. I am of no fixed abode. I have not made myself very welcome in my daughters' homes. I have to pack my belongings over and over again, into ever-smaller suitcases. One or two for all my worldly goods. Mann used to travel with eighteen. All packed by Katia.

I admit I've become rather uncouth in my old age. I blurt things out. I don't do well on someone else's timetable. I don't like being told what to wear. I care about comfort, and texture and color. Not whether something is respectable enough for the bourgeoisie. Perfectly clean is not a quality that I bother with. Alice complained about my unkemptness in her mild way, when she didn't know I was listening. Rosalind told me I was judgmental. I suppose I am. Well, I have standards. They were upset when I dug my heels in about the holiday in Scotland. I was perfectly willing to be here by myself. I didn't need Rosalind to sacrifice herself by staying here with me.

I read Marjorie's letter tucked in Rosalind's desk: "Poor you, I completely agree, she has to go somewhere else before she drives you all mad."

Having already driven myself mad. Having driven myself to Bedlam, no less, where they used to chain the poor loonies to the wall. All right, not Bedlam, St. Anne's Hospital, the very best in London. The very best for crocks like me. Did they think it would cure me? Bedlam never cured anyone. Don't send me back. I won't go.

> *Among the living*
> *none now remains to whom I dare*
> *my inmost thought clearly reveal.*

"She can't look after herself, that's clear"—one of the girls said this, I heard her. I fear that it's true. I seem to be confused these days. And anyway I have no money for a house or even a flat to myself. Not on a translator's meager savings. They point out that I could sell the island house, Charlotte's cottage. It would break my heart, even if I can never go there again. I want the children and the grandchildren to have it. Could I let it go? If I had to, yes. But it would not buy me a home in London.

Pauline would take me in again, if she were alive. My dear Pauline. Ten years younger than me and strong as an ox all her life. Pauline, and now Thomas. I suspect I am next. Or Blanche, a wraith, living on cigarettes.

I don't need much. A quiet room, my nomad's desk, a shelf or two of my books—those that I still have. Where are all the others? So carefully acquired, each one a step in my mind's journey. They've all departed from me, along with my other treasures. My tiles from Portugal. My heavy copper frying pan. My hand mirror with the inlaid back. The little white and blue jug for cream and its matching sugar bowl on the breakfast table every morning. Are they in a box somewhere? Did I give them away?

Elias has my set of all the translations in a cupboard. Proof of my hard labor. I'll get them back some day. I keep a copy of my play at hand, and a few more tucked in a box. I need a means of making tea and the odd meal. A decent bottle of sherry. Do I need company? Most of the time not.

I have to find somewhere else to live. I'll write to Marjorie. "Yes, why not?" says Rosalind, but she sounds dubious. "You could ask her. But you know that you and Irving…" No need to complete the sentence. She points out once again that I could go back to Elias and the Institute. "He's concerned about you, Mother," she says. "He would like to take care of you." I look at her, letting my disdain show on my face. But I know I must leave. I owe them that, these good daughters of mine. I have to take myself off their hands.

Could it be true that Elias wants to take care of me? He would have to let me creep back, if I must, like a skinny old cat who can't forage for herself. I am still his wife. Marjorie would be nearby, and Nicky. I would miss the English grandchildren, though they might not miss me, except Kate.

Elias's probably plotting to pop me into an old-age-home for my own good, somewhere tasteful and well-recommended, of course. There must be a place where they dispose of Institute scholars and their wives when they become gaga. I would loathe that, being shut up with other old detritus.

I must write to Marjorie.

Meanwhile I am a wanderer. I wander. Like that nameless wretch a thousand years ago, speaking his trouble alone before dawn by a bleak sea.

> *Weary mind never withstands fate,*
> *nor does troubled thought bring help*

Poetry comforts me. Reading it, writing it.

54

Because
1954

Because our only spare room is a maid's room, more like a closet.
Because the bathroom off the maid's room is even tinier.
Because the housekeeper uses that bathroom to drip-dry Irving's
    shirts.
Because it wouldn't be fair to Nicky to make him give up his room.
Because my stepson is here every weekend.
Because I'm worried that I couldn't take care of you well enough.
Because you need professional care.
Because what would I do if you break down again.
Because you don't like Irving.
Because he doesn't like you.
Because you're political enemies.
Because I can't bear to listen to corrosive debates at the dinner table.
Because neither of you is considerate enough to be civil for my sake.
Because my days are already busy.
Because you think what I do with my time is frivolous.
Because you judge me for not writing.
Because it would change things between me and Daddy.
Because I'm not selfless like Alice and Rosalind.
Because I can't.

55

Casual Verse
1957

Rosalind escorted her listless mother with her single suitcase back to Princeton. "I hope she settles in," Rosalind whispered to her father, with Helen sitting stiffly at the kitchen table. "And if she doesn't..."

"I'll do my best," he said. Helen had been in England for four years. After the first relief he'd missed her, missed her clever conversation, her companionship. It still means a great deal, he reflected, this long, deep bond between us. Even if we're hardly the contented old couple we might have been.

Day after day Elias observed her sitting by the living room window, upright and motionless, her eyes fixed on nothing. It alarmed him more than her angry outbursts, more than her rambling discourses. When she at last picked up her notebook and pen he encouraged her too fulsomely and she looked at him with contempt and put the book away.

The next time he said nothing, but noted how she was absorbed and more tranquil, bent over her writing board, scribbling something, a poem, a story, he had no idea. It had been a long time, a very long time, since she showed him her work.

But he had an idea. After careful thought it seemed eminently possible. He couldn't think of any reason not to use his connections and money in this way.

He would like to try once more to bring her happiness.

At first she wouldn't even discuss it with him.

"Please, Helen, just listen to me. The poems are excellent. We can and should publish them. I'm offering to organize it. All you have to do is compile them. Do some editing if you want."

She stared at him, surprised and not pleased. "What you're proposing is a vanity publication," she said. "It's insulting. It's unthinkable. I have professional standing in the field."

He let it go but returned to the subject a few days later when they were taking an early evening walk along the avenue of flowering lindens. "Ah," said Helen, closing her eyes for a moment to inhale the scent. Elias decided to speak.

"Helen, about my idea: you mustn't dismiss it because of some narrow concept of professionalism." He'd thought of a tactic. "I'm sure I don't need to tell you the etymology of the word 'publish'." He stopped walking and waited expectantly.

She sighed. "It's from the Latin *publicare*, of course."

"And what does it mean?"

She shook her head but answered, "To make public."

"Exactly, Helen, exactly! So what is publishing? Simply making one's work available to others. The means of publication are immaterial. The scope of the readership is immaterial. Don't you see?"

She did not answer and was silent for the rest of the walk. He couldn't tell if she was thinking about it or not. Later he brought it up once more.

"Helen—think of our daughters, our grandchildren. Don't you think it would mean a great deal to them all to have your poems in book form?" He was pleased with himself for this particular argument. Most of Helen's recent poems—she'd told him—were addressed to the grandchildren. When their daughters were small she'd written poems for them, too. He remembered those tender, humorous little verses. The girls would love to read them again, he was certain.

He said judiciously little about his good friend at the Oxford University Press who had already agreed to bring it out under his own imprint. There would be no reviews, advertising, or sales in bookstores, his friend warned, but that was not the point.

Eventually she accepted. He congratulated himself on his strategy. Helen came back to life as she excavated old notebooks of poems of the past sixty years, pored over them, edited them, retyped them, even read a few aloud to him, including, shyly, an early love poem. Something like warmth sifted back into their quiet evenings.

Casual Verse arrived, eighty pages, attractive in its austere brown cover with her name below the title in graceful italic. Her name only. No one else's. She seemed calmly pleased though not uplifted as he would have liked. She refused a launch party— "No! How vulgar!"—but tolerated a celebratory glass of champagne with Elias and Marjorie and agreed to read a couple of poems aloud to them.

"So beautiful, Mother!" said Marjorie, clapping. "Please read another one!"

"No," said Helen. But she held the little book in both hands and gazed at it with what Elias thought was affection.

Elias, himself delighted with the little collection, wanted to send one to the Knopfs but she forbade him. He found it frustrating. He knew better than to expect gratitude from her but he wished she would allow him to give his gift to its fullest. Why couldn't she be happy with this modest publication? Surely she harbored no illusions, at this point, about being a celebrated writer.

"Have you even told Alfred and Blanche?" he asked. From her silence he gathered she had not, that she did not want the literary world to know that she had been reduced to publishing her own writing, or, worse, letting her husband do it for her.

The book's brief flurry ebbed away, like a wave sinking into the sand as the tide goes out, leaving no trace. Elias no longer saw Helen picking it up and leafing through its pages with an almost-smile. The book had not even prompted more writing, as he'd hoped. I don't understand, he thought. I don't think I've ever understood.

Helen took to retiring earlier and sleeping later, doing little in her waking hours beyond desultory reading. She seemed indifferent to food, let alone cooking. Evening meals, now prepared by the housekeeper before she left each day, were silent.

Elias brought home a new leather-covered notebook and presented it to her.

"For when inspiration visits you," he said with pretended cheer.

But the notebook remained unopened on the coffee table. "What is there to write about?" she asked.

"Life!" Elias wanted to say. "There's always life, Helen!" Her static gloom was incomprehensible to him.

He woke suddenly one night, startled, and realized he'd just heard the front door close. He looked at his bedside clock: 3 a.m. Alarmed, he threw on his bathrobe and slippers and hastened down the stairs, careful not to stumble in his bleary state. He threw open the door. "Helen!" he shouted into the dark. "Helen!"

What on earth is she up to now, he thought with irritation. He grabbed a flashlight from the hall table and shone it in a circle, uncomfortably aware that curious neighbors might be watching. She couldn't have gone far, he reassured himself, conjuring and then dismissing the idea of a full-fledged search party. "Helen! For god's sake! Where are you?"

Nothing. The night air was cold. He ventured down the steps and shone the flashlight around again. This time it caught a ghostly figure fifty feet away. She did not move as he approached her.

"Now, Helen, you must come inside with me." He made his voice gentle though he wanted to shout his worry and anger. To his relief she let him guide her to the house. Her feet were bare and she was wearing nothing but a light nightdress. "Come, dear, come inside."

In the lit hallway he saw that her eyes were blank, her face slack. Was she sleepwalking? Insane? Now he was frightened. How does one look after a demented spouse?

She seemed to rouse for a moment when he led her into her room. "Have you any idea what you did to me, Elias?"

"What are you talking about, Helen?"

She slept for the rest of the night and all the next day, then, to his surprise, appeared downstairs as though nothing had happened.

"You don't remember last night?" he asked.

"Remember what?"

Over dinner she was as mute as ever. She ate almost nothing. He found it unbearable.

Two nights later she wandered away again, this time further, almost to the main road. After that he hid the keys to the front and back doors at night. But he could not look after her all day. The housekeeper made it plain that it was not her job.

"Marjorie," he said on the phone, "I don't know what to do. I can't keep her safe."

"Oh, Daddy. Perhaps it's time. You really tried."

For the last time they packed up her few clothes, her books including the translations and the last box of *Casual Verse*, some small paintings for the walls of her room at Mrs. D's.

"You'll be relieved, won't you?" she'd said, her tone bitter, when he told her that she was too ill to live at home anymore. "It's what you wanted."

"No, no, dear!" But he could not deny an easing in his chest.

56

Confession
1958

Elias didn't come to the front door when Marjorie knocked. She waited, then opened the door and called to him: "Daddy? Are you all right?" He had recently been diagnosed with mild angina.

She found him reclining on the couch in the living room, swathed up to his chin in a green and blue mohair blanket, a book closed on his lap. Subdued chamber music played on the gramophone.

"Are you all right?" she asked again, glancing at the pill bottles on the end table.

Elias waved her in with a tired smile. "Just a twinge or two," he said. "I took three pills. Not too bad." Severity was measured in how many pills he had to take.

"Sorry I'm late," she said. "I stopped at Mrs. D's."

"And?"

"She's...OK. The same."

"Good girl. I know it's not easy."

Marjorie made coffee and brought a tray back to the living room. Elias pushed himself up, grimacing with the effort. She helped him rearrange the soft blanket over his knees and tucked it around his ankles in case there was a draft. He sipped his coffee, staring at the patterned carpet. Marjorie watched him. It was unlike her father to be so motionless and quiet.

At last he looked up. "Your poor mother. I've been sitting here thinking about her."

Marjorie was alert. For all their closeness her father had never confided in her about Helen.

Elias went on. "She has such bitterness. About her work. About me." He reached for a cookie on the tray, then changed his mind. "I have been both ambitious and fortunate all my life, Marjorie. And I believe that good fortune has come to me in part because of my disposition. I enjoy life. I work hard, as you know. I am not easily discouraged. When I have had setbacks—which I have, inevitably—I have made it a point not to indulge self-pity or depression." He looked at her meaningfully.

"And you're saying that Mother..."

"One cannot always choose circumstances and outcomes. But one can choose one's attitude in response."

She was reluctant to argue with him but wanted to defend her mother. "I believe it's been truly hard for her, Daddy. She never did the writing she wanted to do. She wasn't well treated by Mann and the publishers, or the critics. She deserves far more recognition than she's ever had. Don't you think? She's one of the world's great translators."

"I still maintain..." He put down the cup and cleared his throat. "There's something else, Marjorie," he said. "It's not a matter that we've discussed before. I'd like to talk to you about it."

Marjorie was startled by his somber tone. She heard the unvoiced words "before it's too late."

"This is about your mother and me. Our failed marriage." The string quartet played a final cadence and the needle lifted itself off the record. "Her animus towards me, despite all my efforts," he continued. "I have been lying here today thinking about it. The loss. All my unsuccessful attempts to reconcile, to make her happy."

"The little poetry book made her happy, Daddy. That was a wonderful gesture."

He shook his head. "Her pleasure didn't last long, did it? She was unable simply to enjoy it for what it was. I apparently did the wrong thing, yet again." He hesitated. "There was...an incident, more than twenty years ago, that seemed to throw her off

241

balance. When she left me. In my opinion she has never quite been herself since then."

An incident?

"Perhaps it's wrong to talk about this with you."

"Daddy. I am not a child. You can talk to me about anything."

He glanced at her. Then he said, "Do you remember Phoebe?"

Marjorie had not thought of Phoebe for years. She recalled an athletic older girl, confident and amusing, a little bossy. Rosalind's friend. She had fulfilled her ambition to be a popular writer—Marjorie recalled a display of one of her novels in a London bookstore window but had not read it.

"Phoebe Hadley, in Oxford? Yes, sure. What about her?"

"Something happened..." Elias frowned and looked away. "Phoebe was twenty-one or so. Your mother was away somewhere. Phoebe came to our house and approached me quite forcefully and I succumbed. I was a foolish middle-aged man, flattered by a young temptress. It meant nothing at all." He coughed a couple of times and rummaged for a tissue. Marjorie, stunned, handed him one.

"I told your mother, believing she'd understand. I thought she might even laugh with me about it. It was farcical, after all. I made a fool of myself. But she was furious and distraught. I was greatly taken aback. I did everything I could think of to reassure her. But apparently in that one moment I lost her regard forever." He peered into his cup, which was empty, and gestured to the coffee pot. "We'd been married for so long. We loved each other, Marjorie. We were the best of friends. I depended on her."

Marjorie poured him more coffee, stirring in milk and sugar automatically. She could not make sense of it—her father and their friend Phoebe. Marjorie had been fond of her. They all were. Family occasions were more fun when Phoebe was there, as she often was. She remembered a moment in the kitchen: her mother teaching Phoebe to make a soufflé, their hilarious mock-accusations when it came out of the oven solid as a dumpling.

But now Phoebe appeared in a different light, selfish and promiscuous, betraying Helen's kindness to her in this awful way. Goldilocks indeed, pushing her way in and taking what was not hers. And why had her father been so passive? He could have turned her away.

A question occurred to her. "But why did you tell Mother? Why did you think she might laugh?"

Now her father looked a little embarrassed. "This will seem very strange to you, I'm afraid. Your mother and I had an understanding...she was gracious enough to permit me to see other women from time to time, when I was traveling." He paused. "I'm not sure how to say this to you. The fact is I had an unusually strong sexual need, in my prime." He glanced at Marjorie, who was now reeling a bit. "I was grateful to Helen," he went on. "I always told her when I had an encounter. I did not want to deceive her."

"When you were traveling...."

"Yes, you're right. Phoebe was right there in Oxford. But still. It was such a passing thing. Even so, if I'd had any idea of how your mother would react..." He looked away. "I do blame myself severely."

Marjorie was finding it hard to absorb this revelation. She had been on the receiving end of infidelity herself and shrank to recall the humiliation and hurt. And the repulsive idea of her father with Phoebe, almost another sister... But she knew all too well how difficult her mother could be, how critical and moody. It couldn't have been easy for him, being married to her. Perhaps the strain had made him susceptible to Phoebe.

Her father was so penitent, so concerned. He seemed to need her to comfort him. "Daddy, you had no way of knowing that Mother would be so—" she searched for the word. "So destabilized. I'm sure you were very reassuring. You didn't leave her, she left you."

243

He looked up with a sad smile. "Still..."

Marjorie reached her arm around his shoulders. She was struck by how small and thin he felt.

"Thank you for telling me," she said.

"Marjorie dear—please keep this to yourself."

"I'll be discreet," she assured him, but she knew that she would have to share this privileged, shocking revelation with her sisters when she saw them. It was far too delicate to put into a letter. How distressed Rosalind would be to learn that it was her friend who drove their parents apart.

57

Amalie's
1961

Against her own policy Helen waited in the dayroom. The windows were open and the curtains moved with the breeze. She bent to sniff some splendid peonies in a vase before realizing that they were artificial. Perched on the edge of a wicker chair, she tried not to notice the other inmates—"*residents!*"—who looked up from their card games with curiosity since she so rarely emerged from her room. One old woman watched her with a sly smile. Was she the one that Helen heard crying out at night sometimes? "Mama! Mama-a!" But her mother was never going to come.

Helen, in her grey jacket and box-pleated skirt, her black handbag on her lap, was in the dayroom because she wanted to see Nicky the minute he arrived to pick her up. Every now and then some sloth-like person shuffled between her and the door, blocking her view. Helen hoped Nicky would come into the room just for a moment so that the other old crocks could admire her handsome grandson. She wouldn't introduce him: she did not know their names.

But it was young Elias who appeared at the door. Or so Helen thought for a moment, shocked. The springing dark hair, the glasses and bright brown eyes, the vitality. "Grandma!" he cried, striding over to her, and she realized that of course it was Nicky. He leaned down and kissed her cheek. "You look lovely!" She knew she did not look lovely but she was pleased all the same. Nicky glanced around the room, his smile reaching each person like a rapid sunbeam.

"Are you ready, Grandma?" He helped her up and gave her his arm. She was tempted to turn to see all the others gazing after them but resisted.

Nicky's car was in the driveway, small and jaunty red. The sight of it prompted an unease she could not identify. He settled her into the passenger seat and started up the engine.

"Good old Grandpa!" said Nicky, patting the dashboard.

Helen scowled. What did Elias have to do with it?

"Oh, I thought you knew. Grandpa gave me the car, or at least money to buy it. So I could drive down from college and see you both."

Yes, now she remembered Marjorie telling her about Elias's largesse but it was not an item of information that she kept in the front of her mind. Elias's money—all that fertilizer, shrewdly invested so that it had proliferated over the years—was a reproach to her own failure to ever accumulate money herself, despite her years of toil. But he was generous with it—she couldn't deny it and was appreciative, though hated her dependency.

Of course Nicky was devoted to his grandfather as well as to herself. She would have preferred to ignore it. Would Elias ever stop getting in the way?

No, he wouldn't.

Nicky parked on the wide main street. She had not been in town for at least a year, she believed. Fast-moving pedestrians of all ages were out on the sidewalk or crossing the street, apparently unconcerned about their chances of being hit by a car before they reached the other side. Nicky escorted her into a small restaurant with swagged curtains and round tables draped in beige. It was quiet, with only two other tables occupied— either an unpopular restaurant or they were early for lunch. Nicky caught her look. "Is Amalie's all right, Grandma? You liked it here last time." Helen had no recollection of last time but did not want to say so. She didn't care where they went. It was delightful simply to be with her grandson and away from Mrs.

D's. He pulled the chair out for her, made sure she was positioned with enough light to read the menu, summoned the waitress with a quick smile. Helen tried to remember how old he was—surely not more than nineteen, already so poised and charming. She ordered mushroom soup, Nicky a hamburger and French fries.

"A glass of wine, Grandma? I'm going to have a beer." He lowered his voice and winked. "If you don't mind being my beard."

Helen had no idea what the legal drinking age was. She would love a glass of wine and refrained from claiming coyly that she didn't drink at lunchtime.

Nicky raised his glass.

"Here's to my brilliant grandmother."

It was almost too much pleasure for her.

He leaned forward over the table. "Tell me how you are. What have you been doing?"

Oh lord. What can a very old woman say to a very young man? Well, darling, my body is as stiff as a dead tree and probably as rotten, it aches in about seventeen places, my teeth are apparently beyond repair, my digestion a farce, I have heart palpitations and sometimes pain, my faculties are deserting me, my mind most egregiously. Sometimes I seem to forget important things, I forget that you are not babies, you and the other grandchildren. I spend my days shut in my room brooding about the failures of my life. I wish I had been more courageous when I was younger. I wish I could stop wishing. I try to forgive myself. I'm not at all sure anything could have been different, given the era of my birth and my incompatible longings.

"Oh," said Helen, "I'm all right. Not doing much. Nothing much happens at Mrs. D's." She recalled the cunning, failsafe way to deflect unwelcome questions. An infallible strategy, especially with the male of the species. "What about you, dear? What are you up to?"

He smiled, sipped his beer, leaned back, put his hands behind his head. Again she saw Elias, about to tell her with calibrated modesty of his successes. She prepared herself to listen, nod admiringly, murmur astonishment and praise. She was the old granny now, not the naïve young woman dazzled and intimidated by Elias's achievements. Let the child boast. It was just like when he was a chubby eight-year-old, preening in his parents' admiration over his school report cards, his little stories and drawings. Why do boys grow up with this mantle of confidence? She remembered Marjorie's pride in her son since he was an infant, her certainty that he would excel.

"And what about your literature classes?" she asked Nicky after he'd catalogued his triumphs on the student newspaper ("I'm the first sophomore who's ever been deputy editor") and the debating society. She hoped, shamelessly, that he'd say that they'd been studying Mann, in her translations. She pictured Nicky raising his hand in class: "Helen Lowe-Porter is my grandmother."

A stooped old couple entered the restaurant, he with a walker, she with a cane. The manager greeted them and they made their slow way to a table in the corner, not looking around. They've been married for sixty-three years, she hypothesized. They come here to lunch every Friday, or whatever day it is, she cannot remember. They always order the same dishes—easy on the teeth and the stomach—and eat them with concentration. It will take a very long time. They will have ice cream for dessert, their weekly treat. They will crack mischievous little smiles when the waitress offers fudge sauce and whipped cream, and greedily accept. They rarely talk to each other in public since it distracts them from the novelty of being out in the world. Later, resting on their twin beds, they'll reprise the day. They're aware, though they don't discuss it, that one or both of them could die at any moment. Maybe I'll write a story about them, Helen thought, wondering if her little notepad was in her purse.

"She was in my Shakespeare class and I found her comments unusually astute."

"Oh?" said Helen, cross with herself for letting her attention wander. Who was "she"? "What play were you studying?"

"'Twelfth Night,' and we did an acted reading. That's how we got to know each other. Lisa was Viola and I was Feste."

What a lucky girl to earn Nicky's praise for her astuteness, she thought, but kept her sarcasm to herself. I hope he doesn't tell her she has a mind like a man's. Or give her a man's name.

"What do you call her?"

Nicky looked puzzled. "Lisa. Her name is Lisa. She doesn't like nicknames."

"Twelfth Night!" she said hastily, to cover her ill-chosen question. "What fun!" She paused and added casually, "What about Thomas Mann? Do you study him as well?"

Nicky was leafing through his wallet. "What? No, Mann's not in the syllabus. Here, Grandma, look."

She took the photo and peered at it. Nicky smiled at the camera, his arm around a girl who had long hair and an amused look. Helen was reassured. This girl did not hanker for Nicky's approval.

Both were far younger than herself and Elias when they met in Munich. She studied Lisa's face. What was it like to be a bright young woman in the second half of the twentieth century? Would she use her gifts to their fullest? If not her, then perhaps her daughter. Or her granddaughter. Times would change, surely.

"Bring Lisa to meet me," she said.

Nicky looked surprised. "Of course, Grandma. She would love that."

249

58

Assemblage
1963

Helen found herself stretched out on the bed, fully clothed, the light on and her book still in her hands. She lay motionless on her back, hoping to capture her dreams, but they flitted away. She squinted at the small clock on the bedside table—ten past three, which must mean three in the morning since the room was dark. Helen was wide awake and alert, as though she had slept all night. The big house was silent. Her gaze wandered around the room. My prison cell, she thought, where I have been confined for a long time and will no doubt die, probably soon. She sat up and looked again at the book. She heard the echo of her voice reading lines aloud. Her gaze fell on the empty top shelf of the bookcase. Aha, Thomas Mann, you no longer live in my room. I got rid of you. With all due respect and appreciation.

The empty space on the shelf seemed to open and deepen. The back of it was in shadow. It was like a stage, awaiting action. Propelled by an idea, Helen pushed herself to her feet. The shelf was too high for her to reach so she dragged a chair over—quietly now, let's not wake up Mrs. D—and climbed up, her book in one hand. It took considerable effort to lever herself up, though she was not heavy. Her joints were stiff and her muscles wasted. Decrepit, she chided herself. Well, I'm old. Ancient and feeble. She stood the book on the shelf so that the illustrated cover was visible, supported by the sturdy binding.

Abdication, or All is True: a play by H.T. Lowe-Porter. She admired the title yet again, with its layers of connotation and irony. True, factual, faithful, yet not factual, since clothed in fictional times and characters, as Shakespeare himself must have appreciated. A different kind of truth.

There. No more hiding in between other books. Pride of place for you, my lovely. She gripped the back of the chair and lowered one foot down, then the other, till they were both solidly on the floor.

She looked up at the display, liking it. But the book seemed lonely, as though it was not sure it belonged up there, so prominent and visible. Helen looked around. A gray-green fringed scarf hung over the back of another chair. She did not remember ever wearing it. The scarf made her think of Marjorie—she must have forgotten it. Or was it a gift? Her daughter had visited recently, she thought. Helen clambered up again and draped the scarf on the shelf, then placed the book on top of it. The effect was pleasing.

She considered the other book with her name on it, her neglected runt of a poetry book. Did it belong up there? She decided no. Then changed her mind. All things considered, yes. But not upright. Humbly on its side. She peered into the dimness and pulled the book out of the lower shelf, then clambered up again to place it on the edge of the high shelf, its spine just legible from below.

What else, then? Helen prowled around the room looking for ideas. A sherry glass sat on the table—she picked it up and sniffed. It was empty but redolent of sherry—ah, naughty old girl, you've been tippling. The bottle was nearby, uncorked and half-full. She pushed the cork in firmly and carried both the bottle and the glass up to the shelf, positioning them both in relation to the book, the bottle horizontal with its gold-printed label visible. The spot was exactly right. Anywhere else would be wrong. What was that rightness and wrongness? Like finding the right word, the right sequence of words. Like almost-forgotten Ruth with her palette, mixing the right color. Like the dead monk shaping his illuminated letters.

She was seized once again by the familiar excitement of creating something. Not on paper this time, not a poem or a play or a novel, instead something visual and tangible. A sort of poetry of objects, allusive, like a poem.

As though she was a divining rod, Helen let herself be drawn to other objects in the room. A string of amber beads from her drawer. An old postcard from Oxford with a photo of the Bodleian. A rusted button proclaiming "EMANCIPATION!" which she pinned to the scarf. A miniature German dictionary. A smooth oval pebble. She held it in her palm, remembering the island. Four crumpled balls of paper from the wastebasket.

There's a French word for this kind of thing, she thought, and waited for it to come into her mind. Assemblage. I am making an assemblage.

What's its title? A work of art needs a title. But she couldn't think of one.

After a while, tired from the searching and climbing up and down, she stepped back from the chair and looked up at her assemblage. It was almost complete. She was aware of the aesthetic danger of adding too much. But it needed one more thing. She went to the window and drew back the curtain. There was no light in the sky, no glimmer yet of dawn. On the windowsill there was a long iridescent feather. What was it doing there? She picked it up, stroked it across her throat. She remembered: her daughter came to visit and she, Helen, was going to give the feather to her grandson, thinking he was a little boy. She made a mistake. Marjorie was upset with her.

Helen brought the feather back to the bookcase and studied the assemblage. It had meaning, though the meaning was not translatable to language. The feather would complete it. She climbed onto the chair once more and carefully placed the feather so that it was cantilevered over the edge of the shelf.

Still standing on the chair, she leaned back to see the effect. The chair tipped from under her. Her back thumped onto the floor, her head landing a split second later. The feather trembled but did not fall.

She lay still, dizzy and winded, her whole body in pain. One coherent thought emerged from the jumble in her mind: I've finally done it. I've killed myself.

But she had not. After some time—how many minutes or hours she could not tell—the tumult in her head subsided. Her body still hurt but not from broken bones, she was sure. A miracle. She told herself to turn and push up onto her knees. Then onto her feet, holding the bed for support. She took a step or two to test her legs, which seemed to be working.

Slowly, breathing hard, she took off her clothes and changed into her long cotton nightdress, behaving with propriety for once, out of gratitude to her good fortune in not dying just yet. The covers settled around her snugly. The bedside lamp was still on. Helen reached to turn it off, after one more look at the assemblage in the dramatic shadows high above.

I'll dream a name, she thought as she drifted to sleep.

Afterword

This novel is loosely based on the life of Helen Lowe-Porter, who was my grandmother-in-law. I did not know Helen, who died in Princeton three years before her grandson and I met. What I heard about her from family members intrigued me, even more so as I began to read the letters she wrote and received, and the few other writings of hers that still exist. The person who emerges from these letters, poems, and essays is a brilliant, politically engaged, warm-hearted, witty, and perennially self-deprecating woman who adored her family and was committed to her work both as a writer and a translator. Sadly, apart from her one published play and a small collection of poems, none of her creative writing now exists, and we have very little evidence of others' reactions to it. A notable exception is Thomas Mann's letter with warm praise for her final work, a novel called *Sea Change*, presumably destroyed in manuscript after it failed to find a publisher.

Helen's translations of Mann and other German writers have proven themselves. It is due to her thirty-six years of work that the English-speaking world knows Mann's novels and essays. In recent decades lapses in her accuracy have come to light and have drawn savage criticism from some quarters. Some novels have been re-translated. But it was Helen's translations alone that built Mann's reputation in the United States and in England. She succeeded in the immensely difficult task of transforming Mann's dense, erudite, and often deliberately obscure prose into lucid English that felt idiomatic to readers on both sides of the Atlantic, while evoking the style and mood of the original. Her own nonfiction writing, in letters, translator's prefaces to the novels, and her two major essays, is graceful, direct, informal, sometimes funny—in contrast to some of her poetry, where she tended to adopt an ornate Victorian style. Her play, *Abdication*, *or All is True,* is written in astonishingly fluent and beautiful blank verse.

Helen was a writer to her bones, and it is tragic, in my view, that the depth of her devotion to Mann and to her husband and family impeded her own original work. She never gave up, despite repeated disappointments as well as her unremitting self-doubt. Critics and reviewers have dismissed Helen's passionate commitment as an artist by citing her own ironic and wistful remark at face value: "Dr. Mann says I'm a sociological bird, not a literary bird." All fiction writers have to be sociologists. Mann himself certainly was. But Helen was indeed a literary bird as well, to her last days.

There is a spectrum when it comes to fiction based on real-life characters, from novels that faithfully recount a period in the lives of historical characters while imagining their thoughts and conversation, to stories with characters that share some characteristics (and sometimes names) with real-life individuals but are otherwise entirely imagined. *Mrs. Lowe-Porter* is somewhere in the middle. My main characters Helen, Elias, and Thomas Mann are very closely based on what they wrote about themselves and what others wrote or said about them, filtered, of course, through the lens of my own impressions and leanings. Likewise the Knopfs and Einstein. Some other characters are composites or imaginary. Pauline is my invention. There was a real-life "Phoebe," though her personality and thoughts come only from my imagination. (For nonfiction accounts of Helen's life, see John Thirlwall's biography *In Another Language* and Patricia Tracy Lowe's *A Marriage of True Minds: A memoir of my parents, Helen Tracy Lowe-Porter and Elias Avery Lowe.*)

Since Helen's descendants are my own family by marriage I've avoided bringing them into this story. A number of them are unusually gifted and distinguished people, with complex stories that are theirs to tell, not mine. (Boris Johnson, the former prime minister of Great Britain—whose politics would have appalled her—is Helen's great-grandson.) Marjorie shares some attributes and experiences with Helen's daughter Patricia, my late mother-in-law, but is not her. Her sisters in the novel are even further from their real-life counterparts. Nicky does not resemble any of the actual grandchildren. Kate is more or less parallel in the story to Helen's granddaughter Suki, the only grandchild to have had a warm relationship with Helen. (There is a puzzling discrepancy between Helen's fondness for her grandchildren—evident in her letters and poems—and their perception of her as remote and intimidating.)

Most of the key events of the novel are based on events from Helen's life. Other episodes are imagined but could plausibly have happened. Helen described herself as a suffragist (and was an avowed feminist all her life) but I don't know whether she ever attended a suffragist rally. She may or may not have attempted and abandoned a novel when she was young, but she did write *Sea Change* in her late seventies and the manuscript has disappeared, as has all of her other fiction. Was there a fire? No one knows.

Helen's dilemma has always moved me: the dilemma of so many women, then and now, torn between our artistic commitment and the needs and expectations of others, not to mention the pressures of social convention. Would she have been pleased to see this imagined version of her life? Probably not, with her tendency to self-effacement and her intellectual rigor. I hope her spirit will forgive me.

Quotations

Throughout the novel the character Helen at times speaks or writes the real Helen's actual words, taken from her letters or published work. I've also used the documented words of others. Since this is fiction and not biography, I've occasionally rephrased a sentence, omitted a word, or patchworked two letters together. Many of the quotes are taken from copies of letters or other original documents in my possession. Others are from sources listed below. Letters in the text not referenced here are invented by me.

Epigraphs

Letters of Frances Hodgkins, edited by Linda Gill. Auckland University Press, 1993.

Abdication, or All is True, Act IV, Scene 1, by H. T. Lowe-Porter. Alfred A. Knopf, 1950.

Chapter 2: By the stream

"We have crushed the ripe pomegranate..."
From Helen's poem "Consummation" dated 1906. *Casual Verse*, Oxford University Press, 1957, p. 13.

Chapter 11: Hyde Park

"Over the Pass of By-and-By
You go to the Valley of Never"
This suffragist banner appeared in a historical photo online.

"Shoulder to shoulder and friend to friend!"
From the song "March of the Women," music by Ethel Smyth
and words by Cicely Hamilton.

Chapter 15: The Package

Passages in German and English from *Buddenbrooks,* by Thomas
Mann. German publication: S. Fischer Verlag, 1901. English
translation by H.T. Lowe-Porter, published by Alfred A. Knopf,
1924. Literal translation by Janet Salas.

Chapter 16: In the mountain's shadow

"Not a literary bird":
First quoted in "Talk With H. T. Lowe-Porter" by Harvey
Breit, *New York Times Book Review,* June 11, 1950.

Chapter 19: Der Zauberberg

"Extraordinarily sensitive and accomplished—wie geboren,"
he'd written— "as if you were born to it."
Letter from Thomas Mann to H.T. Lowe-Porter, April 11,
1924. *In Another Language,* John C. Thirlwall, Knopf, 1966, p.
4. Mann's letters in this volume were translated by Thirlwall's
and Lowe-Porter's mutual friend Judith Bernays Heller.

"Deeply intellectual and symbolic"
"I would suggest that if any scruples or doubts…"
Letter from Thomas Mann to H.T. Lowe-Porter, April 25,
1925. *IAL.* Ibid.

"I need not say to you, for you know me…"
When Mann wrote questioning Helen's ability to translate *The
Magic Mountain* she forwarded the letter to her husband with a
note written on the back, including this excerpt.

On the Making of the Magic Mountain: The Unpublished Correspondence of Thomas Mann, Alfred A. Knopf, and H. T. Lowe-Porter. Jeffrey B. Berlin, Seminar, 28.4, November 1992. Reprinted with permission from University of Toronto Press.

Chapter 23: The bottom drawer

"Have I any tool at all..."
Untitled poem, *Casual Verse*, Oxford University Press, 1957, p. 30.

Chapter 29: The happiest day

"Why, even a beast hath leave to choose his mate..."
From Helen's play *Abdication, or All is True*, written in blank verse and inspired by the abdication in 1936 of Edward VIII after he was forbidden by the church to marry his divorced American lover.
Abdication, or All is True, Act II, p19, by H. T. Lowe-Porter. Alfred A. Knopf, 1950.

"Ah, gentle friend, betwixt that would and could..."
Abdication, Act III, Scene II. Ibid, p 48.

"A riot of gorgeous, colorful splendor."
From the *New York Times* review of the world premiere in Dublin of *Abdication*, September 28, 1948.

Chapter 36: Taking trouble

"I appreciate your position which is uncomfortable..."
Excerpts from Helen's letters to Alfred Knopf, May 3 and 16, 1937.

"I am reasonably certain..."

Adapted from Helen's letters to Alfred Knopf, August 26, 1946 and November 11, 1943.

The translated sentences are from Helen's essay "On Translating Thomas Mann." *In Another Language*, John C. Thirlwall, Knopf, 1966, pgs. 202-203.

Chapter 39: Reunion

"A plane is over the house..."
Undated wartime letter to Helen from a friend in Oxford.

Chapter 40: The Mann dinner

"...an indescribable sense of freedom."
From an interview quoted in *Thomas Mann, A Life* by Donald Prater. Oxford University Press, 1995, p. 278.

"...the future towards which we can all work together."
From Mann's interview in *Aufbau*, June 7, 1940. Quoted in *Thomas Mann, A Life*. Ibid, p. 311.

"With a movable right arm for heiling"
This phrase appears in Helen's letter in *The New Yorker*, January 18, 1941, with an anecdote about attempting to hex Hitler when she and her daughter were in Germany in 1932.

"To A. Einstein"
Verse quoted in *In Another Language*, by John C. Thirlwall, Alfred A. Knopf, 1966, p. 80.

Chapter 41: Apple trees

"With my love and best wishes for your birthday I send you this plate of fruit...."

Verbatim from a miniature handwritten card from Helen to Elias in 1928.

"Let us not discuss, let me make all the choices..."
Adapted from Helen's letter to Elias, March 31, 1941.

Chapter 42: Mountain House

"Man and His Wife Run Publishing Firm."
This newspaper interview, originally with the headline "Man and His Wife Chief Officers in Publishing Firm," is described in *The Lady with the Borzoi: Blanche Knopf, Literary Tastemaker Extraordinaire* by Laura Claridge. Farrar, Straus and Giroux, 2016 (which also describes Alfred Knopf's newsletter.)

"I was so interested as not to notice..."
From a letter from Helen to Alfred Knopf dated February 6, 1937.

Chapter 43: The island

"How could you do it"
Mann quotes Helen asking him this question in *The Story of a Novel* by Thomas Mann, translated by Richard and Clara Winston. Alfred A. Knopf, 1961, p. 219.

Chapter 44: White Elephant

"I feel there is a risk..."
From Helen's essay "Doctor Faustus" written in 1948 and published in full in *In Another Language*, John C. Thirlwall, Alfred A. Knopf, 1966, p. 160.

"The comment of the most thorough and intimate connoisseur..."

Mann quoted in *IAL*, Ibid, p. 110.

"The loving and extraordinarily proficient hands..."
From a review of *Doctor Faustus* by Alfred Kazin, *New York Herald Tribune* weekly book review, October 31, 1948.

"It is strange that Herr Professor..."
Letter from Mann to Helen, dated January 8, 1949, quoted in *In Another Language*, by John C. Thirlwall, Knopf, 1966, p. 116. The original quote mentions the critic's name, Harry Levin.

Chapter 46: Husband of the playwright

"The Dublin season was great fun..."
Letter from Helen to Alfred Knopf, dated November 3, 1948.

"Women writers over the age...."
Handwritten note from the critic George Jean Nathan to Alfred Knopf, January 21, 1950.

Chapter 48: A distinguished alumna

"Mrs. Lowe-Porter held her questioners spellbound..."
From "Letter to Minerva" by Jane C. Morgan, *Wells College Alumnae News*, April 1950, p. 10. Quoted by permission from the Office of Advancement at Wells College.

Chapter 49: Such human love as this

"Before she sat in the chair..."
Helen was devastated by the executions of the Rosenbergs. These lines are from her poem "Waste" in *Casual Verse*, Oxford University Press, 1957, p. 48.

Chapter 51: In the corner

"I would repeat
That they are truly very sweet…"
Lines from "For Charlotte" in *Casual Verse*, Ibid, p. 66. Written for her granddaughter.

"The reason is perhaps silly…"
In Another Language, by John C. Thirlwall, Knopf, 1966, p. 131.

"…my ending is despair."
From *The Tempest*, quoted by Mann in a letter to Agnes Meyer, in *Thomas Mann: A Life* by Donald Prater. Oxford University Press, 1995, p. 488.

Chapter 53: The Wanderer

The italicized lines in this chapter are from Jonathan Glenn's translation of the medieval poem "The Wanderer," published at http://lightspill.com/poetry/oe/wanderer.html. Quoted by permission from Jonathan and Teresa Glenn.

Sources and References

Berlin, Jeffrey. "On the Making of *The Magic Mountain: The Unpublished Correspondence of Thomas Mann, Alfred A. Knopf, and H. T. Lowe-Porter*." In Seminar: A Journal of Germanic Studies. University of Toronto Press, November 1992.

Brown, Virginia. "E. A. Lowe and the Making of *The Beneventan Script*" in *Miscellanea Bibliothecae Apostolicae Vaticanae*, XIII, Città del Vaticano, 2006, pgs. 27-89.

Claridge, Laura. *The Lady with the Borzoi: Blanche Knopf, Literary Tastemaker Extraordinaire.* Farrar Straus Giroux, 2016.

David-Fox, Michael. *Showcasing the Great Experiment: Cultural Diplomacy and Western Visitors to the Soviet Union, 1921-1941.* Oxford University Press, 2011.

Horton, David. *Thomas Mann in English: A Study in Literary Translation.* Bloomsbury Publishing USA, 2013.

Lowe, Elias Avery. *The Ambrosiana of Milan and the Experiences of a Paleographer.* Transcript of address given at the Morgan Library, New York, 1966.

Lowe-Porter, Helen Tracy. *Abdication, or All is True.* Alfred A. Knopf, 1950.

Lowe-Porter, Helen Tracy. *Casual Verse.* Oxford University Press, 1957.

Lowe, Patricia Tracy. *The Cruel Stepmother.* Prentice-Hall, 1970.

Lowe, Patricia Tracy. *A Marriage of True Minds: A memoir of my parents, Helen Tracy Lowe-Porter and Elias Avery Lowe.* Tusitala Publishing, 2006.

Mann, Thomas. *Buddenbrooks.* Translated by H. T. Lowe-Porter. Alfred A. Knopf, 1924.

Mann, Thomas. *The Magic Mountain.* Translated by H. T. Lowe-Porter. Alfred A. Knopf, 1927.

Mann, Thomas. *Lotte in Weimar: The Beloved Returns.* Translated by H. T. Lowe-Porter. Alfred A. Knopf, 1940.

Mann, Thomas. *Order of the Day: Political Essays and Speeches of Two Decades.* Translated by H. T. Lowe-Porter, Agnes Meyer, and Eric Sutton. Alfred A. Knopf, 1942.

Mann, Thomas. *Doctor Faustus.* Translated by H. T. Lowe-Porter. Alfred A. Knopf, 1948.

Mann, Thomas. *The Story of a Novel.* Translated by Richard and Clara Winston. Alfred A. Knopf, 1961.

Mann, Thomas. *The Letters of Thomas Mann 1889 - 1955.* Selected and translated by Richard and Clara Winston. Secker and Warburg, 1970.

Prater, Donald. *Thomas Mann: A Life.* Oxford University Press, 1995.

Thirlwall, John C. *In Another Language: A Record of the Thirty-Year Relationship between Thomas Mann and His English Translator, Helen Tracy Lowe-Porter.* (Includes HTLP's essays "Doctor Faustus," 1948, and "On Translating Thomas Mann," also published in part in Symposium, Syracuse University, Fall 1955.) Alfred A. Knopf, 1966.

Additional Sources

Unpublished letters between Helen Lowe-Porter, Elias Avery Lowe, Alfred and Blanche Knopf, and other professional and personal correspondents.

Elias Lowe's pocket diaries, housed at the Morgan Library, New York.

Written reminiscences and personal communications from Helen Lowe-Porter's daughter, Patricia Lowe, and grandchildren including Anneke Campbell, Jonathan Fox, Suki Harrison, Charlotte Johnson Wahl, and Sarah Thomas.

Acknowledgments

John C. Thirlwall's biography of Helen, *In Another Language*, documented the milestones of her life and was an important resource for me in writing *Mrs. Lowe-Porter*. Thirlwall knew Helen and wrote the book soon after her death.

I'm full of gratitude to the many people who helped this novel take form:

Suzanne Bennett, Elin Menzies, Debra Moskowitz, and the late Pauline Uchmanowicz read the first draft and offered essential critique as well as enthusiasm.

My astute later readers included Lisa Mullenneaux, Anneke Campbell, Scott Cohen, Rickie Solinger, Kathie Fiveash, and Nava Atlas. Susan MacNeil's heartfelt affirmation came at a crucial moment for me.

As I researched and wrote I was in constant imagined dialogue with my late mother-in-law, Patricia Lowe (Helen's daughter), missing her and appreciating her own writing about her parents.

My niece Miranda Laurence, with baby Ruth in the pram, kindly showed me around Oxford so I could picture Helen living there.

Michael Becker, a literary agent in Frankfurt, loved the book and was working hard on finding a German publisher when he died suddenly. I am deeply grateful for his efforts.

My editor at JackLeg Press, Julian Anderson, has been a delight to work with, both rigorous and kind. Her insights and inspired suggestions have been formative. Mary Bisbee-Beek astonished me by embracing the book from the outset and eventually connecting me with JackLeg. Much gratitude to JackLeg's publisher and editorial director, Jennifer Harris, for bringing my novel into the world.

Jonathan Fox, my husband and Helen's grandson, has been a co-conspirator all along, joining me in countless conversations about Helen and Elias and engaging with my artistic quandaries. Hannah, Maddy, Sam, Rex, Rio, and Anya keep my heart full and my feet on the ground.

My sister Janet Salas, a writer and translator herself, has been an extraordinary companion—across 11,000 miles—during this book's long gestation. Her knowledge of literature and the German language, her research skills, and her loving support have meant a great deal to me.

Thank you all!

JACKLEG PRESS

V. Joshua Adams, Scott Shibuya Brown, Brian
Rivka Clifton, Brittney Corrigan, Jessica Cuello,
Barbara Cully, Alison Cundiff, Suzanne
Frischkorn, Victoria Garza, Reginald Gibbons,
D.C. Gonzales-Prieto, Neil de la Flor, Joachim
Glage, Caroline Goodwin, Kathryn Kruse,
Meagan Lehr, Brigitte Lewis, Jean McGarry, D.K.
McCutchen, Jenny Magnus, Rita Mookerjee,
Mamie Morgan, Karen Rigby, cin salach, Jo Salas,
Maureen Seaton, Kristine Snodgrass, Cornelia
Maude Spelman, Peter Stenson, Melissa Studdard,
Curious Theatre, Gemini Wahhaj, Megan Weiler,
David Wesley Williams

jacklegpress.org

CPSIA information can be obtained
at www.ICGtesting.com
Printed in the USA
JSHW080315250723
45283JS00002B/122